EVERY
HIDDEN
THING

EVERY HIDDEN THING

A NOVEL

TED FLANAGAN

CROOKED LANE

NEW YORK

Published in the United States by Crooked Lane Books, an imprint of The Quick Brown Fox & Company LLC.

Crooked Lane Books and its logo are trademarks of The Quick Brown Fox & Company LLC.

Library of Congress Catalog-in-Publication data available upon request.

ISBN (hardcover): 978-1-64385-764-0
ISBN (ebook): 978-1-64385-765-7

Cover design by Lance Buckley

Printed in the United States.

www.crookedlanebooks.com

Crooked Lane Books
34 West 27th St., 10th Floor
New York, NY 10001

First Edition: October 2021

10 9 8 7 6 5 4 3 2 1

To anyone punching a clock in pursuit
of their place in America.

For God will bring every deed into judgment,
including every hidden thing, whether it is good or evil.
Ecclesiastes 12:14

1

THE BABY CAME on one of those January nights in the city. Warm. Everyone in shirtsleeves. A gap between inevitable blizzards. Cars crept along damp streets shrouded in snow-fog. Black-crusted drifts bounded roads warped by frost heaves, ice forming beneath the asphalt and buckling it, melted water dribbling along underground fissures to a canal dug by Irish laborers two centuries ago.

They were angry men with alien accents. In old photos they had huddled in tents and lean-tos on the muddy hills ringing Worcester while they dug the Blackstone, like an army laying siege. The canal was forever their proudest feat, but it was narrow and when the trains connected Worcester to Providence and onward to a wider world that couldn't care less, they abandoned the canal.

The city buried the thing in the 1970s as part of urban renewal, which had no place in its heart for a waterway that reminded them of the ways progress had failed them. Below the asphalt streets and brick factories built over it, below the

city that rose and fell, over and over, the canal flowed onward.
Out of sight.

Thomas Archer rode in the passenger seat of the ambulance with the window down, his uniform sleeves rolled to
the elbows. He enjoyed the interlude. The night had been
slow. He and Julio Tavares, his partner, had done a handful
of calls, nothing that required more than a smile and a taxi
ride for a few of the regulars.

Even that felt like a gift.

The holidays had started almost two months ago with a
cardiac arrest under a Christmas tree, the dead man's children begging for their father's life even as Archer and Julio
knew they'd lost the battle before the first chest compression.
Plenty of mayhem since. Two fatal fires. A murder-suicide up
on Trenton Street on New Year's Day, and two nights ago
Archer had pulled city boxing champ Leon "Sunny" Matos
from a Corolla the pugilist had driven into a brick wall at
eighty miles an hour.

Tonight, though. A breeze. Easy living. They'd eaten
dinner slowly enough to taste it, sat at their favorite booth
at the Bully, then driven down the hill and flirted with
some nurses at University. The cops over at the Bean
Machine on Highland were still chuckling about Mickey
P, the night shift supervisor, who'd had to let a certain state
rep out of a certain cemetery into which he'd—again—
locked himself by accident, with a woman, though not his
wife. Archer had roared with laughter, thinking there were
no better storytellers in the world than Worcester cops, and
around midnight began to contemplate *the word*. The Q
word. Maybe tonight, he thought. Maybe tonight would be
quiet.

Then, Kansas Street, down by the rail yard, three AM and
a call for the ambulance. Woman in labor.

When he listened to the dispatch recordings later, Archer heard a frantic man on the 911 line, whispering, straining *not* to be heard. The baby was here, he said. Months of poor planning, no planning, all coming to a head, and now here's the baby. He said it was limp and gray and soaking the mattress. He said someone had tried delivering the baby at home.

Archer found them, baby and mother, on a mattress on the floor of a third-story bedroom. Train engines and railcars colliding night after night outside the building shook dust and bits of plaster from the walls onto the floor, so the mattress floated on a sea of talcum scrapes. Lath peeked out in places from hundred-year-old patches of broken and gray horsehair plaster, polka-dotted by black blooms of mold.

The woman, cross-legged and hunched over on the mattress, blew air through pursed lips. She squeezed her eyes shut. Her mocha-colored skin glistened. Pupils pinpoint. She grimaced and chased her breath. Blood and water soaked the mattress, and the baby was still and silent. For a moment Archer saw her as on an altar, the baby a sacrifice.

A man stood to the left of the mattress with his arms clasped behind his back and his eyes wide as he stared into a back corner of the room, not at the baby, not at the woman. He seemed as black as night, and when Archer looked at the man for an extra moment, he thought part of him melted into the back wall, where the light from the bulb faded into shadow.

Julio dropped to a knee at the foot of the mattress, touched the baby's stomach, held his fingertips over the baby's mouth, then against the inside of a bicep.

"Shit," Julio said, then placed an oxygen mask and squeezed air into its lungs. Someone had already clamped and cut the umbilical cord, Archer saw. The placenta lay in a glass baking dish on the floor. Blood trailed in a long tendril from rumpled bedsheets to the dish.

Archer felt the pulse in the woman's wrist banging away, a weak and thready metronome.

"Do you speak English?" he asked.

She nodded. "I work for the city," she said, her voice thick and dreamy.

She panted. The bottoms of the sweat beads on her forehead glimmered beneath the weak yellow light from the bulb above, small planets orbiting in the furrows of her brow. The man to her left unclasped his hands and stepped forward to thrust a stack of papers at Archer.

He scanned.

Hospital discharge instructions.

Yesterday morning.

Daisy Fontana, thirty-six weeks gestation, evaluated for eclampsia, gestational diabetes.

Past history included psych issues, heroin abuse, and asthma. Typical for the city.

"You don't need that," a man behind Archer said.

Archer's stomach seized and his heart jackhammered, like a sprinter's at the end of a hundred-yard dash. He wondered for a moment if you could imagine a voice, because the one behind him couldn't be in the room. The voice he thought he'd heard should still be in a jail somewhere, not here, not now.

Where are the police? Archer thought.

"The paperwork," the man said. "It's not pertinent."

Archer turned to the man. He was dressed in a black suit and chewing the inside of his hollow, pockmarked cheek beneath a wispy comb-over of almost-white blond hair. The shadows under his boxer's nose deepened as he pressed into the ring of pale light. It was a face Archer wasn't supposed to see for another decade. Eamon Conroy, a murderer, though sent to jail for obstruction and not the crime he'd really committed.

Archer grimaced at his own complacency. He'd forgotten the paramedic's reflex: never go into a room you can't get out of.

"This is under control," Conroy said. He pointed to the man standing by Daisy's bed. "Rigo here just panicked. There was supposed to be a midwife."

"Midwife?" Archer asked.

"Ms. Fontana here wanted to take advantage of a natural childbirth," Conroy said. "When Rigo panicked, she was understandably shaken. But everything's fine."

"We're supposed to be at Memorial," Rigo hissed. "No fucking midwife."

Conroy held his hands up in surrender. "I told you we were handling this, Rigo," he said. "I thought I was clear about discretion. You know we'll take care of this."

To Archer, the man's eyes were holes in the light, reflecting nothing. He knew one bedrock piece of truth about Eamon Conroy. There were two types of dangerous: the claimed and the authentic. Conroy was as authentic as they came.

"We should have gone to the hospital," Rigo whispered.

"The baby came too fast," Conroy said. "I've explained that to you. Maybe if she laid off that other stuff, we could have gone a few more weeks."

Archer turned back to the woman. He didn't want to look at Conroy. He didn't want to think about Conroy. About the fact that Conroy was back. About what that meant.

"When did the baby come?" Archer asked. He spoke to Rigo.

"The baby's fine," Conroy said. "He's just taking a nap."

"The baby's not fine," Archer said. "You did this, didn't you?"

"I got here after you did," Conroy said. "That's the story I'm sticking to, anyway. That's the one everyone here who's smart will tell."

The woman pursed her lips. Her eyes shifted to Conroy. Archer looked down and to the left, saw Conroy's shirt cuffs stained pink where they poked out from his coat.

"The heart rate is coming up," Julio said. "He's still not breathing well."

"Earlier," Rigo said. "The baby came earlier."

Archer looked at the blood, the water, the limp baby on the bed. He saw brown dots on Conroy's forehead.

"What did you do?" Archer asked.

No reply.

"Police coming?" Archer asked Julio.

"I heard the sector car sign on," Julio said.

"I canceled the police," Conroy said. He waved a cell phone and smiled at Archer. "The police have better things to do with their time than go on medicals. No one here but us mice."

"We should get moving," Julio said. Archer nodded. Conroy clasped Archer's left shoulder, turned him around slowly, and held out a hand. His suit jacket parted open, and Archer saw the dark metal glint of a pistol in the light-brown leather holster under Conroy's left arm.

"I'll need those papers," Conroy said. "Then I'll be out of here."

The woman screamed and bent over double in the bed. Rigo shook his head and stared at a point on the floor in front of him. Julio slid the bags of equipment closer to him with his foot. Archer stared at Conroy, made up his mind. He reached behind him for the heavy black flashlight hanging from the loop on his right hip. He held it over his head, a hatchet ready to strike.

"You know we're taking the baby," Archer said. "And mom. And the papers. Even you know we have to. You can't keep people away from this. It's us or someone else. Whatever you were trying to do here, it's too late."

Conroy smiled. He flicked the fingers of his outstretched hand.

"I have that same flashlight," he said. "Not cheap. I didn't think you guys made that kind of scratch. Must be good at figuring things out. You must be a genius."

"I'm pretty stupid," Archer said. His stomach clenched, and he tasted the fear that rose on a wave of acid rising in his throat.

"Eamon, you know what happens if things go bad with the baby," Julio said. "You haven't been off the job that long. The state will turn this place upside down. No one can stop that, once it gets going. So far, there's wiggle room. We can be flexible. Who was here, who wasn't here, what the hell was going on. All of it. We can be motherhumping Gumby at the moment. But we need to go to keep things that way. We've got to slide, man. Time to fly."

Conroy considered what Julio said, then shrugged nd stepped back.

"There'll be plenty of time to sort this out later," he said, then pointed a finger at Rigo. "Remember what we talked about. Discretion. Tell the right story."

Conroy straightened his coat, picked a piece of lint off his tie, then walked into the kitchen and out of sight. Julio exhaled. Archer bowed his head and took a deep breath.

"You know that psycho got out of jail?" Julio asked. "Seems like someone should have told us that bit of information."

Archer shrugged. "I had no idea." He looked at the hospital paperwork, then bent down to the woman.

"We're going to the hospital now, Daisy," he said. "Your baby is doing better but is still very sick. Do you understand?"

Daisy nodded.

"Can I go too?" Rigo asked.

"Who called 911?" Archer asked.

"I did," Rigo said.

"That guy try to stop you?"

Rigo nodded.

"There was no midwife, was there?" Archer asked.

Rigo shook his head. "They said there would be. This whole thing is fu—"

"Rigo, no," Daisy said between pants.

Rigo shook his head, a pitcher shaking off a sign.

On the way to the hospital, Archer watched as the baby's color and breathing improved, but it was quiet, listless. A bad sign, Archer knew. A kind of surrender. The silence muted any joy Daisy might have felt, he thought, though he sensed there wasn't much of that here in this corner of the city to begin with. He looked up front, saw Rigo absently eating his bag lunch.

They passed the Pigtown Deli on Shaw Street. The accountant in the office above the place found fat returns for the city's cops and firefighters and medics. The deli itself was a front for a Vietnamese religious sect that recruited takeout customers while they waited with a continuous-loop video of doves floating on sun-dappled skies. The bagels and vegan soups were good enough that Archer thought it was a fair price to pay.

The baby remained quiet, even when Archer flicked the soles of its feet. Daisy only winced when Archer started the intravenous line. She stared into the baby's face with a look Archer couldn't interpret. Was it happiness? Was it love? Was it pain?

* * *

Archer tried to write the two charts—one for Daisy, the other for the baby. He started and stopped. His mind wandered. Seeing Conroy again had brought it all back.

Freeland Street, Archer just a couple years on the job. A single-unit efficiency on the fifth floor of a graffiti-covered box of an apartment complex, not a thing in it except a round table and a refrigerator in the kitchen. The living room had a large television, no furniture. Archer's partner at the time, an ancient medic named Arnold Moonandowski—Moonie—recognized it for what it was.

"Safe house," he said, while they waited in the kitchen.

"Safe from who?" Archer asked.

"Place where the cops can talk to people without having to take them into cruisers, or for people who can't be seen keeping appointments at the police station," Moonie said. He whispered. It was the first time Archer had seen his veteran partner spooked. The door to a bedroom at the end of a short hall off the kitchen was closed, but they could see a yellow strip of light below it, shadows of feet passing back and forth.

And they didn't know much. Dispatch had given them the address, said they were going for a sick person. No other details. When they'd knocked, a plainclothes cop opened it. He was coatless, sleeves rolled up, his badge pinned to a strap on his shoulder holster.

"You fellas mind giving us a moment?" he said.

"You need us to leave, Eamon?" Moonie asked. Archer was surprised Moonie knew the cop by name. Worried because the ever-affable Moonie had gone all stiff and businesslike.

"Nothing like that—it's just some of the men in here need to leave, but we can't have people seeing their faces. Secret Squirrel shit, but if you could indulge us and just turn around, that would be great."

Archer looked at Moonie, and Moonie pointed toward the refrigerator, and a small group of people hustled out the door behind them. Archer heard male voices speaking Spanish in short bursts. He sneaked a sideways glance at the four men passing behind him. They were older. He thought he recognized two of them—one of them drove for Blue Cab; the other owned a bodega on Woodland. There was something about them, an air, a presence. The cab driver caught Archer's eye. Archer wanted to get out of the apartment, as far from these men as possible.

"We have a situation," Conroy said, once they were alone. "I can trust you guys here a bit, right? We got this guy in the back room, a real lowlife, scumball piece of shit. Drug dealer. Diddler. Real shitbag. So, we're interviewing him, and he wasn't being cooperative. Hell, what he was being was downright *un*cooperative."

Moonie and Archer nodded their heads as if they knew exactly what Conroy was driving at.

"And the hell of it is, I think we may have hurt him, and I'm not sure what to do about it," Conroy said. "So one of the guys says, hey, let's call an ambulance. Now, generally, I hate to bother you guys with every little ache and pain suffered by our clientele, but here's the thing with this guy." Conroy leaned in, gathered Moonie and Archer in his arms, pulled them close, huddling, like they were a football team ready to make the big score. "The thing of it is, I'm not sure he's still breathing."

They found him hanging sideways from a metal chair in the middle of the room. Young. Twenties maybe. Maybe younger. Shirtless, connected to the chair by handcuffs. A puddle of water under the chair. And piss. A two-foot piece of garden hose on the ground nearby, its ends covered in dried blood. Even from across the room, Archer could see the man was motionless, his chest eerily still, the absence of rise and fall more noticeable than if he still breathed. His eyes were swollen shut. His chest a canvas of abrasions and scrapes and angry red stripes.

Moonie reacted first, ordered Conroy to undo the hand-cuffs. They laid the man on the floor and went to work. Archer noticed Conroy scouring the room, dumping tools and the hose and a small scale into a duffel bag, then wiping down the counter and table with a towel before peeking over Moonie's shoulder to check out their work, then word-lessly striding out of the apartment and into the night.

Later, they sat on the boat ramp across from the hospital and ate subs from the Portuguese takeout place. Archer tried not to think of their patient, now in the morgue at University.

"What was that?" Archer finally asked.

"What that was, was stuff you'll need to learn not to ask about," Moonie said.

"That cop, you know him?"

Moonie nodded. "Guy named Conroy," he said. "Scary dude. I know we spend a lot of time telling the new guys how close we are to the police, and it's true. The cops in this city, we do anything for them. They'll always be there for you. But Conroy? He's an exception. Other cops keep their dis-tance. He's psycho. I watched him once smack around a preg-nant junkie at the New Star shelter because she called him dickless."

"Did you report him?"

Moonie finished his sandwich, rolled the wax paper into a ball and tossed it into a nearby trash can. The city darkened as the sun dropped beneath the surrounding hills. Street-lights on the river bridge winked to life.

"That's not how this works," Moonie said. "The cops will take care of their own. Everyone knows the score on Conroy."

"What was that apartment?" Archer asked.

"Safe house. Not everyone can be seen talking to the cops, so they'll bring them to one of those apartments and talk to them in private."

"That guy was no informant," Archer said. "I mean, they electrocuted his balls. They killed him. We need to tell—"

"You don't need to tell anyone anything," Moonie said. "Conroy is . . . entrepreneurial. He runs his own crew. Off the books. They'll get him. People know what he's up to. But it's not your job. Do yourself a favor, just keep your head down and stay out of it."

*   *   *

Archer finished the charts, dropped copies off with Daisy's nurse. Her baby was upstairs in the neonatal intensive care unit. He peeked in the exam room where Daisy slept, fluid going into one arm, a unit of blood into the other. Rigo nowhere to be seen.

He thought of Eamon Conroy, how he hadn't taken Moonie's advice back when. For Conroy's fellow cops, the Freeland Street thing was the last straw. They had bitten their lips for years, turned a blind eye to his methods, but killing a man, torturing him beforehand? No one had signed up for that. When detectives came asking, Archer gave it up. All of it.

Later, when he'd finished testifying at the trial, Conroy winked at Archer as he left the stand. They sent Conroy off to jail, and Archer moved on, never expected to see the man again.

Now tonight—Conroy. Materializing in the middle of whatever this was, a bad dream returned and alive in the middle of a dark room coated in plaster dust.

Daisy stirred, opened her eyes, and saw Archer standing by the curtain. A thought came to him, as if hitting a trip wire. The moment before the explosion but after it was too late. Daisy slowly shook her head. *I'm in the way*, he realized. *I'm in the way of a dangerous man.*

2

Lu McCarthy got the call right after Valentine's Day. Kittredge was chummy and warm, which the boss never was unless he wanted something. Come to my office, he said. We should talk. She'd evaded, but only for so long. She knew something was coming, didn't like the way her boss refused to reveal the agenda.

"There's just some stuff we need to go over," Kittredge had said.

Navigating the maze of forgotten hallways in this windowless backwater section of the sprawling newspaper building, its plate metal walls sweating from the little steam heat the structure's ancient boilers eked out against the winter cold, Lu imagined which Kittredge she'd face. Her boss had adopted many iterations over the years, a chameleon whose spots always changed in ways designed to keep Kittredge rising, ever upward—although, as it turned out, those spots could get him only to middle management at a midsize daily that had become a grape, dying on the vine.

There was backslapping Gabe Kittredge, your buddy, the guy who always bought the last round when they shut down the Dinger on election night. This was the Old Kittredge, Lu's bureau mate back in the days when they'd shared two desks in a strip mall office in Emporia, covered dog catcher meetings and school visits by state reps who were feted and greeted like royalty. Kittredge had been looser then, still striving but a good guy, so the bottle of rye he kept in his desk seemed less like a prop than a piece of actual office equipment.

Then there was Imperial Gabriel. This version, high-minded guardian of the eternal flame of journalism, Keeper of the Fourth Estate, had arrived when Kittredge became city editor a decade ago. He ate in the private dining room. He shit in the executive bathrooms. This Kittredge spoke at City Research Bureau luncheons and received the state reps, especially in election years, as if he were a sitting Pope. Since he was the driving force behind the paper's editorial page and the chief arbiter of the daily story budget, only the paper's publisher, H. Robert Galloway, held more sway over public opinion in the city. Lu didn't want to deal with this version of Kittredge today. This version, she thought, was a prick.

For a man who craved power so baldly as Kittredge, she couldn't fathom how he'd ended up in a windowless office hidden in a warren of empty conference rooms filled with mismatched office furniture, old fax machines, listing credenzas missing a leg here and there, and glass-topped coffee tables once coveted by long-dead executives, all of it layered with an inch of old, gray dust.

It was out of the way, far from the newsroom and even farther from the palatial sprawl of Galloway and his executive minions. It was cheap, dirty, old. Lu figured it had to do with power and the application of power. Kittredge liked to move in unseen circles, a perpetual cycle of need-to-know with ultimately only one person in need of knowing it all. Lu also knew it was the only office in the entire building with its own private exit, this one leading to a back alley adjacent to city hall.

In the newspaper's heyday, Kittredge's office had been the studio for a low-watt news radio station the paper owned. It was soundproofed so well you could hear your own heartbeat, or the blood coursing through vessels and arteries. She thought that having Kittredge's job, having to come to this dungeon, so far from people, so far from the world and the bright sun outside, locked in here like a declawed tiger, would have driven her nuts.

It was all too quiet in this part of the building. The presses that once ruled the now-empty basement caverns, the newspaper's former heart and soul, their rolling thrum vibrating every corner of the building—they were gone now. The beating heart had been replaced by fiber-optic cables and keyboard clicks and soft shoes on carpets and, the worst of it all, silence. Soulless, Lu thought. As good as dead.

The radio station went under in the early 1990s, the studio converted into storage, and then last year, when half the *Courier*'s Telegraph Street home had been sold to a health insurance company looking for a bigger downtown footprint, the defunct studio was converted into an office and Kittredge moved in. Lu avoided it as much as she could.

She rapped on the doorframe, and Kittredge, a phone tucked into his shoulder, swiveled his office chair around, held up one finger, then pointed to an empty chair in front of the desk.

"There are other factors at play here that maybe you don't appreciate, different metrics altogether," Kittredge was saying. "You've got to understand that, from thirty thousand feet up, at the end of the day, we're missing out on the low-hanging fruit here. And you're comparing apples to hubcaps."

Lu cringed. When, she wondered, had people in this business stopped speaking like human beings? *We used to make fun of people who talked like that*, she thought. *Now we're assimilated.*

Kittredge chewed his bottom lip like bubblegum and ratcheted his head up and down as he listened. Lu knew the look. It was when Kittredge had arrived at the point where he knew what you were going to say, no longer wanted to wait, had conjured a reply, and now boiled inside with the desire to be done with your opinions and move on to his.

"Write whatever you want, Phil," Kittredge said, "but the official *Courier* position is that we are realigning our resources to be tighter, leaner, and more agile, and going digital first is one way to do that."

Kittredge put a pretend finger gun to his head and feigned pulling the trigger.

"We saw this with the collapse of ad revenue, but that was, what, a decade ago?" he said. "Might as well have been last fucking century. We're talking disruption, now. Technology outpacing tradition. Totally different. We're not collapsing. We're growing. Things are just revenue-neutral at the moment."

Lu settled into the red fabric desk chair and waited for Kittredge to finish the lesson. She could hear the blood rumbling through the veins and capillaries in her head, a background pulse, like water clanging through an old steam radiator. Each breath whooshed like a bellows, her heartbeats pounding a swishing drumbeat. She couldn't fathom how Kittredge survived coming here every day.

"I'm hanging up now," Kittredge said. A pause. "Because you're being pedantic, Phil. It's clear to me that you've got an agenda. Bottom line, this paper will be here a lot longer than your fucking website!"

Kittredge slammed the phone into the cradle, ran his hands through the gray hair on the temples of an aquiline head, long and narrow with large orbits around his eyes and black circles that gave him the perpetual look of a prizefighter who'd just finished sparring without headgear.

"That sounded like fun," she said.

"Phil fucking Bracken."

"Of course. 'Dienewspaperdie.com.' I'm more a fan of 'newspaperdeathwatch.com.' "

Kittredge laid an arm across his desk, sank his forehead into the crook of his elbow, and nodded. "At least those guys seem a little bit sad about the whole mess. Bracken is down-right priapic about it."

"Getting fired publicly will make a man bitter," she said.

Kittredge looked up, a pained expression on his face.

"*We* didn't fire him," he said. "The goddamn *Herald* fired him. You can't file stories from war zones while hiding in your mother's basement."

"That was not a stand-up move."

"That was not."

"So," she said. "You rang, sir?"

Kittredge picked up a plastic cup filled with paper clips. A handful hung on the magnetic lip of the cup. Kittredge bit his lip and pulled a clip from the magnet and unraveled it, straightening the thing into a narrow-gauge piece of wire.

"The paper is facing significant challenges, as you know," Kittredge began. He looked down at his hands. They rebent the paper clip into a new form, an approximation of its for-mer self, only in opposite curves. "We've attempted to stem the tide. We've beefed up our coverage of the outer boroughs,

erected a paywall on our website, started the printing operation for inserts, that kind of stuff."

"Not to mention getting rid of the pension, firing most
of the bureau staffs in those boroughs, eliminating matches
to the 401(k) that was supposed to replace the pension, a
week off each quarter without pay," Lu said.

Kittredge nodded. "True enough," he said. "We've done
all that, plus a lot of things you haven't seen. Ugly things.
Believe me, the knife has cut deep in advertising and circula-
tion and the executive suite. Editorial hasn't borne the entire
brunt. Unfortunately, it hasn't been enough."

A light came on. Not on—more like a dimmer went from
low to high. Or like the moment before a car wreck, Lu thought,
that pause when the collision is inevitable but you still hold on
to the wheel, stand on the brakes. Futility, but it's just what you
do; you're keenly aware of how perfect everything is, your life,
and how it's all about to go to shit, has already gone to shit but
for the playing out of the physics. The whoosh in her ears became
a torrent. Kittredge snapped the tortured paper clip in half.

"We need to make more cuts," Kittredge said, "deep
cuts. Cuts to muscle and bone."

He met Lu's gaze. She braced for the haymaker.

"We have to let you go, Lu. I'm sorry. You're our highest-
paid reporter, and you work the cops beat. No one your age
works cops."

She dried her palms on the knees of her pants. She rocked
a little back and forth. Cleared her throat.

"I can't say it's a complete surprise," Lu said. "Jesus.
Thirty years."

Kittredge reached into a desk drawer, pulled out a box of
tissues, slid it over the desk toward her. Lu pointed at the box.
Sneered.

"You expecting me to cry?" she asked. "When did you ever see me cry? What did I *ever* do to give you the impression that I'm a crier?"

"Sorry, reflex move," Kittredge said. "I've been doing this a lot lately. A lot of crying in here."

He dropped the tissue box into the drawer.

"It was a great run," Kittredge said. "You're a pro. But we've got to stare down the bottom line here. People like us, Lu, we're becoming obsolete—hell, we're already obsolete. It's all about data mining and computer-assisted reporting and getting kids out of Worcester State willing to do twice the work for half the money, shooting their own video, taking their own art. We used to make crusaders, but now it's—it's not that the facts aren't important. It's just that they need to be in service of more than just the truth. The news is a product. Widgets built in a widget factory that exists on a computer screen instead of newsprint. Content drives everything, right or wrong. Being first is the new priority. No one has time to be right too. Gnosticism runs amok."

"Gnosticism?"

"Hidden agendas and secret orders, and everyone hates an expert, which is ironic since everyone is an expert in their own crackpot theories, about life and power, and the press. Especially the press. There's an awakening, Lu, a vile, veiled thing, and there's nothing we can do about it. We live in a time when every hidden thing is both truth and lie. Fact and fiction are the same, as long as you yell your truth loudly enough. I think Mussolini said that."

"I don't think he did."

"Well, maybe not. Doesn't matter, as long as I *say* he did with enough conviction it becomes true. Not totally true, but true *enough*, and that's all that matters these days."

As he talked, Lu followed Kittredge in a rotation of connectedness. He spoke while thumb-scrolling through emails on his phone. Sidled over to the laptop on his desk, tapped down through messages or a feed or some other kind of deluge of information and opinion, the ever-progressing obliteration of fact, of objectivity, of anyone having an opinion they kept to themselves anymore. Even as he took Lu out at the knees, Kittredge kept up with the feed. That was the job now. Feeding the feed.

"The last kid that applied here?" Kittredge said. "Didn't mention a single word about his student newspaper work. Told me all about his 'platform.' Platform, Lu. That's what they're teaching in J-school these days. The news is no longer as important as the package. No one cares about the message as long as you get it to them first and in a hundred different ways. You can be wrong, you just can't be slow. When the mode of the messenger became more important than the message, that was the moment. We were out of a job fifteen years ago, the last nail in this whole fucking enterprise hammered in by some coder in a cubicle somewhere. Death by HTML."

Lu couldn't hear the rushing blood anymore. The office became just another empty, quiet space in a building daily breeding such spaces.

"How long do I have?"

Kittredge winced. "End of summer. Best I could do. You work night cops through July fourth, maybe Labor Day, if I can stretch things a bit; then we can give you a six-week severance, but that's about it."

"The last round of buyouts, they gave people like six months' pay."

"And I got you six months' worth of work," Kittredge said. "Listen, Galloway wanted me to get you out of here with two weeks and a handshake. This is a good deal."

"My ex is years behind in child support, Danny Junior's at BC, I already make crap here. I mean, where's the money going to come from?"

"Dan Senior won't help?"

Lu laughed.

"Maybe if I could find him. But no. He won't help. I've tried."

"I feel bad for you, Lu, you know that, but who encouraged you to take the last buyout? I did. Remember? But you wouldn't fucking listen. The job too important to you. Shit, we could have said sayonara with nothing, but I fought for you, Lu, I did. I told Galloway that you were a legend, that you deserved something. July fourth. Maybe Labor Day. That's the best I could do, and you should be happy for it."

"Please, no preaching."

"All I'm saying is that you should have listened to me," Kittredge said.

Lu thought she might vomit. The room pitched and yawed. She was desperate to go to the Ding Wa, bungee-jump her way through a series of Manhattans and kibitz with Mae, her favorite bartender, who knew how to use just enough Southern Comfort to keep the warmth in her chest glowing long after last call.

"You should have listened to me then," Kittredge said, "and maybe now."

Kittredge stood and walked to his office door, peered up and down the hallway, then closed the door and sat on the corner of his desk. He leaned toward Lu, spoke in hushed tones.

"I may have something for you," Kittredge said. "But it's . . . it's unconventional."

"I'm not in a position to insist on convention."

"I mean, way out there. And it may be a little touchy for you, distasteful even. But there are some serious rewards to it too. Life-altering things. Let me make my pitch, see what you think. You don't like it? *Vaya con Dios*, no harm, no foul."

"Where am I going?" Lu said. "I just got canned."

Kittredge unlocked a bottom desk drawer and retrieved a manila folder.

"John O'Toole's main guy, this former cop you might remember, Eamon Conroy—"

Lu raised her hands.

"You can stop right there. Anything involving that warped psycho, count me out. I covered that thing when he went to jail, followed the trail of bodies dropped by that private gang he hired, all those School of the Americas alumni. Guy should still be in jail, you ask me. And by the way, there are a few questions about how he engineered his release. Some weird timing there, what with the riot and all."

"I thought I said to hear me out."

"I'm just saying."

"I'm trying to help you out here, Lu."

Kittredge waited. She lowered her hands.

"Me and Conroy, we keep in touch. It's good to have connections so close to a guy like O'Toole. So we're having drinks at the Dinger the other night, and he asked me my thoughts on doing a little work for them on the QT, very quiet-like, for a project they've got going in advance of O'Toole's likely run for governor."

"Of course he'll run for governor," Lu said. "Shit, I heard he even rented a warehouse on St. James to store all the signs he's already made."

"We're talking about this thing they need done, and immediately your name came up," Kittredge said.

"I don't do pay for play," she said. "I've got my integrity; at least give me that."

"It sounds like, you do a good job on this, bring home what they want, there may be a city job in it for you, long term. Short term, Conroy said they'll pay. Fifty thousand, under the table."

Kittredge let the number hang in the air.

Lu played poker face, but inside she was stunned. Almost a year's salary. For what? No way, she thought. Working for a murderous psycho? *But how can I say no? Do I really want to? Who's going to tell Danny Junior not to pack for school in the fall?*

"I know it's not your kind of thing, Lu, but it's never bad to have the future governor owe you a favor. And the money. A pension. A life after the *Courier*."

Lu shifted in her seat, scratched the back of her head. Three decades and she'd never written a story she couldn't stand by. And what had it gotten her? Nothing but thrown out on her ass with a month and a half of pay to show for it. And how was she going to pay the mortgage?

Lu stepped on her thoughts. She could hear the blood rushing through her ears again.

"What's the story?" she asked.

Kittredge pulled a sheaf of papers from the folder. She could see from across the desk that it was a police report, although it lacked the usual department letterhead. Must be one of the private files she'd seen a few times in her career, the ones not meant for eyes outside the Citadel, aka police HQ. Lu had had such files leaked from police sources in the past. These private reports were usually full of undistilled truth, or at least a close approximation of the truth. Not lies, not exactly, but the grinding wheel of facts against which a kind of truth could be milled. They were private. The victor always writes the history, she thought, and this was their source material.

"There's this baby, delivered in the projects, those slums on Kansas Street," Kittredge said. "This kid has an, um, *complicated* lineage. Very complicated. So anyway, the kid was delivered by city medics in the apartment, and things went poorly. The baby was deprived of oxygen, some shit, doctors say brain damage. Permanent disabilities. Lifetime care needed. Expensive stuff. This could be bad news for John O'Toole's political ambitions for three reasons. One, the mother, this Daisy Fontana, works in city hall, clerk's office, bit of a heroin problem. Links to some tough hombres in the Posse. Two, John O'Toole has been fucking Ms. Fontana's brains out for a couple years, until recently, and the baby is almost certainly his."

"And the third?"

"The third is the kicker. The medics didn't deliver the baby. Eamon Conroy did. He had this half-baked idea that having Daisy Fontana deliver at Memorial Hospital or Saint B's would attract unwanted attention, get wags asking too many questions. So he promised Daisy a home birth with a midwife, all costs covered, plied her with all kinds of stuff—appliances, furniture, promises of more than that. But the baby came early, the midwife they'd planned to use was instead down at this place on the Cape, drying out from an affection for Wild Turkey, and that left Conroy playing catcher, so to speak."

"Holy shit."

Kittredge nodded.

"*Shit* is right," he said. "But there's nothing holy about it. Conroy screwed things up, damn near killed the baby and Ms. Fontana. Her boyfriend, Rigo Mejia—you might remember him from some Posse court cases—couldn't take it, finally called 911. The resultant mess has simmered ever since. One of the medics on the call, Thomas Archer, has made some noise. Filed a few complaints. Conroy wants it gone. He thinks the best way to achieve that is to make this medic go away."

"Shit. Shit. Shit."

"We covered that already."

"Not that," Lu said. "Everyone knows O'Toole can't keep it in his pants. This medic they want me to go after, this guy Thomas Archer. Any chance he was drunk the night this happened?"

Kittredge shrugged.

"If you know him, and he's got a problem with the bottle, that would be a great angle to pursue," he said.

"I'm surprised Conroy hasn't taken care of this himself."

"It's a big year for those guys," Kittredge said. "They're trying to be discreet."

"Me and this Archer," Lu said. "We have a history."

"I know you've written about him before," Kittredge said. "Back when he and his partner testified at Conroy's trial, that other civil case he was in. So what? This will just be more of the same."

She shook her head.

"It's more than that. It's a little painful. We grew up in the same neighborhood. His mother and my father had a, um, brief relationship. Didn't end well for either family."

Kittredge smiled, held his arms out wide.

"Then this will be perfect," he said. "Maybe it's time to settle some old scores of your own. I feel your pain. I'm part of this, too. I'm going to edit these pieces personally, to make sure they get through the desk intact the way we want them."

Lu had trouble thinking. The sound of the blood rushing in her own ears deafened her.

"What makes you trust me with this?" she said. "I could go to Galloway's office right now and tell him what you're planning. Maybe I'd end up with your job."

"Because I know you, Lu. You're pragmatic. You're no crusader. How many years you spend in those courtrooms, or talking to cops, or breaking bread with gangbangers and wiseguys? This isn't something I'd take to an idealist. But you. You live in the real world. So do I."

Kittredge picked up the folder, waved it in front of her.

"I'm not worried that you'll go to Galloway, try to get me fired," Kittredge said. "I'm worried you'll turn me down and you'll be nowhere, bureau mate. You want to try and make money as a freelancer, go ahead. Have fun bagging groceries to put gas in your car, or telling Dan Junior he's done at BC, time to come home, night classes at the adult-ed center, maybe begin his long career in landscaping."

Lu tried to connect dots she couldn't see, like they were painted in invisible ink on a path that led to the mayor's right-hand man. The connection was thin. Hair thin. Until it hit her with a bright white clarity.

"What's your cut?" she asked. By the shrug and the way Kittredge dropped into his chair, Lu knew it was good, probably bigger than hers.

"I'm being taken care of from a separate account. Plus, you won't be the only one with a job when this is said and done, although mine will likely be in Boston, under the gold dome. Just because it's good for me doesn't mean it isn't also good for you."

She thought of Archer, her de facto stepbrother, although she'd moved out as soon as her father let Archer's mother move in during the divorce. Close but not close. Teammates in mutually assured family destruction. Archer, the screw-up. Unstable like his old man, who remained famous on the East

Side for what he'd done to the McCarthy Thunderbird all those years ago.

But how surprised could she really be? Archer's mother—Lu would never think of her as her stepmother, even after her father married her—didn't go off the rails until Lu came home from college, even before she got her first daily newspaper job at the *Courier*. She spent days on the living room couch, drinking cheap wine, sleeping and crying and talking to herself. Lu kept her distance from this woman she barely knew, didn't want to know. She saw Archer at holidays when she couldn't avoid it, the silence between them so loud her ears rang.

She knew that Archer, still in high school, fed and clothed himself, lived for weeks off a few hundred bucks tossed on the kitchen table each month by her father, who himself would disappear for days at a time.

But Archer was an adult now, and he'd made his mistakes. Lu figured he was old enough to know how to handle himself. She'd even heard about Archer's son and the brain tumors from her father, wondered if that had set Archer off.

"I'll need to meet with Conroy," she said, "before I promise anything."

Kittredge smiled. "That's exactly what Eamon thought you'd say."

3

THIN CLOUDS STRETCHED themselves across the blue sky above city hall, and the flags in the arc of poles beneath the front portico snapped in a hot July cross breeze that smelled of heat and damp concrete and diesel exhaust. A grand half-moon of marble steps led from Main Street into the grand entrance of the aging building, palace to municipal graces. It was a big day in this hill-straddled central Massachusetts city. Even the food trucks out back had closed for the morning.

Mayor John O'Toole looked out on the scene from his fifth-floor office and tried to enjoy the view. They were here for him, after all. But the text that had appeared on his phone an hour ago spoiled the view.

He read the message from Daisy again:

Money too tight. Miguel too sick. You won't return my calls. What am I supposed to do?

O'Toole asked himself again, what would his father have done?

In a city as small as Worcester, it was hard to be related to a legend like the first Mayor O'Toole—the late, great Eddie O'Toole. John O'Toole had wanted to make his own path here, but it had proven difficult. That was the dual nature of shadows, the young mayor thought. Great places to hide, not great places in which to live.

Eddie O'Toole had loved this city, learned to love it digging ditches for Commonwealth Gas when his own father, Orion O'Toole, was its president. Eddie O'Toole liked to tell his son he'd seen the city from the inside out. He used the money he earned rummaging below its streets to pay for his education at Salve Mater College, whose red-brick buildings glowed orange today on the sides facing the morning sun, in the ring of hills that rose high above downtown, the hills upon which the city was built. John O'Toole had gone there too, his being one of the last classes where the Franciscan brothers taught nearly every course.

John had learned important lessons from his father, from the way they sat in a middle pew at Mount Carmel's Sunday Mass, so as not to put on airs, to the basket they donated to the Orphan Mission on Mattson Street every Thanksgiving and Easter. Young John O'Toole thought he must be part of the world's largest family the way people on the street, at the butcher's, at the Riverside, everywhere greeted Eddie O'Toole as long-lost kin, some of them hailing and waving hats from passing streetcars. Those were long gone now too. And his father's agile memory—John O'Toole had always marveled at that, the way Eddie O'Toole knew everyone's name, asked about sick mothers and little sisters and fathers and brothers, like all he did all day was memorize the names and personal histories of every city resident.

Some lessons John O'Toole had learned were ones his father never realized he was teaching. Power was a great thing, an important thing, but only if you knew enough to use it. The elder O'Toole wielded it inefficiently, John believed. He was all velvet gloves and sweet talk. When Eddie O'Toole had a chance to finish off his opponent, he always stopped short.

Once, when John O'Toole was eleven, a city councilor called his father out publicly for closing a city pool in Morningdale. The neighborhood had once been a haven for French Canadian workers from Montreal who'd kept the optics plant on Southside Street humming through the Depression and two world wars and well into the sixties. With the death of the plant, the workers left, the vast complex of apartment buildings where they lived turning into public housing for the city's recent arrivals from Puerto Rico and the Dominican Republic.

The pool at Morningdale was decrepit. Eddie O'Toole wanted to close it as a way to extract federal money to replace it on the same plot of city land. Eddie had maneuvered unseen for months to get the money, knew that the surest way to kill the largess of the urban-renewal folks was to talk about their work openly, expose how the money flowed into the city in brackish streams. Their reticence was an opportunity for O'Toole's opponents, who caught wind of the plans to close the pool and chastised the mayor in the *Courier* as a racist. The city councilor who called Eddie O'Toole out knew all this, but he also planned to run for mayor in the next election.

The morning the article appeared in the paper, John O'Toole ate his oatmeal and watched his father read, a thin smile on his face. The mayor's wife refilled her husband's coffee, placed a hand on his shoulder.

"It isn't fair," she said.

"Never mind this stuff, Bridgit," Eddie O'Toole said. "Grace compels me to take a beating once in a while.

Williamson isn't a bad guy; he just wants my job too much."
Eddie looked at his son, winked. "Maybe I should let him
have it."

Eddie O'Toole never exacted vengeance on his enemies;
he took care of everyone but his own. Everyone but himself.
John O'Toole had been careful not to make that mistake.
John O'Toole had the foundational tricks down, could
remember the names of the supplicants who came to him
daily in need—potholes they wanted fixed, jobs they wanted
found for wayward sons, traffic lights they'd like to see
installed, the million little pieces of lead that underwent an
alchemy on the first Tuesday in November every four years,
ground to powder not by mortar and pestle but by the gravitational force of favors that needed repaying, to be turned
into something better than gold, turned into the one thing a
man like him craved more than anything. They turned, of
course, into votes.

O'Toole the younger kept the books, and not just on
those who owed him but also on people he owed, those
who'd voted against him on the city council, who'd held up
money or delayed pet projects, the names of people who
should have known better than to not appear on the list of
O'Toole campaign donors. Even John O'Toole's father in
all his benevolence had understood that mercy had its place
in the pews of Mount Carmel on a Sunday morning but not
in city hall.

The current Mayor O'Toole knew he had the tools, ones
even his father hadn't possessed. A strong, dimpled chin that
the hired guns who ran his campaigns loved to feature on
billboard ads whose local reach the internet had still not
found a way to surpass. Square shoulders. Hair thick black
with just the right amount of gray at the temples. Blue eyes
that embraced the targets of his attention. He had the gift of

gab. He had been born to pontificate. His driving desire in life was to be voted for. It was, after all, the family business.

This morning he stood in his office's big bay window looking down on the news trucks and the gaggle of press below, laughing at their discomfort at the panhandlers working the crowd. Eddie O'Toole would have sent someone down to move them along. The elder O'Toole loved the press. John O'Toole, he loved what the press could do for him.

John heard a door open behind him.

"We're just about ready," a man's voice reported.

Eamon Conroy dropped the morning *Courier* on O'Toole's desk and began peeling an orange. O'Toole pointed to the crowd below.

"She sent me another text this morning," O'Toole said.

Two park-bench drunks had discovered one of the television trucks. A blond reporter—*what's her name?* O'Toole wondered; *remind myself to give her the first question*—pretended to take intense interest in the crowd around her, which let her look over heads without making eye contact. The two drunks flanked the reporter as if waiting to be interviewed.

"How many for the week?" Conroy asked.

"Twenty. Not counting voice mail. You're supposed to be taking care of this."

"The furniture people are on their way today. A Viking range. Liebherr fridge. Top-of-the-line stuff. All with PAC money, under the table. No one will ever know."

"One thing my father never would have done. Gotten into bed with a junkie."

Conroy shrugged. "How were you to know? She's an undeniable beauty."

"Forty years in this office, a legend, defender of the masses—all that horseshit and yet my father never once attracted a crowd like this," O'Toole said.

"He never ran for governor," Conroy said. "Attracts a different kind of fervor."

O'Toole straightened his tie. "You know what governors become?" he said. He looked over to ensure the office door was closed. "They become president. That's why there's crowds. It's the first time the sycophants smell blood in the water."

John O'Toole, busy eclipsing his father, knew he was at the start of a long ascent that could lead, well, anywhere. He'd worked favors, sprung Eamon Conroy from jail, had him spend a couple years cleaning up loose ends.

Some of those problems walked off from downtown dives like Hoagies or the Cash Club and reappeared as bodies on the side of I-495 in Marlboro, or in Douglas State Forest, or just disappeared. Out for a smoke some Saturday night or walking their dogs in one of the neighborhoods overlooking Great Brook Valley and then, gone, John O'Toole's secrets with them.

The dirty money had been laundered. The laundered money sent away, only to come back even cleaner for the absence. PACs and super PACs and secret committees within secret committees. The money flowed through the campaign like a remote forest river in which the mayor slaked his thirst. Money enough to buy his way out of any problem. Almost.

"About that last thing?" O'Toole said. "Our ambulance-driving friend? I loved the quotes McCarthy wrote for me in the last couple articles, but I don't think we're there yet."

Conroy shrugged.

"We're on it," he said. "I'll check with her tonight. I don't think there'll be a problem wrapping this thing up before the summer's out. McCarthy's motivated. Got a kid at BC. Husband cleaned out their bank account, took off with his secretary. She'll need the money soon enough."

"That's what you said when we started," O'Toole said. He sat in the red leather chair by the window, massaged his temples, his eye still on the television reporter below. "I'd thought this medic would get the message by now, but his complaint is still on file with the city. God knows who else he's reached out to. The *Courier* would never run the story, but we're about to have to deal with the Boston papers, the television idiots, the goddamn bloggers. They won't hesitate. Are you sure we can't just pay the guy to take the heat?"

"We've gone over this," Conroy said. "I know this kid, from before. You need balls to take a bribe, and he doesn't have them. Your exposure is limited as long as Daisy keeps quiet, and that's as easy as keeping her flush with cash, stuff, and dope. No problem there. Rigo's playing ball. He thinks we'll owe the Posse a favor for this. He'll want to cash that one in some day, but that's not a problem now."

"We may have to revisit your original idea later," O'Toole said. He pointed an imaginary gun to his head, mimed pulling the trigger.

"Killing Archer? No longer an option. He's been in the paper. He's starting to become a thing for the local wags to piss and moan about. Archer becomes a body, people are going to ask. People who aren't on the payroll. People who could make our lives difficult."

O'Toole nodded. A knock at the office door. O'Toole's secretary poked her head in. "They're ready for you downstairs, Mr. Mayor."

"Thank you, Nancy."

"The state party people would like a moment with you before you go on," she said. "They're in the lobby."

"I'll talk to them, thanks."

O'Toole's walk down the marble-floored halls and marble-footed staircase inside was a victory lap. City workers emerged from their dens and warrens to shake O'Toole's hand, tell him how proud his father would have been.

Daisy Fontana emerged from the city clerk's office with the rest of them, hands folded behind her back. While he walked, O'Toole looked at foreheads, an old trick, eye contact without actual contact. He couldn't stop himself when he got to Daisy. O'Toole looked into her eyes. She stared at his chin, and then he was gone.

In the lobby O'Toole embraced state party chairwoman Shona Eclair, and they spoke about what high hopes they had for his candidacy. O'Toole strolled into the sunny day canopied by bright blue sky and the smells of the city wafted up to him and he thought of it instantly as his own city. He'd never loved the place the way his father had, but today he waved in genuine magnanimity.

This city had been a burden on John O'Toole, a mantle he'd inherited by divine right. Until now. Looking out over the throng and hearing the drone of news choppers circling overhead and the way the faces below looked up at him in supplication, love even, he was caught up in the moment and he felt a sting in his eyes, like pool water, but he knew it was because for the first time, he felt a little of what his father had for this broken-down relic of a city, an industrial corpse waiting so long to be brought back to life.

He stepped to the microphone and banished thoughts of his father. This was a new day. He was a force of disruption. Governor O'Toole. He liked the sound of that, thought he'd be willing to do all sorts of things to make it happen.

O'Toole opened his mouth to speak. He made eye contact with the blond reporter. They had a moment. O'Toole decided to give her more than just the first question. He moved to speak and a round of applause broke out, along with cheers and shouts of his name.

He raised a hand to the crowd. It got louder. He waved a hand again. A woman on the left edge of the crowd raised her shirt. The drunks clapped. Even the panhandlers stopped their appeals. It was a crowd filled with love. They would follow him, wanted what he wanted.

"Thank you, please, thank you, this is really great," O'Toole said. "Thank you everyone, from the bottom of my heart. I can't—I have a hard time—it's just really super, this welcome."

The crowd cheered even louder. O'Toole looked at the blond reporter, winked, and stared into her station's camera.

"My name is John O'Toole," he said. "And I want to be your governor."

4

H E COULDN'T BEAR to kill the dogs.

They'd been Charlotte's more than his, though he loved them in ways he could never love a human. When Knak put the pistol barrel to Deirdre's head, she fled. Giggles looked at him with disinterest. Both reactions erased what little willpower he possessed, and instead he packed them in the Corolla and drove in the late-morning sun to Drumbeck Park and let them loose. He hoped that by the time they got picked up and people put it together, what Knak had to do that day would be done and someone would give them a new home.

It wasn't a great plan, but that was the thing about plans. Time was a commodity, time was better than money, and until the visit this morning, Knak had thought he had plenty to go around. The organization knew there was a plan, knew Knak was ready to go. He'd meant to give them warning. He knew when he got going the group could be exposed. They'd need time to prepare, melt further into the woods, but time had run out.

He'd been covert about the other things. It had been a few days since he last fired his rifle, then gone about the business of circumspection and lying low. Maybe the neighbors wondered about the gunshots in the woods behind their properties, but this was Monticello. Guns went off in the woods all the time, their reports barely registering over the hum of the central air conditioning.

In the end, it was Knak's own fault. He'd been rash, putting that sign up on his front yard, right there on the county road. He couldn't have been surprised when they showed up, he knew. The real surprise was how long it had taken them.

A roadside marquee, lit bright yellow at night, Knak's sign carried two simple three-word messages:

Fuck the IRS

Don't Pay Taxes

The sign had seemed like a good idea. Three AM and a case of Busch in him, Knak wheeled the thing out from his garage, ran an extension cord to it, lit his words up for the world to see. Charlotte would have approved. Knak with his God-shaped hole, but it was Charlotte who filled him, who'd told him about the Jews and the Federal Reserve, how they'd faked the Holocaust and paid for the chemtrails in the sky above that the government used to poison them, about the mind-control experiments on television and how Hurricane Katrina was a test of some awful machine, that they'd weaponized *weather*, for God's sake. It was Charlotte who'd vouched for him to her father, Avis Locke. And it was Avis Locke who'd set him down the path that led him to today. To the dogs. To what he was about to do to his entire life.

When she told Knak about the black helicopters and then a National Guard Blackhawk just happened to rattle by a couple thousand feet in the sky above, Knak thought the government must have planted wires right inside their heads.

The local cops came first, but they knew Gerry Knak from way back. He'd always been the troubled kid. Smoking, drinking, drugs. He tried them all before anyone else in his grade. There were the summer car chases around Bronze Lake, Knak in his rusty Ford pickup missing its tailgate, the town police department's sole cruiser—a wheezy Chevy Malibu—hot on his tail. It was pointless. Everyone in Monticello knew everyone else. The cops dumped Knak's beer when they caught him, threatened to tell his mother.

Chief Kopeck had first busted Knak in Monticello State Forest years ago, when he was a rookie and Knak made pipe bombs and drank cases of Old Milwaukee stolen from the A&P, where he worked as a bagger. Knak howled at the moon and lit bonfires so big the treetop glow could be seen at town hall.

Kopeck and the older cops had watched Knak through his drunk and wild youth, during his years running the pool installation business, and had their eye on him now as an angry misanthrope grieving the death of his wife.

Local cops shared stories of Knak's new venture, begun two or three years ago, the filing of dozens of civil lawsuits that panned the district and federal courts in Worcester for illusory gold. Town clerks all over central Massachusetts reported an intense man in a baggy brown suit demanding access to land records, fee schedules, zoning board applications. A pattern emerged. Anyone doing business with the federal government in central Massachusetts could expect a lawsuit from Gerry Knak. When he expanded into filing bogus claims on the deeds to strangers' homes, he began attracting attention.

This was the worst version of Knak, the old-timers agreed. Like a child with a gun. He had the keys to the courts, and through them he had an eye into his neighbors, into anyone who did business covered by open records laws.

"Qui tam," was all he'd say when asked by skeptical courthouse clerks.

After the sign appeared, Monticello cops passed Knak's house more frequently. When he went to the store, a Monticello cruiser inevitably appeared. The anxiety was palpable. Knak made them nervous. He scoffed at the surveillance. He'd known the town cops forever, had gone to school with the parents of the new guys. It was entertaining, a diversion.

When the IRS arrived, Knak stopped laughing.

They'd knocked on his front door early this morning, two men in their forties, one tall and fit, the other medium height, a bit doughy. They wore matching navy-blue suits and had bad haircuts, though Knak judged they weren't accountants, not with the bulge each had under the left arm of his suit coat. A Town Land police cruiser sat at the end of the driveway, just in case, Knak figured.

"Gerald Knak?" said the short one. He held up a billfold with a government identification card and ornate gold Treasury agent badge. Knak studied both, saw that the shorter agent's name was Murdock. His partner stood back and said nothing and offered no identification.

"I got the First Amendment," Knak said.

"I'm Agent Murdock," the shorter one said, "and this is my colleague, Supervisory Agent Colfax. We just want to have a chat with you. Nothing official, nothing serious. But we'd love to take just a little bit of your time."

Colfax nodded, then spit into the grass on Knak's front lawn.

"About the sign, that's not illegal," Knak said.

"Just a few minutes, informal," Murdock said.

Knak nodded and led the pair behind his house to a small glass-walled pool house where he kept an office. He sat down at a glass-topped patio table on which sat a case of

Busch beer and a pistol, a Kimber .45 Les Baer model. Expensive. Not much different from what the two agents likely carried. Murdock sat down at one of the lawn chairs at the table, unbuttoned his suit coat, and crossed his legs. Colfax stepped into the room, saw the pistol, and backed out.

"Is that weapon loaded?" Colfax asked. Knak saw his right hand start to cross to his left, the fingertips stopping just inside the coat. Knak liked the way the room flooded with tension. It was why he had the pistol out in the first place, for unexpected visitors. Knak liked to keep people off-balance so that then they had something in common. Knak was always searching for sea legs he'd never quite found.

"In my house, it's not enough simply to *treat* every weapon as if it's loaded. Too trite. Too pat. If you want to bleed less in battle, sweat more in training, you know?"

"So, the weapon . . ." Colfax said.

"Hell yeah, it's loaded," Knak said.

Murdock spoke while Colfax picked up the pistol, dropped out the magazine, and racked the slide. A round sprung from the chamber and rolled along the floor. The agents exchanged glances.

"Does that seem like a wise practice?" Murdock asked. "Leaving loaded guns around?"

"Absolutely. Never had a single problem. But my neighbor found out, won't let his grandkids trick-or-treat here at Halloween anymore. Tried to report me to the police but got nowhere. That pistol there is one hundred percent legal."

Knak pulled a can of beer out of the box and offered one to each of the agents. They declined. He shrugged and popped one open and took a long swig.

Murdock went official, like he was reciting boilerplate at the end of a lottery commercial on the radio.

"Mr. Knak, we are indeed here about the sign," he said. "This interview is informational only. There are no charges being contemplated and there is no legal action in the offing. You're not under investigation, and we are not here in an official capacity. This is just an informal conversation. There will be no reading of Miranda rights, and while you won't need a lawyer, should you at any time feel so compelled, you have the right to end this interview at any time and we'll be on our way. There are, though, some concerns we have, beginning with some of your postings on certain websites, and definitely regarding the messages on your sign out there. Since you haven't seen fit to file a tax return in a decade, I was hoping our willingness to come speak to you in person would demonstrate goodwill. We feel you're inciting people to break the law."

Knak drained the first can of beer, placed it on the floor, and stomped it flat.

"Maybe some laws deserve to be broken," Knak said.

Colfax stood in the open doorway, one foot out on the small concrete patio and his right hand resting on his belt buckle. Murdock sat across from Knak, hunched forward and staring at the man across from him as if seeking in the eyes of a cat some hint of a soul. Knak opened a second can of beer.

"It's not just that," Murdock said. "The things you propose. Vandalism. Bombings. You can see our concern."

"I don't tell anyone to break the law," Knak said. "But I spend a lot of time in courts—not in trouble, but cleaning up other people's messes. People steal from the government all the time. I mean, what is an income tax? What is any tax? I've got nothing against the government, but I just think we need to think about what we're doing when we write these checks. That's *our* money you people can't seem to keep other people from stealing."

"It is an imperfect system," Murdock said. He picked lint off a shirt collar, checked out the office with sideways glances that Knak didn't miss.

"Where were you in '08?" Knak asked.

"Topeka," Murdock said. "Investigating bank fraud."

Colfax said nothing. Knak beamed.

"Bank fraud," he said. "In Topeka? And how many people went to jail from your efforts?"

"You're right," Murdock said. "No one."

"No one!" Knak said. "And that weren't just in Topeka. That was everywhere. Entire world economy shattered by a few assholes who played the system like the craps table at Foxwoods, and you fucking guys couldn't—or wouldn't—put a single one of them away. Meanwhile, what's happening to the rest of us? Losing our houses, losing our jobs. And what did you do? You made it worse! Handed these nitwit bankers billions of dollars, like a long-lost aunt sending a birthday card with a twenty inside. 'Don't spend it all in one place, honey.' So they didn't. They didn't spend a dime. They just whacked it up between them. Spit in the face of hard-working Americans. Took all that tax money, treated it like a lottery winning. Makes me sick."

"It was a difficult time, but no excuse for inflammatories," Murdock said. "Your online posts on all those websites. We monitor them, obviously. We're concerned that you might be thinking of something a little more . . . *involved* . . . than simply civil disobedience."

"Some folks will tell you that the income tax itself is illegal," Knak said. "See, I don't agree. I mean, someone's got to pay to keep the country safe, stop our enemies from coming to take what's ours. But what happens when the enemy is us? What happens when the whole fucking thing becomes a, what, a pyramid scheme? Like Albania. Remember what happened there?"

"I'm afraid I don't," Murdock said. Colfax was looking out at the backyard, probably planning the eventual raid, Knak thought.

"The whole economy became a pyramid scheme. I mean, the whole fucking thing," Knak said. "Everyone had their money tied up in each other's investments in shit that had no value. Like a national lottery. Whole thing collapsed overnight. Entire economy, *poof*, gone. No one had anything. And you know why?"

Murdock shook his head.

"Because no one was minding the store. Albanian government didn't keep track of its money until it was all gone. Then they cared. They cared a lot. And now it's happening here. You ought to spend a day in the courts with me. You guys are getting ripped off at every turn."

"We appreciate that, Mr. Knak," Murdock said, "but you can see our problem, right? What if people started to take your advice? When you suggest violence against IRS facilities, when you post pictures of agents' personal vehicles on those websites, give out their home addresses? Are we supposed to just hope and pray that no one listens? Surely you don't want blood on your hands."

"I am a messenger. I'm not the message. I read a lot about this stuff, probably more than you. You guys must have gone to college, right? I didn't. Self-taught. But it's not that hard. Stuff's all out there. John Stuart Mill, he said I have the right to say anything I want, no matter what, as long as it's, what, my *ethical* conviction. I do that, no one can say shit. I got that."

Murdock nodded.

"This isn't just yelling 'fire' in a movie theater," Murdock said. "We have a duty to ensure not only that laws are obeyed but that our colleagues and buildings remain safe."

"I got my civil disobedience."

"And I've got my marching orders," Murdock said, then stood. "So while this is not an official request, Agent Colfax and I would ask, all due respect and off the record, that you reconsider the messages you put on that sign, and we're going to have to insist you immediately cease your online campaign against the agency and its employees. Trust me, it's for the best. Maybe, and I'm spitballing here, take the sign down altogether and, I don't know, just shut the fuck up and enjoy the scenic beauty that surrounds you. Don't spend so much time online, unless you want us back here. We don't mind driving all the way out here from Boston. I mean, it's beautiful here, right, Agent Colfax?"

"Indeed," Colfax said.

"Indeed," Murdock repeated.

Knak took another swig of his beer.

"I might think about it," he said.

"That would be great," Murdock said. "Because, and I'm off the record here, but next time? Next time we don't knock, there's more than two of us, and things won't go so well for you. Believe me."

"I said I would think about it, but I make no promises," Knak said. "If you investigated how your bosses in DC waste the money you collect, you might be a little hesitant to pay your share too."

"Understood," Murdock said. "I was hoping for an understanding here today."

"I understand a lot of things," Knak said. "I understand more than you know."

After they left, Knak paced around the small oval pool in his backyard. Was he ready? He'd been planning, thinking, not sure if it would ever come down to it, contingency planning taken to its extreme, the worst-case scenario presenting itself to him, at his feet. Question was, did he have the guts? Question was, did he love Charlotte enough? The feds were coming. They would find the guns, the maps, draft after draft of the plan and militia documents, all of it written in his small, tight handwriting.

Knak went to the shed, opened a hidden panel behind the Weedwacker and long-handled pool net, took out the worn Navy seabag stashed in there. He laid out its contents on the shed floor, checked the pistols and the rifle, counted bullets, MREs, the camp stove, and freeze-dried pork and beans, his favorite. Knak repacked the bag and put it in the back of his van, under some tarps.

He knew time was short. He cursed his boldness, his loathings working at cross-purposes, it seemed. But then it was all probably for the best. The IRS and whoever else wanted a piece of Gerald Knak would be back tomorrow or the next day or next week, in force and with warrants. He needed to act quickly. That's what Charlotte would have wanted. Quick action. Decisive.

Knak gathered up what he thought he needed from the house. *Don't forget anything*, he told himself, because once the door on this ratty house in the middle of nowhere was closed, it was all gone. A new life just beginning. Knak didn't imagine it would last long. But he was beyond that now, beyond giving a shit, beyond satisfying anything but his need for—what? Revenge? No. Not just revenge. Justice? Perhaps.

Mostly he just wanted to close the loop, make Thomas Archer account for himself, for the way he had let Charlotte down. To pay. If the federal government forced his hand, so be it. Knak wasn't afraid of the consequences. He was afraid of living another day like this, like some Dark Ages monk plotting revenge he would never take against Vikings who'd burned his library and plundered his chapel.

He wanted to shed his skin. He was fifty-eight. Friendless. Childless. The one person with whom he could stand sharing so much as a single day of his life, Charlotte, gone. He wasn't lonely. He was beyond such a simple idea, because loneliness suggested loss, suggested an unwanted emotion you might try to correct. Never again, Knak knew. It was him now. Just him, Gerry Knak.

He made piles of clothes and mail and junk in each room. Family photos and Charlotte's wedding dress stacked high in the main living room. Two dog beds.

Once more he retreated to the living room, the furniture piled in a tall mound in the middle of the room. He'd torn the drapes down from the windows and topped the mound with them and the rolled-up Persian rug Charlotte had insisted they buy three summers ago at the Brimfield Flea Market. Knak sat cross-legged on the floor and spread the *Courier* out before him. He read the article for the last time, his heart pulsing with the recognition of a mission. Knak recognized the byline, Lu McCarthy, from her coverage of his aborted attempt to sue the city for Charlotte's death. He'd never forget the name tag on the medic who treated her: *T. Archer.* Knak couldn't name with exactitude what it was Archer had done to her, only that he was the one who'd done it, or failed to do it, or just let it happen. McCarthy's name on the story cemented it for him. Charlotte couldn't be the only patient Archer had hurt over the years.

City officials continue to probe the botched childbirth in a South of Main tenement last winter that left an infant boy with severe brain damage from lack of oxygen.

Every time he read it, Knak considered the opening paragraph like the early notes of a Wagnerian opera, perhaps something from the Ring Cycle, Charlotte's favorite. It was one of the reasons he loved her, the way her life orbited like a melancholic planet in a galaxy so epic, her entire being seemed an existential statement. Charlotte was bigger than the parts she comprised. Everything about her—about them—demanded more, required a cosmic energy that she absorbed like new black asphalt on a summer day.

He remembered the first time she'd played it in their house. The yellow globes in the dining room chandelier cast a light that soaked up every molecule in the room, made Charlotte's eyes disappear behind the white opacity of her eyeglass lenses while she sat, head tilted toward the chandelier, toward the yellow light, not moving a muscle for hours. He found overwhelming beauty in the sheer inaccessibility of it.

City Hall sources, who spoke on condition of anonymity because they weren't officially cleared to speak on the matter, hinted that the actions of city night shift paramedic Thomas Archer, 39, in the early morning of Feb. 17 led to the permanent, debilitating injuries suffered by Miguel Fontana, infant son of Daisy Fontana, 26, a clerk in the city assessor's office. Mr. Archer has filed an ethics complaint alleging misconduct at the scene prior to his arrival, but the exact complaint remains sealed with the Ethics Commission and details were unavailable.

McCarthy had been writing a lot about this baby, but it wasn't until the last couple of weeks, when her stories began talking about Archer, that Knak had started paying attention. It wasn't until he'd seen the name in the paper again that he had realized what it was all for, all the hours training, shooting at the range, camping alone in Maine during the harsh winter with no food, no water, forcing himself to live off the land, finding in the hardship a discipline he'd never known; it wasn't until he'd seen once again the name *Thomas Archer* that Knak had understood that Locke had been right all along. The purpose sometimes finds the man.

The IRS agents would be back, tear his house apart, find his supplies. He'd known what to do. He'd known how it would all end, but Knak lacked a spark. Seeing Archer's name in the paper had brought it back. Most of all it reminded him that so much time had passed since Charlotte's death. She was a woman of action. She'd want something to be done, a brick thrown into the plate-glass window that was the system.

The path was clear.

The destruction she demanded would first cleanse the pain of her loss; then he'd avenge her and with it move the cause forward.

Knak rolled the newspaper up and tossed it on the pile.

Back in the shed, he grabbed a ten-gallon plastic jug of gasoline and returned to the house. He soaked walls and floors and tossed piles of oil-soaked rags from his workbench and piles of newspaper into every room, then walked to the front door and lit a rag with a lighter, tossed it into the largest pile of tinder he'd made, watched the chiffon on the wedding dress flare and sputter, and closed the door. A ball of flame blew out the bay window when the back wheels of Knak's van flung pebbles and dirt as he peeled away and off into the future.

5

DIFFERENT SHIFT, SAME debate: where to eat? Time was always short. This could be their only chance all night, and Archer didn't want it to slip away. Julio pitched the Bully, said it had character. He liked that the retired wiseguys ate there, with their pinkie rings and flannel pants pulled up over their stomachs, primary-colored silk shirts tucked in tight. He loved how they spoke close and cupped each other's cheeks when they talked.

"I'm worn out on the Bully," Archer said. "Broke, too. Down to like ten bucks. Not really hungry anyway."

"C'mon, hombre. Who even reads the newspaper anymore?"

Archer shrugged.

"I do," he said. "Nothing worse than seeing your name in it every day."

"You know you can call me anytime, man. Always."

"I'm on the wagon," Archer said.

"I'm just saying. You're not alone."

"I appreciate it. Stop worrying. I've been going to meetings."

The dispatcher interrupted. She beckoned like a Bond villain hidden under a glacier and armed with a million dollars of radio equipment and a burning desire to destroy the world, or at least turn a quiet night into a nightmare. There was a priority at the Fine Arts Cinema, she said, lower Pleasant Street. Possible cardiac arrest.

Julio flipped on the ambulance's emergency lights and pulled into the heavy downtown traffic. Archer turned the radio to the local salsa station, blasted it. He hated the stuff, but Julio's drive, Julio's groove. When he was behind the wheel, it was 1980s hair metal. He liked the music itself, loved that it drove Julio crazy, even after a decade as partners.

"Fine Arts?" Julio asked.

"Isn't that the little theater place attached to Mechanics Hall? Probably filled with fifty doctors out for a night on the town. Nothing better than a code in front of a bunch of fucking dermatologists."

Julio gunned the ambulance down the main drag, pausing at red lights just long enough to check for cross traffic, then hard on the throttle again, the turbo-diesel growling in ecstatic mechanical protest.

"Didn't you work that wedding reception call at the Harwood House last summer?" Julio asked, laughing. He'd heard the story dozens of times, but it always made him laugh and he knew it got Archer going, no matter his partner's mood.

All those articles had left Archer in a foul mood all summer. There'd been so many of them. The baby on Kansas Street, the crazy ex-cop, the brain-damaged infant. Julio had begged Archer not to file a report. He hadn't listened. Soon after, the articles began appearing in the *Courier*. Medics had screwed up. One medic in particular. The mayor was involved. Thomas Archer's name had first appeared last week. Now it was in every article. Worst part, no one was allowed to talk. Not in public anyway. No matter the lies in the paper, Archer and Julio had to take it.

No medic liked being noticed like that, good or bad. And the articles had been bad. No doubt Julio thought a little anger might be good for Archer. He didn't believe in brooding. To Julio, work was a way out of pain, not a trail of bread crumbs into some dark forest.

Archer believed in things too. Lately those truths seemed built on foundations of sand. He'd once believed being good at the job would be enough. That the universe rewarded competence, diligence, a clean heart. But he knew now: he'd been wrong about most of it the entire time.

"Entire wedding party, family, probably the flower girls, all docs, all from Mass General or somewhere like that," Archer said. "Everyone was in tuxes or green satin dresses trying to do CPR on the bandleader, like a bunch of monkeys fucking a football. Why can't I ever just get a wedding full of plumbers or stockbrokers or something like that?"

Julio slammed on the brakes, nearly rear-ended a Subaru at Main and Front. He slashed the ambulance into the left lane, hit the air horn, full throttle then past the car before jerking the ambulance back to the right. Archer gave the driver the finger as they passed—no passion to it, no anger, didn't even look at the car. Just *here's the finger so I know that you know that we know that you drive like shit.*

"It was like a Harvard Medical School reunion," Archer continued. " 'Hi, Biff McBiff here, class of '91. Have you considered epinephrine?' Walk in the door and—bam—twenty assholes telling us to do twenty different things at once—" *Brakes, swerve, air horn, finger.* "Nightmare. I thought Knuckles was going to kill someone."

That was the worst part of calls like that, Archer thought. Fighting to get to the sick. So many people wanted to help, or perhaps better, wanted there to be no sickness in the first place. No matter, physician or not, sometimes emergencies hit too close to home. Archer was sympathetic to the impulse, even if he couldn't understand why, like at last night's shooting on Prescott Street. The people screaming at you to help their loved ones also so often felt the need to punch and kick and spit. They fought you, Archer believed, because you were the only thing left in front of them, the only place they could dispatch their despair in the early moments of what, for some of them, would become lifelong pain.

Julio turned the ambulance onto Pleasant Street.

He counted street numbers out loud as the truck rolled to a slow stop. "Fifty-five. Sixty-seven. Eighty-one. Eighty-seven."

Julio stopped the ambulance. The road ahead was steep and dark and potholed. Alleys ran off both sides, their wet brick walls reflecting the ambulance's pulsing strobes. The three closest street lights were blown, and five further up the slope cast pale and weak yellow pyramids on patches of wet pavement and small mounds of garbage that steamed in the dewy air. They surveyed their destination.

"This . . ." Julio said. "This ain't the opera house."

The ambulance lights sparkled against the glass facade of the Fine Arts Cinema. The street and its buildings had once been home to thriving dry goods concerns, or wool merchants, or mercantile exchanges—Archer squinted to read the lettering in worn paint on the nearest: *Woods & Sons Inc.—Finest Masonry Around Since 1906.*

The plate-glass windows bore handwritten advertisements etched in dried soap. Smudged fliers stuck to the building's brick. The marquee above the narrow front door into the theater advertised today's features: *Wicked, Wicked West, Home on the Ranger,* and *GoodFellatios.* One bit of dried-soap-on-glass bragged that the store also stocked *Massachusetts's largest selection of adult toys, tools and mechanical necessities.*

"You're shitting me," Archer said.

"Mechanical necessities?" Julio asked.

Through the glass, the medics could see a handful of route cops standing in the middle of the store. Their body language—hands on hips, surveying the store in broad turns of their torsos, their feet planted while they leaned and twisted—said it all. This was bullshit. No hearts had stopped beating in the Fine Arts Cinema tonight.

Inside, the lobby was sheer sex, or a simulacrum of sex, a feast of flesh and leather splayed on video boxes, magazine racks, and full-size cardboard cutouts. Julio picked up a DVD from a nearby display and held it up to Archer with a shrug. The cover featured five bald women in overalls reclining on hay bales.

"Put that shit back," Archer whispered.

Julio grabbed another, held it up toward Archer, smiling. Three human forms wrapped around each other, their bodies covered from head to toe in black leather. One wore a nurse's cap and stethoscope. Archer shook his head, smiled, gave his partner the finger.

They climbed a narrow staircase hidden in the near wall behind a display of studded collars and DVDs with German titles. At the top of the stairs, a chest-high wall overlooked a sunken movie theater, its seats sparsely filled with patrons, their heads shifting in the flickering projector light.

In the movie, two women in elaborate Native American headdresses and a man dressed like a cowboy made small talk.

"Are you a *real* cowboy?" one of the women asked. The cowboy dropped his pants. Drums began beating.

Along the short wall stood a half-dozen men peering into the darkness, scanning the seats below.

"Who are these guys?" Julio asked.

"We make sure everyone uses words, not hands," one of the men said.

"Can you get them to turn up the lights?" Archer asked.

"Above my pay grade," the man said.

They walked through an opening in the wall and down to the third row from the screen. Archer saw a pile of clothes strewn around a seat in the middle of the aisle.

Archer turned on his flashlight. A naked man sat in the seat, staring at a point below the screen, his head nodding in answer to a question no one was asking. He had a tattoo of Yosemite Sam on his left arm and some illegible, ornate script on his neck. Archer knelt down to check the man's pulse and felt warm liquid soak his knee.

"Hey, is that puke?" Julio asked, peering over Archer's shoulder, his own small flashlight illuminating a chunky brown puddle on the floor.

"Damn it," Archer said.

The naked guy's pulse was strong and regular. His nostrils flared when Archer waved a penlight into his eyes. The familiar sweet tang of vomited alcohol settled in Archer's nostrils. There was a puddle of vomit on the floor, on the man's muscled chest, a brown smear of it in his black-haired ponytail. Archer took a quick blood pressure and announced his diagnosis.

"Night's first drunk," he said.

"I can smell that from here," Julio replied.

"Hey, buddy, you okay?" Archer asked, shaking the naked guy, gently at first and then harder. "C'mon, you okay?"

The drunk turned his head and looked into Archer's eyes, and Archer let go of his arm. Archer knew the look.

He'd been a paramedic long enough to recognize that specific type of glare and where it came from.

"You see a jail ID anywhere over there?" Archer asked Julio. Julio rifled through the man's pants, pulled out a sheaf of papers and handed them to Archer. County House of Corrections. Angelo Rinaldo. Out less than twelve hours.

The pounding soundtrack transformed into a fusion of disco and war drums. Archer glanced up at the screen and saw a school-bus-sized penis jackhammering from left to right on the screen, disappearing into and out of a vagina as big as the Ted Williams Tunnel. He turned his attention back to his patient.

"Grab the stair chair," Archer said. "Let's get out of here."

Julio stood in the aisle, staring skyward at the screen.

"Dude, you know what a vagina looks like when it's thirty feet tall?" Julio said. "Scary, *papi*."

Julio wrestled with the chair, and Archer straightened and shined his flashlight around the nearby seats. Abundance of caution. Index of suspicion. He knew the man in the seat was simply drunk, but Archer wanted to hear what witnesses had to say. He was afraid of missing something. It was a fear he carried often these days.

Archer illuminated an older couple two rows back, their silver hair shifting in spasms across their heads under the wan strobing of the projector's beam. The man wore a large silver wristwatch, the couple in matching golf shirts and windbreakers. They hunched down in their seats when Archer's beam found them.

"Excuse me, folks, did you see what happened here?"

Silence. Indian music thrumming, faster now.

"Folks?"

Nothing. Archer shined the beam on the man's face. The drums pulsed, beating, faster and faster, so loud now that Archer had to yell to be heard over it.

"Sir! Did you see anything!"

"We didn't see a damn thing!" the man yelled, raising his hands to his face. The woman next to him turned and pulled the collar of her Windbreaker over her face. "Turn off that light!"

The drums stopped. Archer turned off his light. The woman dropped the collar.

"You *are* a real cowboy," one of the women on-screen purred.

Angelo stood up, his fists balled.

"It. Is. Alive," Julio said.

"Are you Angelo Rinaldo?" Archer asked.

"Leave me the fuck alone," Angelo said. "Can't a man get some sleep?"

"You can't sleep here, Angelo," Archer said.

"I can sleep any-fucking-where I want."

Credits rolled across Angelo's bare chest and onto the movie screen above him. No one yelled for him to sit down. Angelo weaved and wavered, his hands still in fists, still ready for anything.

Julio pointed to the stair chair sitting in the aisle. "Angelo, sit down there."

"Why should I?"

"Because I asked nice."

"What if I don't want to?"

"You really want to go back to jail so soon after getting out?"

Angelo shrugged, then dropped to the chair. Archer let out a breath, thankful he wouldn't have to fight with Angelo. There would have been two medics in the scrum, but Angelo looked like trouble. Julio covered him with a sheet and secured him with the chair's two straps. Archer gathered the scattered clothes into a bunch and reached under the sheet to place the pile in Angelo's lap.

"You hold these," Archer said.

The movie continued. A Mafia motif had replaced the Native American setting, all violins and accordions instead of percussion instruments.

"Are you a *real* godfather?" one of the women asked. "Could you whack *me*?"

The Mafia don dropped his pants.

The two medics lifted the chair, Archer in back and Julio at Angelo's feet, now face-to-face with their patient as they prepared to descend the stairs.

"Hey, assholes," Angelo said halfway down, staring wide-eyed at Julio. "Listen to me."

"What?" Julio said.

"I'm gonna barf."

Looking down, Archer knew the staircase was too narrow. There was no room to maneuver left or right, and it was so steep that any rapid movement might send everyone toppling. Julio was trapped.

"Let's back up, to the top," Archer said. Julio nodded. They took a step.

Angelo smiled at Julio. "Sorry, bro." He vomited thick streams of brown liquid mixed with chunks of half-digested french fries, each expulsion landing on Julio's averted head and shoulders with a wet thud. They set the chair down and Julio rode out the storm. With each deluge, Julio cursed in both English and Spanish. Archer watched, helpless.

"Your buddy's pissed," Angelo said later, once he and Archer were alone in the back of the ambulance as it weaved and hopped and bumped to Saint B's hospital. Julio had cleaned up the best he could with a towel and a bottle of hydrogen peroxide, tossed his soaked uniform shirt in a plastic biohazard bag before climbing into the driver's seat.

"Can you blame him?"

"I couldn't help it. I got out of jail this morning, and the first thing I wanted to do was get drunk and look at some pussy."

"First step is always to envision your own success."

Angelo leaned over in the stretcher and took a look at the name tag Archer suddenly regretted wearing. "Could be worse, Arrrr-cher," Angelo said.

Angelo's half grin was framed below two eyes that drifted in opposite directions, caught, then wobbled back to center. Bags under his eyes, faded scars around his lips, rippled ear cartilage and a particular bend at the bridge of his nose—a boxer, Archer thought, or he used to be, now a white-trash pugilist at rest.

"What weight division were you?" Archer asked.

"I could be one of you guys," Angelo said. "That would be worse. That thing with the baby, been in all the papers. I feel sorry for *that* guy. That guy is in some deep shit."

Nausea hit Archer like a rogue wave, unseen and now here and threatening to capsize this little boat of his, bobbing on a vast ocean with no shore in sight.

"Why do you say that?" Archer asked.

Angelo grunted.

"That woman whose baby your guy killed or hurt or whatever?" he said. "Her brother's in the Posse. Way up. Shot caller. I was locked up with him. The Posse, they know his name, they got their orders. Whole crew's out here looking, starting tonight. They figure, after all that press, your boy's going to run. They're going to take care of business sooner rather than later, no doubt."

Archer's heart raced. He felt something—panic? He'd seen plenty of patients having panic attacks. Was this what panic felt like? The sudden realization that control was an illusion. Safety, too. It was like being trapped and set free to wolves all at once. He wanted to run. Didn't want to be around Angelo either. He noticed now the scars on his shoulder, his neck. Those were angular and thin keloid scars with thick folds of pink on top—knife wounds. Several silverdollar-sized bulges on Angelo's stomach—healed gunshot wounds. Archer noticed the ropiness of Angelo's forearms and the spider web tattoos on his elbows. He was coiled, and he was close.

"Think so?" Archer said.

"Shit, I find out who he is, I might take a shot myself," Angelo said. "No offense to you guys, but there's a lot to be gained by doing a favor for the Posse. I don't mind the messy stuff. I don't mind getting a little wet."

Archer watched a cloud pass over Angelo's face—pity, almost, for the unknown medic for whom the wolves already lay in wait. He was glad Angelo was too drunk to make the connection, to pull Archer's name from the recesses of his booze-soaked memory, see how easy it would be to do a favor for the Posse right here, right now.

"Welterweight," Angelo said.

Archer looked out the rear windows of the ambulance, looking for something or someone. On his days off, before he got married, before he had a son, before his son got sick, Archer had often succumbed to wanderlust and he'd drive for hours at a time, and the freedom was like honey on buttered toast. That was the only way he could describe it, as if driving down an unfamiliar country road could have a taste.

"What?" Archer said.

When he drove, he felt like the eagle that circled over the reservoir when Archer fished there, and he'd stop at random convenience stores and buy a soda and a candy bar and want to tell the clerk how good it felt to be alive and in a beat-up pickup truck with half a tank of gas.

"I boxed welterweight at the Ionic," Angelo said. "One-forty-seven on the dot. I could always make weight. All you got to do is stop eating for a couple days and drink lots of coffee and take all the caffeine pills you can find. No biggie."

Now the road was a place of fear, its cracked asphalt mottled by black tar patches like varicose veins, a road map to an end Archer couldn't divine, and worse, he couldn't put a name to his dread. This thing was new, announced by far-off drums. The thing he suspected was coming for him. He wasn't sure if he'd know it if he even saw it coming, then realized he wouldn't. He was open, a free country, just there for the taking.

6

2005

K NAK MET CHARLOTTE in the new courthouse, right after it opened. He sat in the cafeteria eating a stuffed pepper in the shadow of the ten-ton statue of Solomon. She wore a white cardigan sweater spotted with Dalmatians and a pince-nez on a beaded chain.

She dropped her tray on the table. Peeled a hard-boiled egg.

He asked her to pass the salt.

"It's bad for your hypertension," she said.

"What makes you think I have high blood pressure?" Knak asked.

Charlotte smiled over the top of a detective novel she'd picked up. "You just seem a little wound up to me," she said, then handed over the saltshaker.

Curly black hair and hazel eyes that looked through him, that he didn't want to ignore. That had been it for him. Gerry Knak was in love.

They ate in silence. Knak desperately seeking a reason to talk to her.

"I know about you," she said, breaking the quiet.

"I've been in the papers," Knak said. "Some people don't like what I do for a living."

"I know more than you think," she said. "I know some people you ought to meet. They want to meet you."

"People?"

Charlotte nodded. She leaned over the table, wagged a finger. He moved closer, their noses almost touching.

"You see it," she said. "I know you do. You're in these courtrooms every day, fighting, and for what? Waste. Hypocrisy. Against the system's aggrandizement. Against open borders, against people who would hand this country over at the drop of a hat because they don't love this place like we do. There are lots of people who agree with you, who are doing something about it. They see you too. They're watching. You've got their attention, and that's a good thing. You need to come meet these people. It'll change your life."

After lunch, they walked through downtown. Charlotte told him she was a paralegal for a Presbyterian children's defense fund in the city, how she'd seen Knak in the courtroom. She didn't like the way he was treated. Such disdain. She talked about the poor, about the way the court used them as a shield for the rich.

"It's a cover," she said. "You know that. A proxy war against people like us. People in the middle."

Knak nodded.

"I see it," he said.

Charlotte nodded.

"We need to get you up to New Hampshire," she said.

* * *

They dated for several months, then got married by a notary in the city clerk's office. They drove to Wright's Chicken Farm, just over the border in Rhode Island, and feasted on platters of chicken and french fries, arms interlocked, Knak feeling for once what he understood as happiness.

They moved to an apartment in the city, an old cannon-ball factory converted into luxury loft apartments. Knak continued filing as many qui tam suits as he could. Charlotte helped with the paperwork, streamlined the filing process, gently guided Knak away from sure failures. Charlotte had faith in him. She turned him into a vessel for her own visions.

Weekends they would often head to her father's farm, an hour north. There, Avis Locke ran an industrial egg farm, his several thousand hens housed in a cavernous metal shed, their feeding, care, and egg collection handled by computer and close-circuit television beamed into every room of the farm's main house.

At first, Avis made Knak uneasy. He felt the old man's eyes on him, watching every move, appraising him by the way he stomped the dirt off his boots before coming in the house, or the color of his car, or the way he said *nook-you-lar* instead of nuclear. Knak wasn't sure of his place with Avis Locke until the day he noticed the flag.

"I like the Gadsden flag," Knak said one morning while bringing a dozen eggs from the massive henhouse to the main house kitchen. The yellow flag was faded by sunlight, and part of the rattler on the coiled snake was missing. *Don't Tread On Me* was still legible.

"What's the one below it?" he asked.

Locke looked up at the flag snapping in the light breeze. It was white with the jagged green silhouette of a mountain, the letters *MMM* in an arch above. Locke smiled.

"I'm impressed that you recognize that one, even more so that you know its name," Locke said. "The other one is the ensign of the Mount Marne Militia."

"Never heard of them," Knak said.

Locke nodded. "That's the idea. For now. But you will."

"So, militia? Like, Timothy McVeigh militia?"

Locke scowled, waved his hand as if swatting an insect from his face. "Hell no. McVeigh was no patriot. He was a terrorist piece of shit. We're patriots. We love this country. Hate to see the ways she's going."

They reached the porch, and Knak held the door open.

"I get it," Knak said. "My line of work, you start to feel sorry for the suckers who pay into this whole thing. Someone's got their hands in the government's pockets every day. They're robbing us blind."

Locke hesitated before going into the house.

"Some of us aren't blind."

*   *   *

Knak and Locke grew close. Locke took Knak to the gravel pits on the far edge of the property, taught him how to shoot—a .22 first, then a varmint rifle. Then they moved up to pistols and long rifles, then to the military stuff, an AR-15 first, then a tricked-out Remington rifle that Locke said was as close to a military sniper rifle as a private citizen could get. Knak wasn't good with any of them, but Locke enjoyed teaching and was patient while Knak seethed and muttered to himself with each missed shot.

Then there were the meetings. Strange men showing up at the farm, retiring with Avis to a back office. New faces at the gun range every weekend. Knak was flattered that they all seemed to know who he was at their introductions. As if they'd been watching him. He felt like the chosen one from some aboriginal myth, everyone seeing in him a destiny he himself couldn't imagine.

Then one morning three years into the marriage, the middle of the night, really, Charlotte woke up screaming, clutching her head, eyes wide as if a bomb had gone off inside, called out "Gerry!" then rolled off the bed, unconscious, her body quivering and tremorous in what Knak now understood to be a seizure. When the paramedics arrived, there were two of them. Knak smelled one of them from across the room. Alcohol. Knak rarely drank, but the smell reminded him of his youth, of his mother. Name tag said *Archer*, and Knak knew Archer had been drinking.

She died three days later in the neuro intensive care unit. She never woke up. They never took out the tube Archer had put down her throat on the floor of their home, denying her a chance to say good-bye. In rare moments he admitted to himself—even the doctors said it—that there was nothing the medics could have done to change the outcome; that what they'd done, what *Archer* had done, had been within the guidelines, within the realm of the medically acceptable.

But he'd never been able to accept the fact that sometimes effects have causes that aren't connected by threads one can live with. Knak knew himself, and knew he needed to hold someone accountable.

Charlotte's death clarified things for Knak. The way they always screwed his order up at the drive-up and how unfair it was that you paid all your taxes and your bills and you lived a good life and that life went to shit in the blink of an eye, a thunderclap headache, they called it. Goddammit, he didn't care if no one else thought this medic had anything to do with it; that fucker had been drunk, not on top of his game, not ready, not prepared for his wife's moment of trial. Gerry Knak knew, felt it in his bones, knew it as much as he knew the Lord Almighty was coming back in vengeance someday, maybe not in Knak's lifetime, but he was coming, and if Knak had to bring a little of that fire and brimstone himself beforehand, well, that might be okay.

And as he thought, warm tendrils of hate searched out his heart and enwrapped it like the vines of some dark jungle tree that bore no fruit, save a poisonous pistil as fragrant to Knak as a flower.

7

Last summer

LOCKE DOUBLED THEIR time at the range. Called it taper-ing, told Knak it was time to cut the fat from his tech-nique. Less than a year out from the start of things, he said. Knak still hopeless with so much of it, the fieldcraft, the stalking, the indoctrination. It wasn't enough for him to embody the cause. He still needed to find a way to be useful.

Still, Locke knew how to dangle the carrot when needed.

"You're shooting better," Locke said.

"You're a patient teacher," Knak said.

"Charlotte didn't even shoot that well, not until she was in high school anyway."

Locke dropped the magazine from his rifle, tossed it onto the bench in front of him, slid in a new one. Locked and loaded, then fifteen shots, rapid. Dirt kicked up behind the white paper targets at the end of the range, hay bales with pictures of Kierkegaard, Schopenhauer, John Wesley, John Paul II, Eisenhower, others.

Charlotte's father shared a last name with a famous philosopher, took turns obliterating pictures of politicians, religious figures, and philosophers who had disappointed him. Locke put ten rounds into the chest of a photo of Jung, spread the others around. When he was done, he dropped the magazine out, laid the rifle down, and began reloading a pile of loose rounds in a metal box on the bench.

Knak shouldered his weapon, aimed and squeezed. *Click.* Misfire. He cleared the jammed round. Racked the bolt. Pushed the forward assist. Fired again. *Click.*

"You still suck at cleaning that thing," Locke said. He sipped Super Oxygen Factor from a metal canteen cup. The brown liquid stained his white moustache and dribbled in sepia blots onto his chin. "Gas-operated actions require diligence. A single grain of sand and you'll have misfires like that."

Knak dropped the magazine out of his weapon and racked the slide, unchambering a single round. He broke down his rifle on the bench and scrubbed the metal parts with a steel-toothed brush and a small bottle of cleaning oil. He looked at Locke from the corner of his eye, went back to the rifle, then sneaked another peek at his father-in-law.

"I'm ready," Knak said.

Locke loaded rounds into a magazine but didn't look at him. "Maybe."

"How long am I supposed to wait? I tried to do it through the courts, and look what that got me. I'm telling you, Avis, if I wait too much longer, this guy is going to get nailed for something else. I might miss my chance. Eventually the IRS is going to figure out I've stopped paying taxes, and then what? Maybe the come for the house? Maybe I go to jail? Charlotte deserves better."

Locke nodded. "She was extraordinary, even as a girl," he said. "I ever tell you about the time she got kicked out of the 4-H competition at the fair? We raised this enormous heifer, loved it like a member of the family, beautiful animal."

Knak had heard the story before but smiled.

"We go to the Pemberton Fair, fully confident in the win," Locke said. "The judging begins and the judge, this shrunken old woman in cowboy boots and an old-fashioned top hat she must have gotten on sale at a flea market, she comes and squints her eyes, takes about a minute, far less attention than she gave the other three heifers in our class."

In other shooting positions along the range, pistols and rifles began banging away. Knak transported himself to a war zone, imagined conversations with artillery shells bursting around him. He remembered telling Charlotte he wished he could have gone to war, that he wouldn't have wavered, even for a moment. But at the range, the way the pistols and rifles going off around him shrank his courage, made him shake, Knak knew he wouldn't have made it. The thought was depressing.

"The judge lines all four heifers up," Locke said, "and I'm immediately nervous because ours is on the far right, and sure enough, she points at each heifer and starts counting, you know, 'one, two, three,' and we're fourth, last in the class. Before I can stop her, Charlotte, all of eleven or twelve at the time, she stomps over there and gets in this woman's face. She wants to know how anyone could place these other heifers ahead of the beautiful animal we brought, right? So the woman says something like, 'This white-and-black-spotted heifer has more correct legs, and this other one is squarer-rumped,' that sort of thing."

Locke stopped talking for a moment as a shooter behind them switched to full automatic, sending thirty rounds downrange in two seconds. Locke and Knak turned and looked, scowling. Licenses for fully automatic rifles were hard to obtain, and no one at the shooting club possessed one. A goateed man in his twenties waved sheepishly.

"No more," Locke told him. "You think we need that kind of attention around here? We're already under enough scrutiny as it is."

The man shook his head and left the firing line. Locke turned back to Knak.

"Where was I? Right, so Charlotte hears this and freaks out, starts screaming at this woman. I'm trying to get down from the stands where they corral all the parents. When I get there, Charlotte is telling this woman that *her* rump is squared, and how she'd like to break the woman's limbs, maybe help her correct her own legs."

Locke closed his eyes, smiled at the memory.

"Most mad I ever saw her," Locke said. "They gave us five minutes to get the heifer packed and be off the fairgrounds. On the way home we stopped at a Friendly's, had a couple chocolate shakes. Charlotte never talked about it again, almost like, for her, it never happened."

Knak nodded. "She had a way of putting a fight behind her almost immediately. She never held grudges."

Knak remembered a day driving up to northern New Hampshire, to Rudolph's Rendezvous, a Christmas-themed amusement park not far from the Canadian border. It was a beautiful, cloudless summer day and Charlotte endured the ride on Knak's Harley because she wanted an apple cider muffin that the place was famous for. She'd talked about the things for a month until Knak relented, said he'd go up there with her.

They stopped at a biker bar in Lincoln, an hour south, and one beer led to another, time wore on. It became too late to finish the ride to the park. Knak got them a room at a nearby Motel 6. Charlotte refused to speak with him, even when he brought back the six-pack of Long Trail and a pizza. They'd watched an old *Honeymooners* episode in silence, but Knak could sense her softening, the way she leaned her back into him while they lay there. After a while she told him she was tired and they made love and fell asleep, and by checkout the next morning it was as if none of it had happened, and Charlotte never mentioned the failed trip again. It was a capacity for forgiveness that Knak didn't possess.

"I miss her," Locke said. "Every day."

Locke sipped, licked the bottom of his moustache. Took another swig from his canteen cup. Knak put his rifle back together, racked the slide back and forth a few times, admiring how smooth it was now after a little cleaning. Locke remained quiet, still, as if remembering his daughter had drained all the energy out of him.

"I'm ready," Knak said.

"They'll never let you get away with it," Locke said. "You'll get the one shot, and that will be it."

"I know. I should give you the dogs."

"I would, but—allergic," Locke said. "You understand, once you start this, you probably won't survive it."

Knak nodded. "I'm not afraid."

"If you're really going to avenge Charlotte, then you're going to need to be ready to die," Locke said. "They'll do their best to kill you first. This medic, Archer, he's part of the system. The system that lets thieves steal billions of dollars from the government, the system that lets the government steal trillions from people like you and me."

Knak nodded. He took a swig from Locke's canteen cup.

"Big money involved," Locke said. "They're not going to stand by and let you degrade the system. I see it every day.

Immigrants pouring over the border, terrorists coming up from Mexico, jungle diseases arriving on airplanes from Africa, wars and rumors of war, all overseen by legions of silent helicopters and fleets of drones. The system won't like you, Gerry. Not one bit."

Knak popped open a Narragansett beer. Locke pulled up a nearby stool and dropped down with a groan.

"These old knees and hips," Locke said.

Knak offered a beer. Locke declined, grabbed his canteen cup instead, and took a gulp.

"Water," Locke said. "Fluid dynamics. When you go out into the city and put your mission into action, you need to remember that not everything is going to follow predictable data."

"I've prepared thoroughly," Knak said.

He had. Knak told Locke he'd followed city ambulances for months. He knew where they hung out between calls. He'd drilled down into the data and scoped out the addresses they went to most often. Knak had paid a guy who knew a guy, who'd hacked into the ambulance service's scheduling system. He knew Archer's whereabouts for the next six months.

"I've scouted primary and alternate shooting sites, then found alternates to the alternates," Knak said. "I'm ready to do whatever it takes to get this guy."

Locke raised a finger.

"First, fluid pressure is always perpendicular to any surface on which it acts," Locke said.

Knak waited. He tried to understand where Locke was going with this.

"So, when you're faced with a problem, going left or right won't relieve the pressure. You might as well continue forward with the plan. Don't be tempted to let obstacles deflect

you. You're only exchanging one pressure for another. Forward, always forward."

"I'll be like a dog on a bone," Knak said.

Locke took a long swig from the cup and wiped the sweat
from his forehead with the back of a hand.

"Another rule: the amount of pressure at any point in a
fluid at rest exerts an equal intensity in all directions," Locke
said. "Take your time. Rushing off on tangents is a waste of
time."

"I'm focused," Knak said.

"Third rule: external pressure applied to a confined liquid is transmitted undiminished in all directions. In other
words, don't feel boxed in. Limits—as when the police begin
hunting you, which won't take much time—it's like a pressure applied to you, the confined liquid. Welcome it. Embrace
it."

"What more pressure can they bring?" Knak said. "Fucking IRS. Ten years of receipts? Shit. I don't have receipts for
the Denny's I ate this morning."

"They are thorough."

Knak laughed. "I've got nothing for them. They'll take it
all—the house, my truck. I'm going to owe thousands. Tens
of thousands. Charlotte would have fixed this. She had all
those assholes figured out from way back."

Locke refilled his canteen cup and pulled a wallet from
his back pocket. He counted bills inside.

"Let's head on over to that fried-chicken place on the
rotary," he said. "Lunch is on me."

They rattled down the rutted backcountry road in
Knak's dented and dusty pickup truck. Soon they passed
through the unmanned gates of Fort Devens. The fort had
been closed for fifteen years, and various groups still fought
over what to do with it. Meanwhile, the place sank into itself,

a boat settling slowly into harbor mud. Collapse was everywhere—in the empty buildings, the parking lots cracked open by long lines of grass and weeds, the empty guard shacks with the collapsed roofs and missing stop signs, where no one had stood a post in a decade.

Grass on the immense central parade ground grew knee-high and dandelion-speckled, the field now an ocean of pale emerald dotted with yellow-capped waves and dirt patches where nothing grew. Knak passed the massive, four-story brick headquarters buildings, empty and abandoned, boarded windows like missing teeth on the once-grand facade, the white paint on the trim faded and peeling.

"I always love coming through here," Locke said. "I like decay. Provides new soil for new growth. Reminds me not to worry about the feds too much. Nothing they make tends to last."

"Except for the prison hospital," Knak said.

"This place really hummed during the first big war. All those doughboys from Kansas and Oklahoma and Pennsylvania. Shipped here in railcars like cattle, then packed on ships and sent over to the War to End All Wars. Hundred years later, we're still packing them up and sending them somewhere to fight and die, and for what? Corporate greed, the fever dream of the imperialist oil barons."

"Same old, same old," Knak said.

A frisson of time scuttled across the back of Knak's neck. He could feel the thousands of American soldiers, dead now, men like his father, off to war in a place that was as foreign as it could possibly be. He wondered what eighteen-, nineteen-year-old kids from the Midwest thought of Massachusetts. Could they have even comprehended places like Belleau Wood, or the Somme, or Paris? How many had walked these streets and never returned? How many were buried under small white crosses in France, or Belgium, someplace so far from here?

"Of course, this place had the last laugh," Locke said.

"The flu?"

"Not just the flu. The killer flu. The pandemic. H1N1. The bug that killed twenty, maybe a hundred million people, probably close to three percent of the world's population."

Knak knew the story too. Thought of it every time he drove through from the shooting range to his favorite road-side fried chicken joint.

One of the worst disasters in human history. It had gotten its toehold here, on this base, when infected soldiers from Kansas arrived in 1918 in preparation for combat in France. Once it started, a thousand soldiers a day came down with it. First, a cough in the chow hall at breakfast, maybe a fever. Delirium set in. Cheeks turned dark red, almost mahogany, huge spots popping out. Then their skin turned a dark blue, first at the ears and then across the face, so dark that doctors couldn't discern white men from black. Most who got to that point would be dead by nightfall.

Knak drove past the buildings and parade ground and headed down a winding road that took them past the base cemetery. The headstones were covered in brush. No flag flew from the pole that leaned against the open wrought-iron gate.

"Death upon death, Gerry," Locke said. "We're just heaping death upon death. Meaning? We construct meaning ourselves. There is no natural order. There is only disorder, punctuated by interruptions in the chaos, when nature pokes its head in and wipes our slate clean."

The truck passed through the former base's unguarded rear gates and continued down the narrow two-lane. Knak wiped the sweat from his forehead with the back of a hand.

"Is that what you want from me?" Knak asked. "To wipe the slate clean?"

"Not just you. But you'll get the ball rolling."

Knak pulled the truck into the parking lot of Frenchy's Fried Chicken. Locke looked ahead, staring at a family as they ate at a picnic table out front. Mom and dad sat on opposite sides of a picnic table while a young boy and younger girl chased each other around the table. Mom collared the boy, pointed to his plate. Knak couldn't read lips, but he imagined what she was saying.

"I am good at recognizing a type," Locke said.

"Am I a type?"

Locke nodded.

"You weren't hard to figure out," Locke said. "I can always tell people who can handle the covert truth. This whole thing is a sham based on a lie wrapped in bullshit. The names change—democracy, communism, capitalism, Nazism—but the system is the same. The world's power shifts shapes as needed. The system failed to punish the man who let my Charlotte die. By punishing him, you punish the system. And punishing the system is what we're all about."

"I won't let you down," Knak said.

Locke nodded, smiled at Knak.

"I know," he said. "But I'm not the one you need to worry about."

8

"**Y**OU'RE TOO FAR away," she said.

Archer switched the cell phone from his right hand to his left. He stood on the helicopter landing pad outside the Saint Bonaventure emergency department. Julio was inside, scrounging a scrub top to replace his vomit-soaked shirt.

"The mortgage is due this week," he said. "I didn't have a choice."

The constant struggle. Michael sick. Elaine out of work to care for him, and the city no longer willing to advance Archer sick or vacation time. Every day the same choice. Go to work and keep the apparatus up and running—house, cars, cable television he never used anymore—or go to the hospital, keep vigil over Michael but lose out on the pay. It was a way of life now. No money and no time.

"It's bad," she said.

"Worse than normal?"

A scratching sound in the connection. A ruffling, like someone shaking a sheaf of papers. A cough. His wife spoke softly to someone else in the room. He heard Michael, not a moan, but not words either. A kind of language that the chemo created, born of a kind of pain that transcended the senses. It was an animal, a growling thing with teeth.

It tested Archer's ability to believe, this agony of Michael's. Belief was a luxury, a choice, Archer thought, the way faith occurred only to people who had the space and time to weigh options, to refute things seen and unseen. His son's agony was the center of Archer's galaxy, the sun around which he orbited, only now a year took an infinite number of days and felt like it might never end. Archer couldn't remember when it had begun.

He thought he had seen people pushed to the edge. Watching his son, Archer knew he'd never touched but the surface of what hurt could be. For the thousandth or millionth time since the diagnosis, Archer wished he could take the pain himself. What he wouldn't pay to make that possible. Love wasn't about what you'd do for your kids, Archer thought, but about the how little you wouldn't do for them.

"Elaine?" Archer said.

"Yes," she said. "It's worse than normal."

The ninth floor of the hospital in Boston was less than forty miles away. The phone put Archer right in his son's hospital room, but he had never felt so distant. No, not distant, but forced forward, like a crewman on one of Cortés's burned ships. No way back, only forward, uncharted. Archer liked to say they were learning more about brain tumors every day, but it was like being on Mars. New discoveries daily, but every day, still an alien.

The boy was transparent now. Archer often traced the blue veins on Michael's head while the boy slept on his chest, as if they were a map he could use to discern what was going on below them. He could not. When Michael was an infant,

Archer had loomed over his crib at night and worried. He couldn't name his fear, thought it was probably just a part of being a new father, loving this thing, this piece of you, whose mechanics you didn't yet understand. Now, Archer wondered if his premonition was evidence of a wider perception. Had he known Michael would be sick? Had he somehow caused the sickness with his worry?

The medicine seemed to be working, and it was a race now, trying to kill the tumors before the medicine killed the boy. Articles of faith ruled Archer's life these days, and this was one he clung to with the most tenacity. He couldn't be sure of anything, none of it visible to the naked eye.

The machines and doctors told him Michael was sick. The machines and doctors told him Michael was getting better. Michael looked like shit, and the doctors told him not to breathe easy just yet. There was still plenty of time to lose this thing. But we're winning, they said. Archer chose to believe them, because what other choice did he really have? Sometimes he doubted, and the doubt felt like betrayal, and he knew that if Michael died, if they lost, Archer would blame himself.

"Did he get his shots yet?" Archer asked.

"Amy said she'd come by soon," Elaine said. "One of her other patients is getting electrolytes. She's busy with him."

"Don't let them wait too long," Archer said.

"I won't."

Silence. Archer wanted to tell his wife that what she was doing was an amazing thing, that he couldn't imagine how he would perform in her shoes. He wanted to tell her that he'd loved her since the day he met her in the parking lot of what became their favorite restaurant, Cactus Jack's, when he jumped the battery in her dead Impala, then had the presence of mind to ask for a phone number. He wanted to say they were in this together, like he'd said the day the doctors called to say they'd seen something on Michael's MRI, that they didn't want to discuss it on the phone.

Instead, he said, "I'll try to be there first thing in the morning, as long as we don't get a late call. You should be able to get some sleep tomorrow."

"It feels like it's been a month," Elaine said. "That can't be right. But it seems like that. It's been a few days, anyway."

"You must be exhausted," Archer said.

"Exhausted would be an improvement. I just feel, I don't know. Spent. Wrung out like a dishrag. If I could, I'd just go to sleep for a year and not wake up. And when I woke up, I'd be someone else. We'd just be home, all of us, this would all be one big nightmare that I'd wake up from and rub my arms and just be like, whoa, that was a bad dream."

"Remember Winnipesaukee, that summer where we had the sundaes from that all-you-can-eat place and then we watched that electric parade on the lake, the one with the blue dragons?" Archer asked.

Elaine chuckled. "Mikey had the entire thing smeared on his face," she said.

"And then he dragged his hands all over the seat of my truck, when it was new."

"That was bad."

"Seemed like the end of the world at the time," Archer said. "Thing about it is . . ."

"The thing about it is, you'd give anything to let him do it again," Elaine said.

"I would."

"What made you think of that?"

"I'm ready," Archer said. "I'm ready to get back to a life where the little problems are the big problems."

Elaine breathed deep. He heard a door closing, the click of the mechanism into the hasp. She'd gone into the small bathroom, which Archer and his wife did whenever they didn't want Michael to hear.

"Did you hear about the Delaneys?" Elaine said.

Tommy Delaney was Michael's best friend on the neuro-oncology floor. He was sick like Michael, four years old like Michael, on the same protocol, but he'd had different results. Tommy's mother, Sheila, and Archer's wife were close, fox-hole buddies. Tommy hadn't handled the chemo well. His kidneys were failing. The two boys had spent the afternoon together two days ago, drawing in Red Sox coloring books. Tommy had looked haggard the last time Archer saw him. His skin was thin like parchment and yellowed. He panted between words.

"Don't tell me," Archer said.

"Today," Elaine said. "Right after lunch. The room was full of people, and Sheila was outside crying and they made her stand in the hall with the child life specialist and a chaplain. For an hour, maybe more. Then it got quiet, and Shelia's been in there ever since."

Archer was sad for the Delaneys and scared for his own son, and the fear ratcheted up the guilt. The hospital world was a web, with every string somehow pulling at Michael. A break in the web in the Delaneys' room down the hall only made Michael's existence more tenuous, and Archer hated that he thought this way, but he did and there was no way to stop. Elaine said Dr. Monroe had come by afterward to say they were considering changing Michael's protocol, given what it had done to Tommy.

"He said they can't prove that everyone who gets the metal drugs will live," Elaine said, "but they do know no one with Michael's tumor who *hasn't* gotten the metal drugs—carboplatin, I think—has survived."

"Hell of a choice," Archer said.

"It had to be his kidneys," Elaine said. "Dr. Monroe wouldn't be specific, but it had to be. I want Michael's tested before we decide."

"Is that what's going on tonight?"

"His breathing is bad, real bad," Elaine said. "He's seeing things. Talked about angels visiting his bed this morning. The attending keeps coming in here every five minutes and eyeballing the code cart. Dr. Monroe has been holding them at bay, says he's seen far worse, but it can't go like this forever."

Archer thumped the door panel with his fist.

"I shouldn't be here," he said.

"We could lose the house," she said.

"But I need to be there."

"We all need to be somewhere else."

"I'm coming," Archer said.

"No."

"I'm on the other side of the world."

"I've got to go," she said.

"Wait."

"The doctors are coming in."

"Stay on the line."

"I'll call you later. I've got to go. They're looking for me."

Archer heard the dispatcher on the radio, calling his ambulance. The connection to his wife went dead. He was alone. He was an arctic explorer, frozen in the ice with months on his hands and his boat crushing under the pressure. He could feel the coil of his life unwinding. He thought about turning off the radio, leaving his narc keys on the dash and walking away. Instead, he blacked out his cell phone's screen and picked up the radio, and it felt like a surrender.

9

DAWN. THE CITY'S eastern neighborhoods waking to a red button sun. Angelo Rinaldo long ago tucked into bed in the ED at Saint Bonaventure's, the remainder of the night an incessant crush of the sad and mildly ill. Archer pulled the ambulance to the curb, put it in park, and gave thanks that the night was nearly over, that he'd likely escaped having to dispense any real medical care for an entire weekend night.

The narrow-fronted modernist ranch house on South Florence Avenue showed little to the road. A white vinyl fence hid a sprawling complex that flowed into the woods behind it in ways the facade didn't suggest. Archer thought it looked like a flattened McMansion, spun out like pizza dough so that it melded with the patch of old-growth forest that surrounded it, one of the last slices of true nature left in the city.

Julio curled in the passenger seat in a position a cat would admire, his boots on the dash, a baseball hat pulled over his eyes.

"Tell Ann I said hello," he said.

Archer stepped out of the ambulance and took a deep breath, enjoying the air on this side of the city. It was a quiet enclave of comfort and leafy sidewalks occupied by midlevel civil servants, cops who doubled their salaries with detail pay, and firefighters who worked second jobs as carpenters and painters and machine shop foremen, all of them married to teachers or human resources reps or nurses. Unwilling to leave the city, they worked themselves to the bone to belong to it. Archer envied them. They'd understood early in life how to make this happen. He'd grasped the concept only recently, and felt his grip loosening.

Religious statuary filled the front yard—marble and balusters and dead saints and a dozen different renderings of the Holy Mother. A crucifix in yellow-stained marble dominated a small pebble garden. Jesus in his ecstasy and his misery topped a small fountain and pool into which other visitors had tossed small change.

The front door opened before Archer could knock. The woman who opened it wore a simple white button-down blouse, a lint-speckled black skirt, and sturdy black shoes. A gray sweater that exactly matched the gray streaks in her dark hair. She smiled. He stopped at the bottom of the small concrete staircase and bowed slightly.

"It's a good thing I don't sleep anymore," she said.

"Good morning, Ann. Is it too early?"

"It's never too early and never too late, but I worry about you," she said. "All this wakefulness."

"Is it okay for a visit?"

"A short one. Evangeline isn't feeling so well today. But I do have something for you."

He stepped into the dark hallway and handed Ann a bundle of cellophane-wrapped roses he'd bought at Teddy Mart during a break earlier in the morning.

"I brought these for Evangeline," Archer said. "I didn't want to come empty-handed, not today, but I never know what to bring."

"It is a terrible day," Ann said, "and yet, the most wonderful day."

"Eight years."

"Seems like yesterday."

The living room was a shrine, filled with statuary and replicas of Russian icons and paintings of the Holy Mother and her legion of saints, an explosion of religious ecstasy and hope, and in the middle of it all, Evangeline. Her hospital bed was set in the bay window that looked out onto South Florence Street, out into a world Archer was pretty sure she'd stopped comprehending almost a decade ago, but which her mother was convinced her daughter had been born to serve, born to bear pain for in pursuit of purification.

White Christmas lights framed the window and bathed the supine Evangeline in a soft glow now softening more in the creeping daylight until she reflected it, her skin so white against white sheets and her white sleeping gown. Archer noticed the pinkness of her cheeks, the drops of perspiration on her earlobes, because they were the only things besides her hair that weren't white.

Archer and Ann stood over the girl. She had long black hair, now wet and matted down to her head, and her skin was a pallid gray color with those streaks of red on her cheeks. Her eyes were half-open and her mouth was slack. The tube at her neck pulsed every time the ventilator behind her headboard pushed a rush of air into her lungs. The gauze that covered the tracheotomy hole was stained in the middle by slips and bits of yellow mucus.

"She looks uncomfortable," Archer said.

"They can't find the infection," she said. "This is the third one this year. The antibiotics don't seem to be working."

"Are you taking her to the hospital?"

Ann pulled the sweater down from her shoulders and dropped into a nearby rocking chair. Outside, an elderly couple approached the window, the man tall and bent and laboring across the yard with a walker, the woman next to him holding him by the elbow.

"I don't want to," she said, "not today, at least. Dr. Marcus thinks the vancomycin will work. He's an optimist. We just got back from the trip down to Pennsylvania and upstate New York. Saw almost fifty thousand people. It was glorious, but she must have caught something from all those people touching her. Bound to happen. Her gift is also her burden."

Ann said she had something for Archer and disappeared down the darkened hall. Archer stood with his hands behind his back and looked at Evangeline's face, wondered what she thought of all this, if she even thought at all. So still except for the machine pushing the air in, nature sucking it back out. Outside, the woman knelt on a stool in front of the window, and her mouth moved as she twisted the rosary beads in her hand. The man remained standing, holding on to the walker with shaking hands. After a minute, the woman rose and the pair turned and began their trek back to the street. Ann returned and handed Archer a small vial of dark glass with a black plastic cap.

"I was praying for you yesterday and Evangeline started coughing, so the respiratory therapist had to suction a lot of mucus up, and I was looking at the statue of Saint Adolphus over in the corner and he was bleeding from his eyes and the stigmata, and there was so much oil that I had to get a vial," she said. "I thought you could bring it with you. When you visit your son. Saint Adolphus was a healer. He looks out for all healers. He's the saint of paramedics. Also janitors, I think."

Archer turned the dark vial over in his hands and held it up to the light. It was like molasses, dark and syrupy. He rolled the vial, and the liquid hesitated before it slid down the sides of the glass in a spider web of veins. Archer thought of expensive wine draining down a crystal chalice. He tucked the vial into an inner pocket on his jacket.

"I'm not sure what I expected when I came today," Archer said. "It's a big day, but it's also kind of like every other day."

"She's so sick. It's part of the joy, though."

"Father Pat?"

"Asleep in the quarters. The other one, too, across the hall."

"You don't like the new guys, do you?"

"It's not that they're new. It's just that they're so sure of things. I haven't been sure of many things for the last eight years. Except how I feel about you and dear Julio. Our miracle begins and ends with you two."

"I will always wonder," he said.

"She'd been in the pool too long."

Archer pinched his forehead. "She's growing," he said.

"She is. That part is fine."

"What should I do with the oil?"

"Saint Adolphus was a great healer," she said. "Father Pat told me you should apply it in a cross to your son's forehead every night before he goes to bed."

"I work nights."

"Your wife, then."

"She'd do it."

Archer walked closer to the side of Evangeline's bed. He took a hand and caressed the back of her thumb. Archer often wondered what Evangeline might have been like as a little girl. Was she a happy child? Did she watch television? Did she eat her vegetables? Was she, like his own son, a Muppets fan? What would she be like now if she hadn't fallen into that pool? Would she be a good kid? Would she be normal? What the hell did normal even mean anymore? Would Archer find her on a Saturday night on the front steps of the Olympian, stoned out of her gourd, nose bloodied in the mosh pit and crying into the shoulder of some rat-faced teenage boy's Norwegian death metal sweat shirt? Unknowable things, Archer thought. The respirator clicked and whooshed, and Archer brushed a lock of hair off Evangeline's feverish cheek.

Ann tapped him on the shoulder and pointed to a rocking chair next to the fireplace on the other side of the room. He sat, Ann next to him on a faded ottoman with her elbows on her knees. Neither spoke for a time, and then Archer pointed to a marble statue on the mantel, a robed figure pointing toward the sky, long beard flowing behind him, his bald pate thrown back in anger, or pain. Maybe joy.

"Is that Adolphus?" he asked.

Ann smiled.

"Striking, right?"

"He looks like a man with a purpose," Archer said.

"He was a great man," Ann said. "He was a victim soul. Just like my Evangeline."

The ventilator hiccupped, an alarm chirped, and Evangeline's chest heaved, then relaxed. The alarm stopped.

"She gets agitated when she's sick," Ann said. "She bucks the vent and coughs, and that horrible thing goes off all hours of the night. It would be very annoying if I still slept."

"How long has it been?"

"Eight years and a day, since the night before the accident. It is my penance. 'Rejoice in my sufferings for you, and fill up those things that are wanting of the sufferings of Christ.' My favorite verse, from Colossians."

"Don't you miss it? I go three, four days sometimes without sleep. By the end, I'm desperate. I want to go to bed the same way people want to breathe. By the time I get to bed, I'm so tired, it's like being drunk."

Ann shook her head.

"It's a privilege. And a burden, but a burden I carry with joy. Our family has been chosen by God to endure more than our share of suffering, to take on the pain of the world in communion with our Savior. We thank God for that yoke."

Archer said he didn't understand the nature of suffering. He saw it every day. Work. His son and his hospital. So much pain carried by so few, and yet he saw plenty of people go through life untouched by it all.

"It doesn't seem fair," he said.

Ann pulled the sweater over her shoulders and tied its arms in a loose knot in front of her.

"Evangeline's father was afraid of justice. That's why he's gone. That's why he's not here to be a part of all these miracles we witness every day."

Archer fiddled with the volume knob on his radio. He looked over at Evangeline's bed. The girl's head leaned toward the big bay window. In the growing light, Archer's ambulance looked almost like another piece of statuary in the yard.

An old Chevrolet Malibu with blown shocks waddled by on South Florence Street, its muffler scraping against the pavement when the car bottomed out. He didn't want to be lumped in with Evangeline's father, Reggie, who'd left Ann not long after the accident and now supposedly ran with a motorcycle gang somewhere in southern New Hampshire.

"I'm afraid of injustice," Archer said. "I'm afraid of that."

"Justice is good," Ann said. "It's the highest calling. And punishment is part of justice, so punishment is good."

"It feels like I'm being punished all the time."

Ann put a hand on Archer's knee.

"Society raises people to hate all punishment," she said. "It's an error in the spirit of the age. When God punishes someone, you should be on God's side. Don't react against it. Bear what others have difficulty bearing. It's more Christlike, which is rewarded in heaven. The saints themselves, like Adolphus, they approve. Back in high school, at Notre Dame, we learned Aquinas—'that the saints may enjoy their beatitude and the grace of God more richly, a perfect sight of the punishment of the damned is granted them.' "

"What did my son do? What did Evangeline do? What are they being punished for?"

Ann patted Archer's knee.

"It's a broken world, Thomas," she said. "Don't think too much on why. Just rejoice and be glad that there are people on this planet who will bear your pain, suffer for sins known and unknown. By His stripes we are healed."

Archer wasn't sure. He was waiting for a cure, and yet his son got worse every day in that hospital in Boston.

"Put the oil on his head every night," Ann said. "I touched the bottle to Evangeline's forehead. That's the good stuff. That's where you need to be."

10

Three years ago

KNAK AND SUPER Oxygen Factor. The first swig of the oily brown liquid went down in three spasms. Knak lowered the recycled plastic gallon jug from his lips and considered vomiting right there on the floor of the Marlborough international trade center.

Then the heat, a cloud of it, uncoiled from below his sternum and wrapped itself around his heart like a warm hand towel at the Hibachi Grill, where he used to take Charlotte, then rose through his clavicles and upward, where it eddied behind his ears before mushrooming at the top of his skull in a roiling mass so intense he thought it might explode. When it was over, Knak didn't know if he felt better or worse.

"You handled that well. Not everyone can take it first go-around," Avis Locke said. "This is made by a fellow militiaman, good for the soul."

Knak pursed his lips and sought the skylight above. When they'd first married, Knak confided to his wife that the elder Locke unnerved him. She'd suggested that he accompany Avis on "one of his shows." Knak was nervous. Avis made him feel that way, like he possessed the riddle to some mystery about Knak that even Knak himself couldn't divine. Avis either hated Knak or loved him like another son. Knak would believe either.

The vast hall was windowless and tall ceilinged, and the roof stringers disappeared above into the dim lighting provided by row upon row of fluorescent bulbs. A cranky ventilation system struggled in vain to vent the heat and musk of moist flannel and woodsmoke and fresh popcorn and oases of mulch.

SurvivoCon attracted a type. Survivalists. Preppers. People ready to bug out and cut bait. Knak wasn't sure what he was looking for but had a growing sense it was here, among these people.

The few times he'd gone with Charlotte and Avis to militia training sessions, he'd come to realize that he was among his people. They talked about guns, the World Bank, the Bohemians and the evil of Jews, Papists, the Federal Reserve. In their talk of conspiracies and shadowy leagues accumulating power in dark retreats far from public light, Knak took refuge. The world was mysterious and conspiring—his own father dead by the shores of a Korean reservoir during the war there, sacrificed in the service of the United Nations. Knak felt like a refugee who'd discovered a neighborhood in the big city where the tribe spoke his language.

At SurvivoCon, the end of the world was on sale. Table after table filled by circumspect purveyors of all manner of apocalyptic accessories. Freeze-dried food. Generators that ran on cellulose and rotten vegetables. Knives and hatchets and bomb shelters on the installment plan, just ten easy payments. Knak wilted under the End Times commerce, by

Armageddon turned into a late-night infomercial for the latest slicer, dicer, and refrigerator deodorizer.

Then he'd found the booth in the back with its pyramid display of cloudy plastic jugs filled with a brown concoction. Locke beamed, put his arm around Knak, and introduced him as his son-in-law to the one-armed man in camo pants and a leather vest who ran the booth. Knak shook hands with his head lowered so that no eye contact was possible.

Locke introduced the man as "Mr. Limber." Limber wore a cheap black digital watch on his left wrist and a Kimber semiautomatic pistol on his right hip. Knak couldn't imagine how Limber would draw the thing, his right arm missing below the elbow. Limber pivoted on the balls of his feet, and every time he turned, Knak heard the tinkle and jingle of coins, pens, film canisters, and whatever sorts of things a man like that carried with him on any given day. The possibilities were endless.

Knak hadn't planned on taking a drink. The smell was overpowering, of mint and disinfectant, and he didn't like the way its head foamed orange. The smell crossed over the narrow folding table from the stack of sealed jugs. Knak also detected hints of bacon and periwinkle, maybe a touch of bug spray. Limber said he thought Knak might benefit from a drink. Said it helped people like him.

"What kind of people is that?" Knak asked.

"In need," Limber said.

It was arithmetic, he said, and popped the thin plastic cap off the top of the nearest jug and held it out to Knak.

Knak demurred at first. Not interested, he said, doing just fine. Locke shook his head.

"I can see into men like you," Limber said.

"Nothing to see here," Knak said.

"You don't come to many of these things," Limber said.

"First one!" Locke offered.

Knak shook his head.

"You're not sure what you're looking for," Limber said.

Knak shrugged, pretended to sort through the pamphlets on the table. Somewhere a PA system clicked and squawked to life, someone tapping on it as a test, the thumping shaking Knak's chest. Then a woman's voice announcing that the ax-throwing demonstration would begin soon. Limber waved Knak in, scanned left and right, leaned close.

"I think you know what you're looking for, don't you?" Limber said. "You want to know the secret ingredient of this shit? Tabasco. And a sprinkle of gunpowder. Not enough to make you crazy, of course, but it packs a punch."

Knak didn't know what to make of the concoction. He didn't want to disappoint Locke, but he didn't like the idea of drinking gunpowder. He knew he'd drink it. He could never disappoint his father-in-law.

Locke reached down behind Limber's chair and returned with a bottle of Macallan.

"Not to disparage the source of your lucre," Locke said to Limber, nodding toward the pyramid of jugs. "But this is much better."

He poured a couple fingers in three plastic cups and handed one each to Knak and Limber. He drank from the other. Knak thought Locke's lips turned an even paler shade of pink. Spittle pooled at the corners of his mouths.

Knak tossed back the Macallan, then chased it with a shot of the foul-smelling brown drink Kimber placed on the table between them. . His chest exploded in fire. He was dizzy and nauseous and elated simultaneously. His heart pounded in his chest, and he had trouble catching his breath. And then, then it was like he was a jet pilot breaking the sound barrier, the controls smoothed out, clouds flew by so fast he could see light bent and broken into all colors and yet none. Knak's head swam, and he thought he knew what an out-of-body experience must feel like.

It was over quick. Knak wanted more. He played cool.

"What do you call this stuff?" he asked.

"Super Oxygen Factor," Limber said. "It's an ass kicker, right?"

They talked for an hour. Tongues loosened—Knak's from the foul brown liquid, Limber's and Locke's from the Macallan's. Limber's booth had few visitors. He neither made a sale nor seemed worried about it. Locke said Limber had a doctorate in anthropology but had never done anything with it.

"It guides me as a torch in the struggle," Limber said.

"That's it!" Knak said. "The struggle. At least you have that. I'm after something. I just don't know exactly what it is or when to take it. I don't know how to . . . do it . . . exactly. I don't know if I have the courage."

Locke clapped him on the shoulder.

"You'll find it," he said. "Right, Mr. Limber? How long was it after your accident that you finally came upon the idea for this fine concoction you're selling here?"

Limber wiped his mouth with the back of his hand, squinted an eye, and looked at the ceiling.

"Let's see, tractor rolled over on me in March of '97, started brewing in 2000," Limber said. "So minus the time in the hospital, call it three years."

"Pain is not resolved quickly," Locke said.

"Not for me, anyway," Limber said.

Knak returned home late that night, laid a camouflage poncho on his living room floor, and arranged the things Locke had helped him buy. After they'd left Limber's table, Locke and Knak had bought some fudge from the Pentecostal end-timer two booths down and wandered the tables with Knak, pointing out things Knak would need.

Five thousand dollars later, left to right: a Kimber Les Baer 1911 .45-caliber pistol, just like Locke's and not unlike the pistol Knak's father might have carried in Korea. Four eight-round magazines. A thigh holster. Binoculars. Two bags of trail mix and a power bar. A carton of powdered soy milk for the lactose intolerance. Handi Wipes. Imodium tablets. Poncho. Poncho liner. ALICE pack from the stoned military-surplus guy at the table with the homemade soap on a rope. A machete. A brown fishing vest stuffed with nine thirty-round magazines for the best purchase of the day, a .223-caliber rifle made by the Articulate Arms Co., an up-and-coming weapons maker based in a retooled vacuum cleaner factory in upstate New York, swapping cleaning machines for guns, where the margins were broader and consumer demand never higher.

Knak opened the manuals for the rifle and pistol, laboriously followed their instructions on how to disassemble the weapons, oil the actions, reassemble them. He tried on his fishing vest and tested the rifle's electronic scope against a wall in the pitch-black of the downstairs furnace room. He screwed the silencer onto the threaded end of his rifle barrel, an aftermarket piece of gear Locke had assured him was legal. Mostly.

Then he was alone and the house was quiet and Knak packed everything into a brown canvas seabag he'd bought at the show and went out to the shed behind his pool and popped out a fake wall panel in the back. He stuffed the bag in there and closed it up and went back into the house.

He sat in a recliner and turned on his favorite news channel on the television, then switched over to Animal Planet, watched a documentary about male penguins guarding the eggs of their offspring, about how penguin fathers would cross the Antarctic ice with eggs balanced on their flippers and protect them until they hatched. Knak chewed his lower lip and twisted a roll of skin above his right kneecap. Pain to avoid pain. The usual.

Charlotte was away at a conference. Knak ran out to his Ford Ranger and pulled back the tarp in the back and grabbed a jug of Super Oxygen Factor—Avis had hinted it was crap, but he'd loved his first experience with it, bought a dozen gallons—then gulped it down right there in the driveway, not wanting the awakening to stop, to disappear like every other impulse he'd ever had in life. Back in the recliner he sank deep into the leather, drifting off to sleep, adrift in a universe he was starting to believe might make some sense. A wife he loved, a mission he deserved, a guide like Avis Locke. Gerry Knak fell asleep certain that this was the beginning he'd sought, come late in life but welcome all the same. Time to make things work. All the time in the world.

11

L U LOVED HER desk. Close to the newsroom's communal kitchen but not so close that colleagues could visit without going out of their way, which suited her fine. Without leaving her ancient wooden desk chair, Lu could see the row of her bosses' glass-walled offices, got advance warning of their comings and goings.

She was devoted to its spot, to the real estate. They'd tried to move her every time a new managing editor ascended to the throne and reorganized the departments according to the latest trend in organizational philosophy. Lu had fought them off each time, which explained her various stints sitting among arts and business reporters, not to mention the interminable year listening to the paper's two metro columnists argue the minutiae of city politics and power rankings.

Lu suffered it all. This desk, after all, had once been Joe Randone's.

The newsroom was empty this time of night on a Saturday. In an opposite corner of the room, pasty-skinned copy editors scraped the last of their leftovers from

scratched-bottomed plastic bowls or spritzed their varie-
gated philodendrons with water, skimmed the pages of yesterday's final edition. Half the fluorescent lights that filled
the drop ceiling in ranks sat dark, the desks below them
unoccupied. The police scanner chattered and squawked on
the desk next to Lu. She listened enough to know nothing
out of the ordinary was going on.

Tomorrow was a big day, not least because of a fact that
had begun to gnaw at Lu in recent days: come tomorrow
morning, Lu's desk would be unclaimed for the first time in
over sixty years. Her runway at the *Courier* had run out, Kittredge out of ways to keep her around any longer. She'd seen
the org chart. No one waited for her spot.

She'd owned the desk for thirty years. Before that, Randone for thirty-three. Randone was what the *Courier* used to
be, when the city paper meant something to people here.
Randone had grown up in the city, gone to its schools, started
working at the *Courier* in obits, then on the rewrite desk.
World War II broke out and Joe Randone found himself in
North Africa and Sicily, waded ashore at Omaha Beach and
onward, not quite to Germany when a mortar shell took off
his left hand in a dark and dank stretch of Belgian woods.

Lu had started at the paper on the Monday of Randone's
final week. She'd been terrified to meet a living legend. Especially when they'd told Lu she would be the retiring Randone's replacement. She'd never met the man, expected
something from *The Front Page*, a gnarled old newshound
who took his whiskey neat and called women *gals*, complained about lazy kids and Jimmy Carter, remained pissed
off about Vietnam. She'd worried how he'd feel, handing off
his desk and beat to a woman.

When she met Randone, the first thing she noticed was
his height. Randone was short. His suspenders stretched taut

over a belly that threatened to pop the buttons off his maroon button-down shirt, and his wide, plaid tie was speckled by coffee and newspaper ink. Close-cropped gray hair and florid red cheeks made Randone look as if he'd always just come in from the cold.

"So you're the new kid they told us all absolutely nothing about," Randone said. He smiled, held out the stump of his left hand as if to shake. Lu started to extend her left hand, dropped it, started to extend it again, stopped, then, for reasons even Lu couldn't quite comprehend, bowed. Randone laughed and extended his right hand, which she shook. "That one always gets people, first time. Joe Randone, welcome aboard."

"Lu McCarthy."

Randone dropped into the seat at his desk, pointed Lu to one next to it. An IBM Selectric hummed on Randone's desk.

"Nervous?" Randone asked.

"A little."

"No need," Randone said. "This is the easiest job you'll ever have. Where were you before this?"

"*Blackstone Valley Tribune* last couple years. Before that, I was in school, at Worcester State. I grew up in the city, over in Morningdale."

Randone beamed.

"A local! I love it. There aren't enough of you folks. The *Trib* is an excellent paper. Lots of folks here started there. You must know my buddy Davey Matheson."

Lu nodded. Matheson was an old *Courier* reporter who'd left the paper under murky circumstances and ended up at the small weekly, specializing in articles about local history and school sports.

"He was a good man," Randone said. "Just covered city politics too long. Got to him. You want my advice? Don't ever leave the cops beat. Best beat at the paper, because when the shift's over, you leave it behind."

Randone slid a black rubber glove over the stump on his left forearm. An upside-down, unsharpened number-two pencil was glued to the palm of the glove, and as he talked, Randone typed, using the pencil and glove to tap the keys his left hand would normally work.

"Work mostly nights, get to know where all the bodies are buried, don't have to deal too often with the flacks," Randone said. "Great gig. Plus, most of your stories, you write them and they're done. None of this long-term futzing around."

Randone finished typing, pulled the sheet of paper out, handed it to Lu. Names and phone numbers.

"I know all you young reporters want to be Woodward and Bernstein, and that's all well and good, but here there's no point in exposing the corrupt," Randone said. "They ain't hiding. We all know who they are and no one cares, as long as there's parades on St. Patrick's and Memorial Day, fireworks on the Fourth, and parking downtown stays cheap. Cops, crime, courts. That's the best job for an ink-stained wretch in this town. In and out, one and done."

Lu nodded. "I'm excited to get to it. You're leaving big shoes to fill."

"Nothing to it. Follow a couple simple rules."

Lu pulled a narrow notebook from her back pocket and opened to a blank page.

"Number one, always take good notes," Randone said. "See? You're way ahead of the game. Two, if you're not trying to get a free lunch every day, you're not working hard enough."

Lu smiled.

"That's no joke," Randone said. "You know how many press conferences and roundtables and how much other assorted nonsense goes on in this city every day that includes a catered food table? Or at least some pastry?"

She wrote *food*.

"Underline that twice," Randone said, pointing to the notebook. Lu underlined twice.

"Rule number three—this is the big one. You major in journalism?"

She shook her head. "Art history."

"Good, so you haven't had your mind warped by all those social science types, trying to break down the rules of journalism like they're splitting the atom or observing gorillas in the mist, or whatever. Because here it is, the most important rule of the whole thing, the one piece of advice you must follow even unto the grave, if, that is, you want to do this job correctly: you must not trust."

Lu wrote *must not trust*.

"Remember this saying, maybe tattoo it on your forehead in reverse so it's the first thing you see in the morning when you wake up," Randone said. "Remember this: if your mother says she loves you, check it out."

Mother loves, check it out, Lu wrote.

Randone tapped the notebook with his gloved stump, the pink eraser abrading the notebook paper, roughing it.

"If you don't remember anything else, remember that. Someone comes to you with a story idea, or a tip, or a need, they're coming to you to coerce you. They want something done, and the paper is the way to get it. Never get in fights with people who buy ink by the barrel, maybe, but better idea? Get the people buying all that ink to do what you want without their even knowing it."

It was the first of many lessons she had learned from Joe Randone in the first week of her job here. Randone took Lu along to meet all the watch commanders at the police department, the shift sergeants, the route cops. She met fire-fighters and deputy chiefs and battalion chiefs, nurses and doctors in the emergency rooms of the two city hospitals. He explained the list of phone numbers.

"That's a down payment on your Rolodex," Randone said. "I'm taking mine with me. You need to build your own, only way to get credibility with these people. I've given you a good start, but the rest is up to you."

Randone retired a week later, but he called Lu often those first few years, usually in the middle of the night, reruns of *Bonanza* or *Ironside* in the background. He checked on Lu's progress, pointed her in directions she wouldn't have found on her own, prompted her to dig stories out of the paper's morgue that enlightened current issues. Always Randone the teacher, Lu his star pupil.

Until one night. Lu couldn't wait for Randone to call. A scoop—someone on the inside had called *her*, had trusted her enough to pass on a tip. Lu was exhilarated. She was part of it all now, this great play, the stage curtain pulled back just far enough for her to see backstage.

"Johnson, on the city council, he's a tax cheat," she told Randone that night when he called. "He's going to lose that plot of land at the corner of Gates and Summer to a city tax auction."

She waited for Randone to praise her, offer congratulations. *Shane* played in the background.

"Who gave you the tip?" Randone asked.

"Mayor O'Toole's kid, John, his press guy," she said.

Randone chuckled.

"What?" she asked.

"Eddie O'Toole," Randone said. "Man of the people. You know much about him and Philly Johnson? You read the morgue files?"

"No," she said, starting to think the tip wasn't so hot after all.

"Johnson backed Ragosh Amarosian the last time Eddie O'Toole faced a real threat in a primary," Randone said. "This is payback."

"He's still late with his taxes, which as a city councilor . . ."

"You actually go look at the tax records?" Randone said.

"I talked to Johnson, and all he had was a 'no comment.' "

"Which you took to be admission of, what?"

"If he had nothing to hide, he would have denied it."

"Is there an actual tax auction date set?" Randone said.

She paused. "I don't know."

"What did I tell you about your mother?"

"I'll check it out."

Randone had been right. Johnson wasn't behind on his taxes and no auction had been set. Randone theorized later that O'Toole—the son, John—wanted to use the paper to force Johnson to sell the land at a loss and perhaps scuttle Johnson's political future in the process. Money and power— O'Toole wanted to strip his father's enemy of both. Nothing less than total eradication. The earth scorched, then salted so nothing would grow after. Not here, anyway.

"If the paper makes Johnson look bad on the front page, then exonerates him a month later on B20, which impression is going to stick in the public's mind?" Randone asked.

Tonight, three decades later, Lu McCarthy heard the voice of Joe Randone echo in her mind. Randone was long dead, had expired fifteen years ago of a heart attack at a land-locked dive bar called the Yacht Club, the same joint where Babe Ruth had drunk a beer in 1917 on his way back home to Sudbury, which was the kind of thing people in the city remembered, these infrequent glancing blows of immortality. But Lu heard Randone as if he still sat at the desk, tapping away at the keys with his rubber glove and pencil.

John O'Toole was mayor now, like his father. A would-be governor with an ego that supported plans grander than that, she knew. Everyone had an agenda, and Lu was now an agent of the young O'Toole's. The nagging truth ate at her. She hadn't done her job. She'd been a leaf floating on a swift, shallow river. A dead and brown leaf.

Lu had checked out none of it.

She'd been blinded by the money and her own needs.

The need, more than any other, to keep it all afloat. To survive it all, even without the alimony, not a penny of child support since her husband ran off with his secretary, such a fucking cliché she could puke.

The bigger problem: how to find something with meaning to do after this was all over, after she left the desk Joe Randone had given her like a birthright and they replaced her with nothing, a bare spot of industrial carpet, brighter than the threads around it. Lu eking out her days while they wrote her obituary, certain the first word would be *failure*.

She couldn't name the force that made her pick up the phone. Fear, nostalgia, a last shred of professional pride. It was a stupid move, would cost her big money, probably a lot more than that. When Big Dan left, last thing he'd said on his way out the door was that Lu was no crusader. Said she was too comfortable orbiting the fight, chronicling other people's battles. Lu, since this was her trademark move, had only agreed, then watched as he pulled away in their Volvo.

She picked up the phone and looked at the number Conroy had given her. She dialed. A woman picked up on the fifth ring.

"Hello?"

"Ms. Fontana?"

A pause. "Yes."

"My name is Lu McCarthy. I'm a reporter from the *Courier*. Eamon Conroy gave me your number, said I should call."

"I've been waiting for it."

"Can we meet?"

"Tonight is a bad night. There's a block party going on. Some people up from New York. Tomorrow would be better."

"I really need to talk tonight," Lu said.

"It could be dangerous. No one in or out on nights like this."

"I'm on a real tight deadline."

She sighed. "I can't promise you'll be safe."

"This is the last chance I'll have to tell your story. I'm done at the paper tomorrow, and I can't get through tonight without talking to you."

12

THE WAITRESS DELIVERED scrambled eggs and bacon, refilled Knak's coffee cup.

"You know why I like breakfast so much?" he asked the waitress.

Irish girl. Cape had been awash in them the past couple summers. He could tell by her accent. Solid and freckled, she smiled and refilled his coffee cup.

"Who doesn't like breakfast?" she asked. "Most important meal of the day."

Knak nodded. "I like it because it's like the way the sun rises in the morning, no matter how shitty a night you had. Everyone gets a fresh start."

He peppered his eggs, squeezed a dollop of ketchup into the middle of the pile, and stirred. He chewed openmouthed and stared out over summer-busy Hyannis Harbor. Dark water under blue cloudless skies, like a postcard, with the high-speed ferry backing away from its pier, horn blast echoing across the flat calm of the harbor's dogleg entrance.

Knak hated that he loved it. The serenity. Indulging in it was countenancing weakness, but he couldn't help it. It wasn't perfect, though. All those fucking loud talkers in SUVs with New York plates strolling around in boat shoes and golf shirts, the women with their striped handbags made of discarded boat sails, the men in Yankees hats and Crocs. He tried not to think of his burned house, of the dogs.

The yuppies didn't eat at the Majestic Egg, thankfully. Long-net fishermen, some nurses from Cape Cod Hospital, ferry crews. No one on vacation. Workers. Knak a worker too. Of a kind. At least that was something. Whenever he came here to smell ocean air and get away from the mud and crabgrass of Monticello, this place was his first stop. It grounded him. Set his head straight.

He'd driven down last night, pitched a tent at a campground overlooking the Cape Cod Canal. Knak figured the cops at home had put two and two together about the fire and the dogs, assuming they'd been found already. He needed to go somewhere unexpected. They'd look for him north, in the hills of New Hampshire or Vermont, seek him among the professional hermits and assorted vagabonds with reasons to avoid the police. Knak instead headed south. Hide in plain sight. It wasn't the first time he'd come to the Cape after a house burned.

* * *

First time had been with his mother, Gloria. The bicentennial year, 1976. A Crock-Pot malfunction had burned their house to the ground. They moved in with a sister of his mother's boyfriend and attended this nondenominational church in an old one-room schoolhouse on Route 68, the last building before the New Hampshire line. Pastor Lionel, who also owned the local paving company, preached about the end of the earth and being ready with a pure heart and mind for the

End Times, which had arrived. There would be no 1977, Pastor Lionel said, except that which they experienced in glory.

Gloria and the boyfriend, Glen, attended every night except Friday, which was set aside for drinking. Knak ate TV dinners freeze-packed in tinfoil trays, read books on World War II incessantly, sometimes watched television on a tiny black-and-white that picked up one fuzzy Albany UHF station.

Knak thought his mother a hopeless case the longer she stayed with Glen. On Fridays they'd come home drunk, then argue all night before putting themselves together for the Saturday noon service. Pastor Lionel mandated time apart. Knak and his mother spent a weekend in a cabin in Wellfleet owned by a fellow parishioner. Pretty soon, it was a regular thing. Then Glen was gone, they moved out of his sister's house, but their trips to the Cape continued. It became their respite. First from Glen. Then from life. From the way their lives had turned out.

Charlotte had seen that in him. A yearning. Knak was never settled. Even the act of relaxation filled him with guilt.

*   *   *

The waitress refilled Knak's coffee mug a third time. Dropped the *Herald* on the table. He scanned the paper, not expecting to see news of his arsoned house in it, still disappointed when his expectation proved correct.

Knak pulled out his phone. Opened a new text message.
Looks like I've made my escape.
Two minutes. A buzz. Knak read:
All quiet up here. Charlie Mike. We stand behind you.
Knak smiled. Avis Locke. *Charlie Mike.* Continue the mission. He finished his coffee, dropped a twenty on the table, and walked outside. Sea gulls cawed. A buoy bell tolled. A replica pirate ship filled with cheering kids and their

exhausted parents, gamely smiling and pointing at it all, motored through the mouth of the harbor and into the bay.

He'd planned to bug out some day, leave a mark on the world then disappear, like Elijah. Knak remembered the songs they sang about the Prophet, these simple, sappy things that ignored the reality of Elijah, a man who slit the throats of five hundred prophets of Baal because Baal had not appeared when called. Being with Charlotte hadn't slowed that plan down one bit. He'd had to double his supply runs to factor in his wife, but she agreed with him. The world was doomed. Her father had told her so, and she'd listened.

I'll give it a couple days. Then back to Worcester, Knak typed.

He stretched out in the back of his van in the parking lot, locked the doors, then cleaned his rifle. He counted the ammo. Made sure the settings on his scope hadn't changed. He soaked small cotton swabs with cleaning fluid and swiped the barrel, Q-tipped the bolt. Knak broke the rifle down, reassembled it with his eyes closed. His phone buzzed.

Please advise prior to operation. We have people need to go to ground. Sic semper tyrannus.

13

Two years ago

CONROY HAD SLOGGED his way through the first half of a ten-year jail sentence in administrative segregation. Solitary. His cell one of a dozen in a windowless basement corridor, each housing either the incorrigible, the crazy, or the marked. No one more marked in here than an ex-cop with a reputation.

Conroy spent twenty-three hours alone in a cell. The hour he got in the yard occurred long after his fellow inmates were locked in for the night. He showered alone. He thought alone. He didn't mind that the only human contact he had, other than with the corrections officers, was with fellow ad seg inmates at chow and chapel. Conroy only had use for the chow, but he went to services anyway. He liked the smell of incense.

Two years in, his first parole hearing had come and gone. The board rejected his appeal like a piece of bruised fruit at the Price Chopper. Violation of public trust, they found, mandated more years behind bars. Word through back channels was, plan on doing the entire dime bid. No early release, not for Eamon Conroy, not while the current governor held the keys to the empire.

In the years since he'd first come to ad seg, Conroy had slowly entered the social scene of the unit, such as it was. Inmates communicated by tying string to notes folded tightly into triangles, then slinging the notes under their doors and across the floors of the unit to other cells. Conroy used the system to play games of chess with two inmates in particular, Raymond Fiore and Patty Regan.

Fiore was the former head of the rail yard signalmen's union. He lived in a cell diagonally across the hall and was doing a bid for embezzlement. Early fifties, taciturn, medium height, a rotund, formless body and wispy black hair he unsuccessfully swept in a comb-over.

Regan was gregarious, great hair, great teeth, son of a politically connected Irish Catholic family of great width and breadth, genealogically speaking, that included several members of the governor's council, more than a few state reps and senators, and at least one comptroller. He was also Mayor O'Toole's former chief of staff, now jailed for attempts to lure high school girls to his house for sex.

Regan trafficked in prison gossip. If it happened in the jail, he knew about it. Who was about to be sprung, whose wife had left who for a guard, which guards were square and which ones had pills to sell, which prisoner had the best hooch. He and the mayor were still close. O'Toole himself visited from time to time, often after official visiting hours were over.

"He knows he has to," Regan told Conroy during the sermon one Sunday in chapel. Conroy had asked about the visits. Regan was careful to not actually use the mayor's name, lest a guard overhear. "Hizzoner knows he needs to keep me happy. Lots of info floating around in this head of mine."

Fiore just played chess, avoided the gossip. He sent over moves, played the game, and that was it. No chitchat, nothing frivolous. All chess business. One day, Fiore stopped playing. On the way to chow that night, Conroy noticed Fiore's cell was empty. Fiore not in the line of ad seg prisoners marching to the dining hall. At dinner, Regan sat across from Conroy.

"You notice Fiore's gone?" Regan asked.

Conroy nodded. He scooped a spoonful of cold mashed potatoes into his mouth. Old sensors came to life. For the first time in three years, he once again heard the banging and yelling that was the soundtrack of life in the jail. He knew most of those making the noise would gladly slit his throat if they could.

"I knew it was going to happen a month ago," Regan said. He looked left and right, then checked his six, just to make sure no one was behind him. "They moved him to general pop. He's getting out this weekend."

Conroy shrugged.

"Good for him."

"Maybe. But bad for other people. You know what Fiore was in here for, right?"

"Ripped off the union."

Regan nodded. He dragged a piece of limp white bread through the puddles of gravy on his tray. He talked while he chewed.

"Seven hundred fifty thousand, thereabouts," Regan said. "But that's not the important thing. Guess whose reelection campaign received about half that money?"

Conroy was at full alert. He knew Regan wasn't making idle conversation. Conroy had started many of these talks himself. Always someone wanting something.

"Just get to the point and ask whatever you want to ask."

Regan put a hand to his chest, feigned insult.

"I'm just making conversation is all."

"You're working up to a question. You've spoiled my dinner; don't insult my intelligence too."

Regan checked his perimeter again, then leaned over the table.

"O'Toole said you're a smart son of a bitch. Okay, so here's the deal. How bad you want out of here? Like, pronto?"

Conroy held his hands up.

"How bad you think?"

"What if I told you we could make it happen in three days?"

"I'd say Fiore's release is involved somehow."

Regan popped another piece of gravy-soaked bread in his mouth, guzzled the glass of lemonade on his tray.

"How'd you like to go to work for the mayor?" Regan asked. "He needs something done that's risky. Dangerous and absolutely necessary. If it goes wrong, you could be in deep shit."

"What's the *but*?"

"But he's tight with the governor," Regan said. "Tight enough that Johnny's the governor's choice to replace him when he retires to the lecture circuit before the next election cycle. The governor just wants to join a few boards of directors, do whatever those guys do to turn their public service into personal fortunes."

"Who would I be reporting to? I'm not interested in being low man again, and I don't do well with supervision. Put me on an org chart taking orders from some dipshit with a pinkie ring, and I'll pass. I'd rather just do my ten and get out on my own terms."

"It'll just be you and the mayor. The salary will be handsome, but it'll come in brown paper envelopes and stacks of cash, if you know what I mean. This ain't IBM. There's no 401(k), no health or dental. He knows there are a few things that need . . . *cleaning up* . . . before he makes his actual campaign. You don't get to become mayor without rolling a little in the dirt. Now he needs a cleaner, and you were the first person he thought of."

"The first person," Conroy said. "I didn't realize I was that notorious."

Regan smiled.

"Your first job is right here in this jail. You take care of it, the mayor's ready to have the governor pull the trigger on a pardon for you that's already written. Just needs a signature and you're out of here. After that, you two work out the job description together. But know one thing, John O'Toole is the only reason you'll be getting out of here. Without him, it's another seven years in that box."

Conroy scratched the side of his nose with his fork.

"What's in this for you?"

"I get a pardon too, just for having this conversation. Mine comes a little later. But we need to move quickly."

"Because Fiore gets out Sunday."

"Saturday," Regan said. Then he smiled. "And that can't happen. A lot of the money Fiore took ended up helping the mayor. Fiore's been telling his wife he's consumed with regret, that he never meant to become a thief, blah, blah, blah. He's been saying the same thing to some assholes from the Ethics Commission in Boston. Nothing comprehensive, but channels have been opened that could be really bad for John O'Toole, future governor."

*   *   *

Timing was everything. Getting Conroy released into general population had been the easy part. Deputy Superintendent Jameson had seen to that himself two days ago. The trick, Conroy knew, was keeping himself alive long enough to do the deed and then get released. It was Friday morning. He stood against the fence near the handball courts and watched Fiore, who crouched on the other side of the yard, his back to the concrete housing block. He kept his head on a swivel, eyes wide. Conroy checked his watch—11:15. Five minutes and the diversion was supposed to begin. He wanted this over already. A few members of the Posse over by the weight benches were eyeing him already, trying to remember why Conroy looked so familiar.

He began his walk. The plan he'd worked out with Regan had him stopping by the concrete picnic table over by the running track. From there he'd wait, but once the diversion started he'd have just a few seconds to get it done.

At the table, Conroy made sure he wasn't being watched by one of the few COs in the yard, then looked up to see if the guard in the tower was watching. He had his back to Conroy, who reached under the seat and found the long metal blade taped there. He pulled it out, then slid it quickly into the right cuff of his jacket. Fiore was watching a small scuffle at the handball court. Conroy walked slowly toward him. He stopped about ten yards away, leaned against the housing block.

Fiore turned and saw Conroy. He stood, was about to speak, when alarm klaxons blared as a brawl broke out across the yard. Ten Hispanics and ten whites clubbed and clawed at each other. Tear gas grenades burst. The four COs in the yard rushed over. The one in the tower shot a warning round from his twelve-gauge into the air, then pointed it down at the crowd. Voices over the PA system blared instructions. Fiore turned to look. Conroy dropped the blade into his right hand and covered the distance to Fiore's back in a few quick steps, grabbed his head with his left hand, pulled back and to the left, and sliced the blade across the length of Fiore's throat in one swift motion. Blood arced out from Flore's neck and splattered on the gravel path nearby. Conroy dropped Fiore and had started to walk away when someone grabbed him from behind and threw him against the building.

Two Hispanics, vaguely familiar. Both medium height, muscled, one holding him against the wall while the other brandished a shiv.

"Remember us?" said the one with the shiv. "We're in here because of you. We know who you are. Time for some pain."

"Who taught you how to hold a knife?" Conroy asked.

He kicked the one holding him in the groin, broke his left arm at the elbow with a quick shot from his forearm, then shoved him toward the attacker with the shiv. As they recovered their footing, Conroy sliced his blade across the face of the attacker, turned, spun the blade in his hand, plunged it into the chest of the one who'd pinned him to the building, pulled the blade out, grabbed his reeling partner by the hair, lifted his head up, and sliced his neck from ear to ear.

When he was done, Conroy wiped the blood from his hands, dragged Fiore's body over near the other two, dropped his own blade, then walked slowly toward the fight.

That night, prison officials were busy putting the pieces together on the two fights that had resulted in the death of three inmates. The whole jail was on lockdown. In the middle of it all, a fax arrived from the governor's office. Ten minutes later a guard appeared at Conroy's cell.

"Grab your shit," he said.

"Where am I going?" Conroy asked.

"Home. The governor issued a pardon. We're a little busy here, so hurry up, grab your shit, and let's go. There's already a cab waiting for you."

14

J ULIO TOOK THE right off Main onto Franklin Street and they saw him fifty yards away, under the statue. He turned off the siren and emergency lights and coasted to a stop against the new granite curbs the city had installed last month. Archer dropped his stethoscope on the dashboard.

"Won't need this," he said.

"There's a combo," Julio said. "Turtle Boy and LD. He's fully reclined. Must have been hitting the good stuff today."

Archer handed a pair of gray examination gloves to Julio, who held them up with a quizzical look.

"Trust me," Archer said. "I did three LD runs on Thursday, and he'd pissed himself every time."

LD was a local legend, a sublime and legendary drunk, and Archer could smell him the moment they stepped from the ambulance. It was the smell of the city as Archer and Julio knew it—stale cigarette butts and worn concrete sidewalks and bus exhaust and the hot dog vendor over by the Empire who steamed the vilest sauerkraut he'd ever encountered. LD was part of that olfactory smorgasbord, bringing to the table piss and wet sweat pants.

LD was known for his inebriation throughout the string of towns that connected the city to Boston. When Archer first got on with the city ambulance, there had been a game in which the medics who first found LD drunk on a given day would put him on the local commuter train with a note—*Tag! You're It!*—on his chest. The goal was to see how many round trips LD could make between the city and Boston before either he woke up or some well-meaning cop somewhere pulled him off and locked him up in the drunk tank. The record was twelve.

LD never gave his age. Archer decided on sixty-two. No reason; he just had to choose. LD was tall and potbellied, something Archer found odd in a man who lived on the street and drank his meals. He wore golf shirts and chino slacks with boat shoes. He had thinning white hair and bushy sideburns that stuck out of his scally cap at random angles.

His dark eyes and prominent brow gave him a regal bearing, like some dissolute minor duke. Or a retired investment banker, just reeking of piss and body odor. Maybe a Worcester Country Club golfer who'd happened to survive—barely—getting hit by a WRTA bus.

When drunk, LD could be an ornery grouch who dined-and-dashed and faked heart attacks in churches during morning prayer and fell down in front of city buses for the slip-and-fall money from a local chiropractor. What drove Archer and the other medics most insane was LD's penchant for calling for an ambulance, accepting transport to a hospital, then exiting the emergency department, only to do it again ten minutes later.

Archer also knew a better LD, a sober LD, a genuine gentleman. He would appear in local emergency departments with flowers for the nurses. For weeks at a time, his clothes were clean and his speech clear. He'd stop ambulance crews and thank them for caring for him. He'd operate an intermittent mobile car detailing operation that was regarded as the best in the city. At these times, anyone who saw LD walking down the sidewalk could be forgiven for mistaking him for a retiree on his way to spoil the grandchildren.

But as they approached tonight, Archer and Julio could see from the lump supine against the base of the statue that it wasn't Gentleman LD who awaited their arrival. He was snoring. His clothes were soiled and rumpled, arms splayed out as if he'd fallen while trying to hug the statue. Alcohol sweat lingered in the air, and the half-full bottle of white-label vodka lay next to his right hand. A melting ice cream sundae with M&M's on top rested on the granite base above LD's head.

"We need to talk about this," Julio said.

Archer and Julio turned away from the snoring drunk and walked far enough away that he couldn't hear their conversation.

"I can't do it," Julio said.

"What?"

"I won't. I'm so fucking sick of this guy, *Madre de Dios*."

Archer turned around to look at LD, then up at the statute.

"You really ought to have more respect," Archer said.

"For that motherfucker? I have more respect for shits I've recently taken."

"For the statue. It's pretty famous."

"You're crazy," Julio said. "You see what that little prick is doing to that turtle? That ain't right."

"They're out for a swim. That there is Greek mythology, my friend. That's art straight from the wellspring of the democratic ideal. That young man is simply out for a ride on that majestic sea creature."

"He's riding him, all right."

Archer shook his head. The statue was a source of grim humor in the city. Archer laughed as Julio spat on the ground. "Ugliest thing I ever seen," Julio said.

"Man who did that?" Archer said, pointing back to the statue. "Same guy who made the Lincoln Memorial. That's real art, amigo. Not one of those velvet matadors you used to hang on your wall."

"I don't know anything about what Turtle Boy is or is not doing, but let me tell you, paleface, that's one surprised-looking turtle right there. And that was Elvis. Not a matador."

Both men laughed.

"Seriously, though," Julio said. "What are we going to do with LD? We bring him in this early on a weekend night, and every ED nurse in the city is going to want to kick our asses. I can't say I blame them."

"Want to call the wagon? Think the PD would take him over to the tank? He doesn't seem that drunk yet to me— maybe they can."

Julio said he thought that was a capital idea, and Archer leaned into the microphone clipped to his left shoulder epaulette and keyed the radio.

*   *   *

On the rooftop across Main and looking down Franklin, Gerry Knak screwed the silencer onto the rifle barrel, then peered through the scope, saw the two medics and the unconscious bum. The homemade silencer weighed the barrel tip down, and Knak had trouble steadying his aim as the rifle bobbed under the gravitational pull and weaved against his heaving shoulder.

He saw Archer. He and his partner had their backs toward the bum and seemed to be discussing something. Bad angle between him and Archer. A trash can, dying sidewalk tree, a tough shot at best. Knak didn't want to kill the drunk but knew it was one of those necessary things he needed to do to get the real target out in the open. He'd shoot the bum, and when the medics came running, he'd have a clear shot at Archer.

Shoot one to get the other. Simple. For months, Knak had prowled the city, following ambulances. He knew how they worked, where they congregated. When he'd found the statue on the city common, the one with the young boy riding the sea turtle, seen the bums reclining against its marble base day after day, it had been like finding a pile of apples left in the woods to attract deer.

Knak centered the electronic sight's red dot on the bum's chest. The aiming point made a lazy figure eight over the scene, following the rhythms of Knak's own beating heart and breathing. He recited Dr. Locke's instructions. Breathe. Relax. Aim. Slowly squeeze. Knak timed the trigger pull within the sea swell of his heartbeat and breathing, trying to fire in that brief moment when both paused, adding an extra steadiness to his aim.

Knak felt the moment arrive and was surprised by the rifle's hop and jump. *The best shots are the ones we take when we're not expecting to shoot*, Dr. Locke always said.

The shot was gone.

Knak felt sure of everything.

*   *   *

LD awoke. He spotted the vodka bottle on the ground next to him, rolled to his right to grab it. His fingertips reached the base of the bottle when it exploded. Glass flew like shrapnel, leaving small cuts on his face. LD's eyes were stung by spraying vodka, his face now lathered in the cheap potato alcohol and rivulets of blood. LD rolled back, wiped his cheeks with the tails of his shirt, and stood.

When LD marched by Julio and Archer, head down, covered in booze and a dozen small cuts, they jumped in surprise.

"Where you going?" Archer called out. "Your ride's almost here. What happened to your face?"

LD stopped and gave the crew the finger.

"Screw you and your rides," LD said. "I'm going to get a coffee."

* * *

Knak recentered the red dot, his breathing ragged gasps. The view through his rifle's scope jumped and bucked with his hammering heartbeat. He saw legs and a stomach, the bum's face for a moment. He lowered the rifle, looked for Archer, too much of him hidden still behind the granite planter. Not enough to hit.

Knak lifted the rifle again, caught the bum's chest in his sights, and jerked the trigger. The view disappeared and the world detonated in a flash of orange and then darkness. Eyes closed, he lowered the rifle and laid his head against the cool concrete.

* * *

It took Archer a moment. He'd been to dozens of shootings, never been there for the moment of impact, never seen the victim spin like a top then fall, arms and legs no longer under control. LD still had his middle finger up and pointed in Archer's direction when a puff appeared in his stained gray sweat shirt. Eyes wide, a quick spin, and LD went down.

Archer heard the gunshot echo off the walls of the buildings surrounding the small green oasis where LD now sprawled, a crimson pool slowly emerging from under his shoulder blades. He crouched below the granite block and yanked the radio from his shoulder. While he talked, the granite seemed as light as the air around them. Inconsequential. He couldn't shake the feeling. The bullet that ripped through LD's chest. That bullet had been meant for him.

*   *   *

Knak peeked over the low concrete brow and saw the bum, supine, a red stain on his chest, a lake of red spreading out from under his back. He couldn't see Archer at all, assumed he'd hidden behind the planter. The volume of sirens careening this way convinced Knak that Archer had called it in. No time for a third shot. A miscalculation. Knak broke the rifle down, stuffed it into his canvas bag, and trotted from the roof.

*   *   *

The streets filled with cops. Guns drawn, they searched rooftops and doorways, kicked under benches, rousted a few junkies in the bushes, but no one had seen anything and soon they let Archer and Julio approach LD.

He was lifeless, eyes open, no pulse, no breathing. Still. When Archer cut away his shirt, they found a dime-shaped hole, center mass, the heart centimeters below where Archer's gloved fingers traced through fresh blood. LD was cold in the arms, cooling over his stomach, his chest. The blood pooled in a kidney-shaped bruise behind his pectorals, the backs of his thighs, the sides of his stomach. Julio called University on his radio, confirmed with a doctor what the medics had already decided. LD was dead. He wouldn't be transported.

Archer and Julio scanned the surrounding buildings, an unease settling between them. They'd arrived at plenty of shooting scenes over the years soon enough after the incident to smell the cordite in the air, or on frigid winter nights to see the warmth of the organs below the wound rise in tendrils of steam from the neat entry wounds.

This was different.

It was the feeling Archer had experienced with Angelo earlier. The sensation of being hunted, of a city prowled by an unseen force let loose just for him.

"You get the feeling LD wasn't really the one these shots were meant for?" Archer said.

"Who would they be for?"

"I don't know. Me? Us?"

Julio waved him off. "Lay off the overtime for a while, man. It's making you paranoid."

*   *   *

Knak had to move. His car was parked three blocks away. He knew he remained free only as long as he remained mobile. He'd scouted plenty of other spots in the city, and the night was young. He knew where Archer would be, would *have* to be. This wasn't the end, just a bad first step. Knak looked across the street one last time, then climbed down the fire escape and loped back to his car. He pulled out a map of the city. He'd get another shot.

As he jogged, Knak smiled. Too easy. He wasn't sure what he'd expected to feel. It was his first kill. They said the hardest thing about training soldiers was getting them to actually pull the trigger in a firefight. He knew humans at the genomic level were supposedly unsuited to killing one another. But he was a student of history, and for Knak, history was a catalog of two kinds of people: those willing to do what needed to be done for a higher principle, and those who resisted them.

Knak knew his place. Shooting the bum had told him everything he needed to know. When Archer was in his sights tonight—*tonight*—Knak knew he'd pull the trigger, and Charlotte would be alive again, almost, a piece of her returned to him by the settling of this debt. Knak ran, and as he ran, he knew that Charlotte would have approved.

*   *   *

The cops still hovered, stretching crime scene tape and tracing paths with a measuring wheel. They'd found two shell casings on a nearby roof. LD's body was long gone, yellow spray paint marking the spot where he'd died. Julio sat in the ambulance, still on the phone. Archer kicked at a piece of glass from the shattered vodka bottle. No longer feeling anonymous. Beginning to feel like a marked man.

"Been a while, Tommy," a woman said.

Archer didn't answer, just stared with narrowed eyes. The woman stopped a few yards away. She kicked at a piece of glass on the ground, looked at the scene. An old Chevelle peeled out on Main, racing toward the turnaround at Highland, out cruising. A group of teens on skateboards rolled between them and off toward the common.

Archer turned to walk away.

"I know you're not happy with me right now," Lu said. "I don't blame you. But we really need to talk."

"After all those things you've written about me the past few months?" Archer said. "No thanks. I never needed to talk with you, even before this."

"You do this time, believe me. It's serious."

Archer faced Lu. "Why don't you come into Boston sometime, you want to see serious."

"I know. I should have gone when I heard. I didn't. No excuses."

"I didn't expect you to," Archer said. "How long's it been? Five years? Ten? I stopped counting."

A cherry bomb went off on a side street above downtown; the hills that ringed the city echoed with the report. Pigeons scattered from the city hall dormers. Archer looked into the hills. Their round tops. An optical illusion. When Archer drove on them, he never found the top. Uphill in both directions, then down, and no idea when one became the other, up into down.

"They shitcanned me, the paper," she said. "I got the word in February. Two weeks and I'm done. I've got a chance to make some money, though. Interested to know how?"

"Not even on my list."

"It involves you," Lu said. "Bringing in the big kill."

Archer nodded. "I noticed. Lot of me in your stories lately."

"I need the money," she said. "But maybe I don't. Depends. I want to hear it from you. You tell me this is fucked. Give me something. I want to do the right thing. Anyone in the middle of selling themselves out wants to know, wants to be sure she's hollowed out before she gives up. I want you to tell me that you hurt that baby, that you screwed up that delivery. You say that, and I can keep this up with a clear conscience. But . . ."

"There's no absolution coming from me. You wrote all those stories, you made my life a living hell for the past six months. You're on your own. I can't give you what you want. I wasn't even there for the delivery. I'm a paramedic. Maybe not a great one. Maybe I'm burned out and sick of the bullshit, but I help people. I don't hurt them."

Lu looked at the yellow outline where LD's body once lay.

"You ever get used to it? The dead?" she asked.

Archer followed her gaze.

"You get used to not feeling anything," Archer said. "This call, this guy getting shot and killed? This is just the first call of the night. He won't be last. We came, we tried to help, then we pack up and put ourselves in service. That's the job. No stopping, no hugging, no crying, just get back in service. The city needs a good mopping, and I'm the janitor."

"Whatever the story really is," she said. "I need it. Otherwise I keep the stack of money they gave me and I write the story I've got and you and I never talk again, because believe me, you think you're mad now, wait until you see what I'm writing. I won't be in a position to do the right thing again. After this, I'm either pumping gas or maybe one of them. But we'll never talk again."

Archer scratched at the curbside dirt with the toe of his boot. "Remember that picnic? The thing with our parents? Things have been messed up a lot longer than the last six months. Why stop now?"

"What happened with the baby?" she asked.

"You see enough horrible shit, it becomes just another ache. Sore knees. Sore back. Nightmares. Angry all the time. Just a different kind of ache."

"I know you. I know you've had your problems, but what they're saying—it doesn't check out. Why? Why you? You're alone. They're coming and I'm bringing them, and if there's any reason to stop them, you've got to tell me; otherwise we're both fucked."

Archer spread a small pile of glass shards. "You never cared before. At least your father left some money."

"We've got things to worry about now," she said.

"I kind of knew. Still, those small piles of twenties that turned up on the kitchen table whenever Mom disappeared or went to rehab, they came in handy. I'd have gone hungry without it. But you never called. I could have used someone to talk to besides the dog."

"I don't want to be wrong," Lu said. "Not anymore. You say the word and I turn this ship around."

"You had no problem writing all those articles before this," Archer said.

"You're right," she said. "I had my reasons, even if I'm not exactly at peace with them at the moment. I can't stop what I've started, but I can, at least, I don't know, do it *right*. That probably doesn't make sense. You ever want to make amends with anything?"

"I have a list," Archer said.

"When you delivered the baby—"

Archer scowled, waved his hand, swatting at an unseen bug. "You and this baby. O'Toole and his fucked-up press conferences. I already said I didn't deliver the baby. I didn't deliver *the mayor's* baby."

Lu stepped back. "So it really was O'Toole's?"

Archer laughed. "Are you telling me the big city reporter doesn't know O'Toole is fucking everything in city hall, has been for years? Don't you actually talk to anyone over there? Cops have been joking about it for years."

"So you didn't do the actual delivery?" Lu asked.

Archer shook his head.

"The baby was already on the mattress when I got there. Me and Julio. We show up and there's this unresponsive new-born on this scummy mattress on the floor, placenta in a glass baking dish, blood everywhere and mom sick as hell, and who walks out of the kitchen but Eamon fucking Conroy, and he announces that we're not taking anyone anywhere."

Archer looked over at the ambulance. Julio still on the phone.

"Write what you want," Archer said. "It doesn't matter. None of this matters. You say I'm fucked, must be true. Not sure I care anymore. Losing my ticket, my job? Might be a blessing."

Archer started walking back to the ambulance.

"There's one question that's nagging at me," she said. Archer kept walking. "Why just you?"

Archer stopped.

"You ever wonder that?" Lu said. "There were two of you on that call. There's two of you on every call. Why aren't they sending the hounds after your partner over there? Why are they paying me fifty thousand dollars to go after just you? I can't figure it out. It never used to bother me, but my curiosity is like an itch you can scratch, it just itches all the same."

"Julio is too smart to talk about it," Archer said. He raised his arms in a questioning shrug. "Me? Eamon and I go way back. You remember what he used to be like. Nothing much has changed. That son of a bitch ruined that baby for life, but nothing new there. I made a stink about it. I filed an abuse-and-neglect report with state child welfare. Mysteriously never got anywhere, not once the mayor's office got involved. I guess the future governor is worried about dirty laundry."

Lu scratched the back of her scalp with a pen cap. She remembered summers on the shore and looking for sand dollars so hard that eventually she saw them everywhere, mirages really, and when she reached down, only handfuls of sand came up. Her mother used to say that the truth was something you saw only when your hands were as hard at work as your eyes.

15

NIGHT CAME ON. The city hit its lull. That was the way of weekend nights. Fireworks first, then an interlude. Sometimes summer nights reexploded in the wee hours, sometimes they quietly slipped into tomorrow. The sun announced itself in the mornings as a purple parabola of heat rising over Lake Quinsigamond to the east, the wet sidewalks steaming in a gray dawn.

Lu leaned back in the chair at her newsroom desk, considered Archer's claim. It confirmed her theories. The baby. The mayor's baby. Delivered by a bagman who'd screwed things up. A bagman with a vicious history. She cursed. She'd known from the start, months ago, seen it clear as day, but consumed with her own fears, Lu had ignored her instincts.

No more.

She found old articles in the *Courier*'s computerized morgue.

Eamon Conroy, son of a widowed and lifelong city bureaucrat. Joined the police force late, almost thirty, not long after a hero's discharge from the Army. Earned a Silver Star during a firefight at Omar Torrijos Airport during the Panama invasion in 1989. Early articles focused on the local-boy-makes-good angle.

A few clicks and it didn't take Lu long to find darker citations. Conroy's name a regular anytime police abuse was alleged. She cursed herself. How could she have forgotten? How could she have gotten mixed up with a guy like this?

Soon, Conroy no longer the golden boy. Lu remembered other cops steering clear of him. She remembered the off-the-record stuff, the rumors, not believing them. Then Freeland Street and *enough is enough*. There was a trial, Conroy off to jail, supposedly for a dime bid, but here they were less than five years removed and he was back in the city, up to old tricks.

Lu logged off. It was time to go meet Daisy Fontana of 33½ Kansas Street, knowing nothing good happened at the halves.

She was almost out the door when the metro editor, Emily Daigneault, called to her. She was one of Lu's favorites. Never butchered copy, handled deadline stress with aplomb, seemed born with the conviction that the day's paper would always come together.

"Lu! You have a second?"

Lu walked over, tapped her wristwatch. "Time is money," she said.

Emily put down yesterday's risotto and picked up a piece of paper from a tray. "Could you do a quick hit for tomorrow's briefs?" she said. "Nothing special. Couple grafs for the morning and I'll have the day crew follow up."

It was a press release from the police. It outlined another shooting that had just taken place, a couple of cops targeted by an unknown gunman. No one hit, but police were seeking a white male, early sixties, average height, average build, who might have been spotted fleeing from the city water tank across the street.

"I heard about this," Lu said. "I'll write it up later. Got an appointment to get to."

"Your sources don't have any weekend fun planned?" Emily said.

"No rest for the wicked." She smiled, tapped Emily's desk, and walked across the newsroom and out the back door.

Kansas Street was a short dead end adjacent to the rail yard. The street had once been a paved road, but now most of the pavement had been chewed away by time and neglect and the road was a rolling mess of potholes the size of artillery blast craters. Lu bounced down the road in her beat-up Saab, its shocks and springs groaning in agony over every mountainous bump.

There were three buildings on Kansas—a small office space for the railroad, a garage, and a triple-decker at 33½. A large crowd gathered in front of the building. Salsa music pounded through the air; someone had filled a kiddie pool with a bright-blue liquid. Lu saw partiers approach the pool and dip in red plastic cups, then walk away, sipping. There was dancing. Bottle rockets burst over the office.

The women ignored her as she weaved through the crowd. The men stared her down, gave her the once-over she knew so well after almost four decades in these neighborhoods. Lu knew a crowd on the edge of blowing up. She walked slowly, knew that bumping shoulders with the wrong person, prolonged eye contact, something as small as a muttered word could get her hurt.

It wasn't a smart idea to come down here alone in the middle of the night like this, she knew. Lu heard a crash, turned around to see glass from the passenger's side window of the Saab tumble to the ground. Two teenagers ran away, yelling, hands over their heads.

Lu cringed. Too far to turn back. She continued navigating to the front door. The crowd parted more slowly the closer she got to the front door of the building. The bonfire flames rose above the abandoned warehouse across the street. She thought about moving her car, but part of her wanted it gone, like a totem gone bad. The old Saab leaked oil from the valve gasket and the automatic tranny switched gears so roughly she sometimes lost grip on the steering wheel.

She walked around to the rear entrance, found a rusty mailbox nailed to the wall. It said *Fontana, 3rd floor* in magic marker scribbled on white electrical tape. Lu pounded on the door. She waited. Pounded again. Nothing. She tried the knob. It was unlocked. Lu stepped inside the vestibule and climbed the staircase slowly, two at a time, looking up the whole time.

The top of the staircase was shrouded in shadows. The lightbulb above the door was dead. The only light came from the second-floor landing, and the shadows stretched up toward the ceiling. She took a deep breath. She shifted her weight from foot to foot, trying to squeeze out the anxiety she suddenly felt in the pit of her stomach. She rapped on the door.

"I'm not coming to the party," a woman said from behind the door.

"Ms. Fontana?"

Lu could see the shadow of feet beneath the wooden door, heard someone lean against the wood, probably checking her out through the peephole.

"Who are you?"

"My name's Lu McCarthy. I'm a reporter from the *Courier*. We spoke earlier. I'd love just a few minutes of your time. I know it's late. I'm very sorry, but I wouldn't have come if it wasn't important."

Lu heard the rasping of a chain sliding, the ratchet of two locks coming undone. The door opened halfway. A young Hispanic woman in a light-blue T-shirt and gray sweat pants peered out. Lu noticed a baseball bat in her left hand.

"You have bad timing," she said. "I warned you. A lot of strangers in the crowd out there. It's probably not safe for you around here tonight."

"I'm not entirely sure I'll make it back, and I'm pretty confident my car won't be there, but this is important. Please. Just a few minutes."

Daisy opened the door wide.

They sat on a vinyl-covered couch. Daisy rested the baseball bat against a love seat nearby. The room was redolent of new furniture, sharp and tangy, chemically clean and unused. Lu left her notebook in her back pocket. She wasn't sure what she'd expected of Daisy Fontana. She thought she'd be broken, meek, crushed by the weight of her baby's illness. Instead, she looked at Lu with steady eyes, fearless.

"Mr. Conroy said I should talk to you," she said.

"I want to talk about your baby," Lu said.

"Mr. Conroy told me."

She nodded. "I know he was born here, and that things didn't go . . . well, they didn't—"

"It was terrible. What that paramedic did to me. What he did to Miguel. What he's trying to do to the mayor. He ought to be in jail, not out on the streets in an ambulance."

"I don't want to reopen any wounds," Lu said.

"That's why you're here, right? To open wounds. Mr. Conroy said you were writing about what happened and how it was this paramedic's fault."

Lu nodded. She noticed the sixty-inch flat-screen television on the wall, saw the box it had come with on the floor below, against the wall. The couch cushions bowed upward, toward the ceiling. The coffee table was new, the stainless-steel refrigerator in the kitchen the latest model, its plastic store protective sheathing still on its sides.

"There's an old saying in my profession: 'comfort the afflicted, afflict the comfortable,' " Lu said. "What happened to your baby—"

"Miguel."

"What happened to Miguel, that was a great wrong. I want to know more about it. You live in this city, you have to trust the people who come to take care of us, our cops and firefighters and medics."

Daisy stood and walked to the kitchen. She took a scratched plastic glass from the sink, rinsed it out.

"Would you like something to drink? I have lemonade."

Lu nodded. Daisy pulled a second glass down from a cupboard. Beyond her she saw a bedroom, and through the open doorway an elegant king-sized bed with a dark-wood frame, a pair of new night tables on either side of it. The bed stood on a dark-wood floor covered in what looked like chalk stripes. The house reverberated with a boom. Dust fell from the ceiling, covered the blades of what looked like a brand-new ceiling fan.

"The trains," Daisy said, before Lu could ask. She sat down on the couch, handed Lu a glass. "Twenty-four hours a day. They slam like that when they put the trains together. You get used to it, living here, but when I first moved in, *Dios mio.*"

Lu sipped.

"My husband, Rigo, left right after Miguel was born," she said. "He wanted to name the baby James, only he didn't want to pronounce the name the American way. He wanted it to be 'Ha-mez.' I told him that was ridiculous. Rigo never really took to Miguel."

"The name?"

"None of it. He didn't like the name. He couldn't handle Miguel. So much work. Rigo lived a simple life, and Miguel won't be simple. If only that paramedic hadn't been so bad at his job, Miguel would be a normal boy and Rigo would be here with me."

Lu looked around, noticed a lack of toys, of baby equipment, of any sign of a child at all. Daisy cried, she saw, but something about it wasn't right. Like a defendant mustering alligator tears in court. Lu knew you could fake it all except the eyes. Daisy's were hard even while the rest of her face contorted.

"Where's Miguel tonight?" she asked.

"He doesn't live with me," Daisy said. "I cannot run the machine that breathes for him. He's up at the special hospital in Lyme, where they have nurses that care for him all day and night."

Lu scratched her chin. "Seems odd, though. Man leaving his son like that, especially after what happened to Miguel. And to you. Have you talked to him lately?"

Daisy toyed with a butterfly pendant on a thin gold chain. She looked at Lu as if divining, a dowser looking for a well on some destitute farmer's land. Lu held her gaze.

"Not since the night he left. He's around, but we don't talk. Sometimes he leaves me money, or flowers on the doorstep, but he won't come in. Don't think bad of Rigo. This was just too much for him, even from the beginning. The people, John's people. As soon as I got the bump, they started coming around, asking if we needed anything."

"John?"

Daisy smiled. "You know who I mean."

"I don't."

"Then you are stupid. You should go. Have fun with your new friends out there."

Lu took out her notebook, wrote. "So John O'Toole," she said. "Why would he care?"

Daisy sipped her lemonade, caressed the necklace. Lu's pen died. She scribbled harder, but no ink came out. Daisy bent forward, plucked a cheap ballpoint off the table, and handed it to her.

"The mayor is very close to those who work for him," Daisy said. "I work in the city clerk's office. The mayor was just concerned for a subordinate."

"The night Miguel was born, how did the paramedic seem?"

"Seem?" Daisy asked.

"You know, how did he act? Did he seem normal? Did he slur his speech, stumble at all, anything like that?"

A bottle smashed against the side of the apartment, near a window. Lu jumped. Daisy remained still.

"They know you're up here and they've been drinking," Daisy said. "There are some people in that crowd. My brother's people—the Posse. They're drunk and a little pissed off at the moment. As for the medic—he seemed, I don't know. Out of it. Like not all there. Like maybe he'd been drinking or something. I was lucky Miguel made it out alive at all. Thank God for the other one, Julio Tavares. If it weren't for him, Miguel would be dead."

"So Archer delivered Miguel? You're sure?"

Another bottle. Daisy shook her head.

"You don't forget that sort of thing."

The crowd below was chanting, singing. The bonfire flames rose higher so that Lu could see the licking peak of the flames through the window.

"So there was no one else here before the medics?" she asked.

"I don't know what you mean."

"Was there someone here before them? Someone who may have actually delivered Miguel? Anyone? What would Rigo tell me?"

"These aren't the questions Mr. Conroy said you'd be asking," Daisy said. She rose and paced the kitchen in tight circles, rubbing the butterfly. "You need to leave Rigo out of this. He's taking it hard."

"These are the questions I need to ask," she said.

"You shouldn't have come."

"Ms. Fontana, there's not a lot of time."

Pounding at the front door. Yelling. Daisy walked to the couch, grabbed Lu's arm, and hustled her through the kitchen, through her bedroom, and to a narrow door in the back corner of the apartment.

"You've got to go," she said. "Follow the stairs to the basement; they'll let you out right onto the train tracks. Hurry."

"Someone else delivered Miguel, didn't they?" Lu asked. "Was it Eamon Conroy? I need to know. I don't care what they gave you. I need to know."

Daisy pushed harder. Lu jammed her feet into the doorframe, grabbed Daisy's wrist.

"Rigo isn't the father, is he?" Lu said. Fists banged at the door on the other side of the apartment. She could hear wood splinter with each strike. "Just tell me the truth. Tell me what happened."

"Please! Just go."

"Tell me."

"This isn't what Mr. Conroy said you'd ask me."

"It was Conroy," Lu said. "For god's sake, just say it. It was Conroy who delivered Miguel. Where is Rigo, really? He didn't leave, did he? He's scared—just like you."

Daisy stopped pushing for a moment. Her eyes filled with tears. Real this time, Lu saw.

"These are not the right questions," she said, then pushed Lu through the door and locked it.

Lu crashed down three flights of stairs and burst out of a short basement door and through a weed-filled garden onto a vast field of train tracks. She ran as fast as she could and tried not look back. But like Lot's wife, she did.

A crowd danced around her car, aflame now, their faces flickering in howling red-faced stop-motion, reflected in the fire itself, contorted and hot continents like the flames, Lu's car a burning bush, the crowd waiting for it to speak to them. Smoke rose toward the sky and the hills around the city. She remembered learning once that burning was a process of transition, heat applied to a thing and the thing becoming vapor and the vapor burning not exactly the thing itself but a new version of it, transformed, word made flesh, water into wine, ashes to ashes and dust to dust.

Lu bent over with her hands on her knees and laughed. The car was gone. It was another absence in her life she'd have to learn to live with, at least for a little bit. No car. No job. No nothing. She was getting used to it. So many things she no longer had.

Lu made her decision. She let go of the fear she felt at losing her job, about losing the things she'd devoted her life to, family and work. She saw that, by taking his money, she and Conroy were one and the same. Of all the things she could live with, this was not one of them.

In darkness spreading out in a circle from the flames, a carless and nationless Lu McCarthy set her jaw and marched across the empty train yard, hands by her sides in balled fists. With each step she was further on her own, in a land that separated the loners from the pack and picked them off, one by one.

16

Last summer

SALVE MATER COLLEGE football field. Even this far above
the field, Archer could tell it was her. She'd grown, but
she hadn't. They'd put the platform at the fifty-yard line.
Evangeline Vacca lay supine on a canopy-covered hospital
bed draped in altar linens. Her white dress glowed in the
midday sunlight. Cloudless sky above. A breeze fluttered the
vestments of the clergy behind her bed. Bishop McInnis himself presided. A nurse tended to the ventilator and monitored
Evangeline's condition.

From his aerie, Archer examined the bleachers. Organiz-
ers expected a full house. It would be Evangeline's first
appearance in the city in months. The buses in the parking
lot came from New York and Pennsylvania, North Carolina
and Florida. The folding seats arranged on the grass immediately below Evangeline's platform were filled by people with
canes and walkers. A corral to the side held the phalanx of
wheelchair-bound supplicants.

He looked over at Elaine. She held Michael close to her chest. He'd just gotten home from his first operation. The scar at the base of his neck was red but healing well. The vomiting had almost stopped. There had been only a handful of seizures the past week. Archer held his sleeping son's hand and caressed his thumb.

"Thank you for coming to this," Archer said.

Elaine rubbed her son's back. "We said we'd try anything," she said.

Organ music piped through the football stadium's PA system. A voice interrupted. "Individual audiences with Evangeline will commence in fifteen minutes."

Archer looked at his ticket. They were in the first group to go. He stood. "We probably should get down there," Archer said.

Elaine looked down at her sleeping son. She rose and they descended the stadium stairs.

"Thank you for doing this with me," he said. "I know it seems a little . . . odd."

"Nothing seems odd anymore. Everything seems possible. Bad. Good. It's all the same."

Archer had adapted to his son's diagnosis. Brain tumors. At first, he'd tried to will their old lives into existence. As if he could ungrow the cancer in the back of his son's brain. Then he'd tried to learn all he could about brain tumors. It was like saying he was going to learn all there was to know about Mars, but in a month.

He quit, decided to trust in the team of doctors and specialists working on his son. It was humbling and terrifying, the loss of control. The loss of any meaningful input. He felt shame for breaking down during the conference with Michael's neurosurgeon the night before the first operation, begging her to fight for his son. That wasn't like Thomas

Archer. He never begged people to do things he knew they'd do naturally, as if there were any question that the surgeons would do their best for his son. But he was discovering that there were adjustments to be made. Begging for his son's life was just one of them.

They descended the stairs and took their place in the long line snaking its way across midfield and to the stairs at the bottom of Evangeline's platform. In front of them the procession limped and lurched to the stage, some carrying small children or offering their arms to elderly pilgrims. One by one they ascended the stairs, approached Evangeline's side, crossed themselves, sometimes touched small bags or artifacts to her arm, then hustled off the other side and back onto the field.

Archer saw a few, overcome by either the heat or emotion or maybe a higher power, collapse in the grass on the far side. Volunteers tended to them. A few shook, others cried.

"Why do they touch things to her?" Elaine asked.

"They believe anything that touches Evangeline has healing powers."

"So those bags?"

"Usually full of coins, or buttons," Archer said. "Things they can hand out."

"And bring to sick people?"

A man in front of them about-faced. Midforties, thick beard, gaunt, wearing a red Windbreaker and clutching rosary beads in white knuckles.

"Stardust," he said.

"Excuse me?" Archer said.

Elaine took a half step back. It wasn't his eyes, she thought, though they set off alarms in her mind. It was the rosary beads. Elaine had noticed lots of people holding them, reciting prayers she didn't recognize from her Methodist upbringing. This man wasn't praying, though Elaine thought he held on to the beads with the fervor of a believer.

"This is all bullshit," the man said. "Statues bleeding oil. Stigmata. Bullshit. You know what they found when they tested the oil? Extra-virgin. Yeah, and I'm not talking about the Holy Mother. The oil coming from the statues was olive oil."

Archer shrugged. "Where does it specify what kind of oil a bleeding statue should produce?"

The man laughed. The line moved forward a step.

"You believe this whole thing then?" he asked.

"I've heard crazier things, so maybe," Archer said. "Maybe not. I don't know. Our son is very sick. I know there's been things surrounding Evangeline that no one can really explain. I'm in no position to turn my nose up at anything. What the fuck are you doing here?"

The man squinted at the field. His eyes had a look in them Archer had seen often. Proximity to death. Maybe the man's, maybe someone he loved. People like him, witnesses, bearers of burdens most didn't want to contemplate, Archer knew, they had a wide-eyed calmness to them. But not peace. Calm sometimes came from pressure, everything pressed flat.

"That wedding ring you're wearing, is it gold?" the man asked.

Archer nodded.

"You know where gold comes from? Exploding stars. That ring on your finger? The gold in it is probably billions of years old. That's where we come from too. Dead stars. Bereft of energy, they collapse on themselves and explode, filling the universe with carbon, hydrogen, oxygen, nitrogen. Shit like gold and silver, the stuff we kill each other for. All of it stardust. A bunch of fleshy sacks sewn together by the atomic links of long-dead stars, standing in line to be saved by a comatose god girl. Can you see the cosmic irony here? This magical bullshit? Might as well believe in the Easter Bunny."

Another supplicant fell prostrate on the ground on the far side of the platform. Two volunteers rolled the woman onto her back, fanned her face. A sea gull buzzed a table of bananas and pastry, cans of juice and bottled water, donated by the college cafeteria.

"If you don't believe, why are you here?" Archer asked.

"Believe, don't believe. What is belief? I mean, what if I told you I didn't believe in disbelief? Maybe I'm a gambler and these are odds I'm playing. The house always wins, right? The house always wins."

The man gripped the beads tighter, rocked from toes to heels. The man's turn arrived. He spun, thrust the beads out at Archer.

"Take them," he said.

"You keep them."

The man's eyes were red and teary. He grabbed both of Archer's hands in his. Archer tried to pull away but the man held tight.

"I'm begging you, take these," the man said. "We're stardust, but in case we're not, I don't want these. I don't want anything."

Later, when Archer and Elaine stood next to Evangeline, he touched the rosary to Evangeline's contracted and bent right hand. Her unseeing eyes stared up at the sun-brightened canopy. Her mouth agape. A modern martyr, Archer thought. The ventilator whooshed. The bishop nodded solemnly. Elaine dipped Michael. His hand touched Evangeline's arm for a moment. The world spun along, unchanged. *Believe, don't believe*, Archer thought. *The house always wins.*

CHAPTER

17

L AST APRIL.
     The first.
Fool's Day.

Julio gazed at the small Cape in Northborough and thought of the possibilities. The snow was gone except for a few stubborn patches under a grape arbor behind the in-ground pool out back. The lawn was green, even now. Flat. Surrounded by woods on three sides.

The small white fence in the front yard, something to paint someday, maybe teach little Jacob how to do it, when he was old enough. The school down the street like a temple. Room to breathe, not like the condo where he lived now, under high-tension power lines that brought hydroelectric power from Niagara Falls all the way to central Massachusetts along a narrow and cracked asphalt road teeming with cars and noise and the odor of trash, diesel, body odor, and cigarette smoke.

A life, he thought. *This is a place you could have a life.*

He wanted out of the city. Born and raised there, Julio'd had enough. Enough crime and grime, the constant noise, trains banging away along tracks in the culvert below his condo complex, the downshifting tractor-trailer trucks at all hours on the nearby interstate. Neighbors who blasted their stereos and howled at the moon. Breaking glass. Graffiti that reappeared as fast as you washed it off the siding. He wanted grass to mow, a driveway to shovel, wanted to come home from a night shift on the city ambulance and float in the pool, adrift on crystal-blue waters, suspended as if in flight above the diamond-patterned pool liner.

Maria and Jacob were inside with the real estate agent.

"The schools," Maria repeated every time Julio brought up the price, which was just beyond their ability to afford.

He'd made a feeble last attempt to object to the cost when they pulled up to the curb this morning.

"Smell that?" Maria asked. "That's lawn. Freshly mowed lawn."

He thought of the schools. He also thought of the gunshots he'd heard in the complex parking lot last night. He thought of the skell who whistled at Maria every time she walked Jacob to the playground. He thought of the hypodermic needles she'd found under the slide last time she went there.

Julio no longer cared if he couldn't afford it. He'd get a side job, maybe at a private ambulance company, maybe driving an airport limo under the table, with tips. Knuckles had a good gig doing that. Maybe he'd just take every overtime shift available, grind himself to a nub against the city's sick and injured. He was willing to barely be around, as long as he knew Maria and Jacob were here while he worked.

Julio was standing on the curb doing math in his head when the Crown Vic pulled up. He knew who was behind the wheel. Eamon Conroy had left a note in his mailbox last night, while Julio was at work. He'd found it this morning when he got home. Didn't tell Maria. He didn't know the man, had met him just the once, on Kansas Street. That one meeting was enough to convince him that Conroy was not someone he wanted following him around.

"That," Eamon Conroy said, pointing to the house, "that's a place for a man to sleep at night."

He held out his hand for Julio to shake. He didn't move.

"Julio Tavares, right? Come on, shake my hand. I won't bite."

They shook hands. Julio ignored the damp smoothness of the other man's hand, looked into the gray pools of his irises and thought of a circling shark, emotionless and predatory, sleek and dangerous in its torpor.

"I know this is awkward for you. Wondering how I knew you'd be here, right? And last time we talked, that was a fucked-up situation, no? What with the baby and everything."

Julio worried about Maria, wondered who else Conroy had brought. The city seemed too close again. Escape impossible.

"Well, I'm paid to know things," Conroy said. "It's what I do. What can I say? Some people are meant to be golfers or doctors or whatever. I'm good at this. Let me ask you something. What're they asking for a house like this?"

Julio looked up and down the street. No other cars. Just suburbia. Green lawns and leafy trees. The line of identical Cape homes glinted in the sun up and down the block. The black seal coating on each driveway reflected heat like mirrors.

"Don't worry, I'm not looking to buy," Conroy said. He laughed. "I'm city through and through. Plus, I've got the other place down on the Cape, in Dennis Port. Nice down there. But I'm just curious. Place like this. What're they asking?"

"I think it's four twenty-five," Julio said.

Conroy whistled.

"Whoa! That's a lot of ambulance shifts, right? You medics must be making good cake, be able to afford a place like this on your salary. What with the kid at home instead of day care and Mrs. Tavares not working. Money's got to be tight."

Anger cut through the fear.

"I'm not scared of you," Julio said. "I know where you come from. You got the rest of them squirming, but you don't scare me. You never did. If you think you're going to scratch up a couple facts about my life—facts like a thousand people know—show up here like some kind of mind reader or whatever, and I'm going to go all weak-kneed? You've got the wrong guy."

Conroy held up his hands. "Hey, whoa, I never meant to scare you," he said. "I know who you are. I know you don't scare easy. I'm just saying. Money must be tight. I look at this house and I think, the man has taste and a plan. I respect that. I want to see you do well, I really do. And, to take it a step further, I think I may be able to help."

Julio saw Maria and the agent strolling by windows inside the house. He didn't want Maria to see him talking to Conroy. He didn't want the guilt by association. He didn't want to have to explain a visit he could not explain in a million years.

"I think you should probably get going," Julio said. "I've got nothing to say to you."

"Four twenty-five, that's a tough nut," Conroy said. "What if I could get you a hundred, for the down payment? A gift. No need to repay. And all you have to do is sign something, maybe meet with a city lawyer for twenty minutes? Go on the record to help out someone who, oh, by the way, will probably be the next governor. Light lifting, just help us out."

Julio looked at the house. Through the big bay window in front he saw Maria swinging Jacob around by the arms. The boy laughed. Maria beamed. She looked weightless and young, like a decade had evaporated overnight. Nearly twenty years together and he loved her the same way he had the day they met at the MDC pool on Gates Avenue. He'd bought them both freeze pops and they'd talked about music. He wanted nothing more than to give her this house, this life.

"I don't know what I could possibly help you with," Julio said.

"I think you do," Conroy said. "Your partner, Thomas Archer, he filed a complaint against the mayor about that baby call on Kansas Street last winter. Made all kinds of crazy accusations. The complaint needs to go away. There's an election coming up, and we can't have certain things going public."

"I won't help you go after my partner. Might as well stop this conversation right here."

"Once the investigation gets going, they're going to be asking you what happened. Who was there. What went down. Those sorts of things. Now, there's a couple versions you can tell. You can tell Archer's version"—Conroy pointed to the house—"and this house remains just a fantasy. Or . . ."

"There's no other version. Never was. Never will be."

"Or if you help us out, just a little," Conroy said, arms spread in an embrace of the tidy Cape in this tidy town, as if to prove to him that he could take it all away or grant it with a whisper, "you can say good-bye to that run-down shithole on Coover Street and come home every morning to your nice house in a great town, throw your little boy around in that beautiful pool back there. You're a realist. I've done my homework. This is a simple decision. Archer's already made his own bed, and he'll lie in it. Only question is, you want to end up there too?"

The thought began as a grain of sand.

An inkling.

A pebble in his shoe.

First step—allowing the thought in the first place.

Why am I protecting Archer? Julio wondered. He'd told him not to file that complaint, that they weren't there to solve the world's problems. Who cared if it was the mayor's baby? Who cared if Eamon Conroy or the mayor or Mickey Mouse had tried to deliver that baby? By the time they'd got there, the worst had happened. No amount of complaints or accusations was going to undo what had already been done.

Medics kept their heads down. That was the way they all survived in the city, he told himself. Cops, medics, firefighters, the nurses at Saint B's emergency department. Keep your head down, do your job, leave the crusades to the crusaders. He'd begged Archer, told him over and over that the complaint was a bad idea. That was Archer, though. He fired first, then aimed.

The Big Question: why should Julio deny his family this house, this life, to defend a guy who'd spent a career making bad choices?

He said the words before he realized the truth announced by that first pebble: that he'd already turned on Archer, and there'd be no going back.

"Tell me," Julio said, "how this would all work."

CHAPTER

18

Two weeks left. Labor Day on the horizon. Lu marveled.

Six months, gone in a blur. Writing those stories about Archer, making that dipshit mayor sound like JFK, taking orders from Conroy—it had become like digging her own grave, and now Lu wanted nothing more than to crawl in and let the undertaker bury her in dirt.

And now, with the end so near, Lu headed once again to the Ding Wa. The first time, Conroy had slid a manila envelope fat with cash across the bar.

"First half now," he said. "Rest when you deliver."

Most of that money had disappeared to pay Danny's college fees and to buy another beat-up Saab.

Lu was meeting Conroy there tonight. Status update of sorts. The bar at the Ding Wa waiting for them, their dark energy camouflaged in a room filled with the sources of the city's real power.

The Dinger itself had many charms. A thatched-hut ceiling over the dining area. The long bar of dark wood that reflected the tin ceiling tiles above, except in the spots where the water rings never quite scrubbed off. The checkerboard white-and-black tile floor. The small parquet dance floor that Lu had never seen anyone dance on. A corner jukebox. The Keno machine above the bar, framed with bubbling electric-orange liquid lights. A buzzy atmosphere charged with clouds of cheap cologne and the sweet tang of fried lo mein noodles.

Two steps in and Lu saw her patron over at the big table by the window, where the city's power players preened most nights. John O'Toole held court before a throng of strivers. He gave Lu a wave and a smile and returned to his Scotch, leaning over first to whisper into the ear of Eamon Conroy, who sat to the mayor's left. Conroy tracked Lu as she crossed the room on her way to the bar.

A few more steps toward the lounge and she saw Stony Forrester. The police chief commiserated with four beefy, flushed-faced men in their early to late forties, all in cheap, off-the-rack suits she imagined they'd bought on layaway at Spag's. The dinner companions were balding and double chinned, their noses like red-vined road maps perched over gabardine and polyester two sizes too small.

She made them for cops, maybe chiefs from the outlying suburbs, the ones who liked to come into the city and net-work with Forrester and his guys, or perhaps local FBI agents, banished to this crumbling outpost away from the buzz and aura of crime fighting in Boston. Here the agents' careers died slow deaths as one day melted into the next, running down check kiters and small-time embezzlers or housewives who financed internet gambling addictions by pilfering from PTA bank accounts.

"So I says to the guy, buddy, this can go down one way or another, I could give a fuck," said the nearest man, taller than the rest, round chinned and with an extra floridness to his face, his sandy-haired comb-over more overt than the others. "I'm still not giving you back the goddamn doll!"

The group erupted in howls. They slapped backs, clapped the table so hard the flatware tinkled first, then crashed like someone rattling a shoebox of broken glass. They rocked their chairs and dabbed with their ties at the tears of laughter on their cheeks. Stony Forrester remained cross-legged, motionless. He laughed without sound, so that it looked to Lu as if mirth pained him.

Stony gave the impression of a man weighing options at all times, panning the mud before him in the hopes of finding flecks of gold. Conversations with the chief always made Lu intensely self-conscious, as if there were some secret sin she would cop to under the intense gaze of Forrester's gray eyes—or were they blue? or green? No matter the color. You couldn't help but notice them. His eyes weren't the soft underbelly of his soul. You couldn't divine anything by looking into them. Instead, it was almost like they weren't there, or they were blast doors from a factory furnace, steel and cold and belying nothing behind them.

Forrester's physical fitness was legendary. The chief kept a seventy-five pound dumbbell in his office that he would casually toss from hand to hand while he spoke. It was said Stony didn't sleep, they just plugged him in at night. Tonight, Lu noted, the platter of kung pao chicken in front of him sat uneaten. The chief's eyes followed Lu as she walked. She was certain he nodded at her.

She suppressed a twinge of sadness as she surveyed the scene. This was the last time she would come to the Dinger as a member of the small tribe that ran the place, find herself welcomed into the city's communal power source. She wasn't one of those who pulled the levers, but as a reporter she'd moved the people who did, and her observations meant something to those people.

Being a daily newspaper reporter in much of America no longer meant what it once had, but here it still carried weight. People here—particularly those in the public sector—still cared what the paper said about them, even as they professed not to give a shit. She didn't know how much longer that would last, but it didn't matter. In a couple weeks, when there was nothing to be gained by knowing Lu McCarthy, she would be as absent from it all as surely as if she'd died.

That's how they would talk about her, too. Gone. A vapor, someone who'd been here and now was evaporated. Jimmy might put her picture up on the wall behind the bar, but it would be like one of those old daguerreotypes funeral parlors once made, of the dead posed as the living and appearing only the more deceased for the effort.

Lu knew what it was like, to be remembered. She'd been around for the toasts that nights like this at the Dinger produced, when the crowd got drunk and misty-eyed and everyone slapped each other on the back and raised shot glasses to Fitzy or Jonesie or whomever and tilted their drinks in honor of the departed, who, if they were lucky and had played their cards right, if they'd been wise enough at the right times to make the correct zigs and zags over a few decades of work, would be at that very moment sitting in a condo on Marco Island, relaxing in the caress of some soft coastal Florida winds, remembering when.

At the bar Lu waved and raised two fingers at Mae, the Dinger's best bartender. She'd been there a decade, knew little English beyond booze.

"Southern Comfort Manhattan," Mae said, "straight up, very dry, with a twist"—which came out as *tweest*. Lu nodded.

Lu couldn't place the accent. Jimmy Minh, the owner, was Vietnamese, had moved here as a child and bused tables at the old El Jabbar up the street, where he'd saved and scrimped and collected enough coins and sold just the right amount of dope, and only to the right people, that he was able to buy the Ding Wa right about the time Lu McCarthy got her job as a reporter at the *Courier* and John O'Toole and a hundred guys like him took over from their fathers. Time moved on so steadily that none of them noticed when they became their fathers, right down to the barstool.

Lu's Manhattan arrived. Time to stabilize, she thought, find some equilibrium. Find a steady state for the hard work yet to come. Soon it would all be new. She'd be a different kind of player this time next month, next year, whenever. She wasn't sure how much time it took graft to work. This was her first try at it. But before the new path, a walk down old and worn grounds was needed.

She thought back to the other old-timers at the *Courier* who'd gotten the heave-ho, took stock of their landings. Sikes worked at the Tech as an editor in the communications and PR department. He'd doubled his salary but was miserable, the job boring him beyond tears. A few others were freelancing. Lu couldn't see herself doing any of that. She couldn't see herself doing anything.

So this was what it had been like for horse whip manufacturers when Henry Ford did his thing with the automobile, she thought. Whole professions disappearing overnight.

The Dinger wasn't hopping yet. It was early. Jimmy glided between the maître-d' table and the booths behind the bar. He was in his sixties and regally overweight, which was in line with his bearing. He wore fine silk suits and kept his hair slicked back in deference to Humphrey Bogart. The checkerboard tiles made him look almost weightless as he walked, like his shoes touched nothing but air. Jimmy stopped and wrapped an arm around Lu's shoulder, close but not touching.

"What is this bad news I hear?" he asked.

"It's a farce," she said.

"It is no farce to lose your job. *Tsk-tsk*. When all is said and done, come see me and I'll take care of you. I always need help busing tables."

"I could tend bar."

A gunshot laugh. "I'm your friend, but I'm not stupid. Have you ever tended bar?"

"I speak better English than Mae," Lu said.

"Big deal," Mae said from down the bar, giving her the finger and smiling. "This isn't as easy as it looks. You've got to be good to get the tips."

"I could restock the maraschinos," Lu said. "Or the pretzel bowls."

Jimmy clapped her on the shoulder. "It occurs to me that if I hired everyone who no longer works at the newspaper, I'd go broke."

She couldn't refute the logic. There were a lot of them, and there were more on the way. Probably even Gabe Kittredge himself, if future political ambitions didn't pan out. She'd like to see Kittredge with a mop.

"You are forgiven," she said to Jimmy's back as he laughed and disappeared into the crowd growing around the bar.

She sipped at her Manhattan, ordered another. Conroy hopped onto the stool to her left. Lu fought the urge to slide to the right. Conroy unnerved her, which wasn't that unusual; the former police detective unnerved everyone. But unlike most people, Lu could put a name to her unease.

She'd been to Conroy's trial a decade earlier, heard about the things he did to make his bones. She'd heard the stories about Conroy's personal squad. She'd seen bodies no one claimed. The crime scene photos displayed at trial. His brand of police work was . . . unconventional. If Conroy's existence had shaken McCarthy's faith in law enforcement, that the police excommunicated him from their ranks had renewed it.

"That one's on the mayor, and I'll take a Guinness," Conroy said to Mae.

Conroy leaned close enough to her that their shoulders touched.

"I'm a beer man, myself," he said. "Guinness. Can you stand it? What a fucking stereotype. A mick and his Guinness. But I love it. You've got to love a beer that you have to eat with a fork and knife."

Lu stared into the mirror that backed the bar. "I'm working on the big finale," she said.

"No doubt."

"Names will be named."

"And the woman's address?" Conroy asked.

Lu nodded. "It was in the police report you sent."

"Have you talked to her?"

"I have," Lu said.

"And?"

Lu sipped her drink. "Enlightening. As advertised." She finished off her Manhattan and asked Mae for a water.

"Smart move," Conroy said. "That's what causes the hangovers. Dehydration. Funny thing about alcohol. It's like, imagine a liquid that leaves you drier the more you drink it. Counterintuitive. Unexpected."

"A little trick my father taught me from his Army days," Lu said.

"Body's three-quarters water," Conroy said.

"Glass of water for every drink."

Conroy smiled. "An Army family, eh? You come from a line of patriots?"

"Not really. Torn meniscus not long after boot camp. He got out on a medical."

Conroy sliced the overflowing head off his beer with a butter knife, put his lips on the edge of the pint glass without picking it up from the bar, and slurped. Lu thought of an anteater plunging into an ant hill on some *National Geographic* special. Conroy rose, wiped foam from his upper lip with a cocktail napkin, crumpled it into a ball, and tossed it onto the floor behind the bar. Mae bent over and scooped it up. Conroy looked at her, one eyebrow cocked, nodded toward Mae's ass.

"About the second half," Lu said.

"After the last story. I'll find you."

"When do we talk about longer-term solutions?" she said. "The job?"

"Don't get distracted," Conroy said. "Keep on digging about this Archer kid. The mayor has a job picked out for you. We were thinking you'd be great as his personal communications assistant. Seventy-five thousand a year. City pension. City perks. Make your own hours and get to know personally everyone in this town worth knowing. But we need this other thing first."

"Okay."

"But it's almost not worth talking about at the moment . . ." Conroy said. He reached into an inner pocket of his suit coat and pulled out a buzzing cell phone. He read for a moment, put the phone back.

"It appears I'm needed back at the table," Conroy said.

"Why is it not worth talking about?" Lu asked.

"Keep grinding. You're almost there. And when this is all over, you won't have a care in the world. Even if you *do* have to bring the hammer down on your stepbrother to do it."

Lu fought for a poker face, lost. Conroy stared into her eyes, the smile disappeared for a moment, and she felt what it must have been like to be in an interrogation room when Conroy had you cold and there was suddenly nothing you could do about any of it. He had you, and what he wanted done was what would be done. The smile reappeared; Conroy clapped her on the shoulder.

"Kingdoms rise and wane," Conroy said, "but the church of Jesus will remain. I know what you're thinking, but the answer is *no*. This is the mayor's call. Our mutual friend Archer cost me my career, but I have no desire for revenge. He earned this all on his own."

And then he was gone. Her hands shook. She wiped beads of sweat from her forehead with a handful of cocktail napkins. Mae brought her a water pitcher and a fresh bowl of pretzels.

Fat Larry climbed onto the stool next to her.

"Who was that creepy motherfucker?" he asked.

Larry Potemkin had covered high school sports for the paper for almost as long as Lu. He was short and weighed three hundred pounds, had bushy black hair, sideburns, and a beard, and wore the same uniform to work every day—black pants, a white short-sleeved button-down shirt, and a black tie.

"Just a city hall guy, a source," she said.

Unlike Lu, Fat Larry had a future at the paper. Sports had been spared the budget ax because no one had yet figured out how to give away local sports coverage for free on the internet. Fat Larry knew his days were numbered, but no one had started counting just yet.

"End of an era, Lu. I fucking hate it." Larry picked up a handful of peanuts.

She scowled at Larry over the top of her glass. "Aren't you allergic to those?"

Larry reached into his pocket for a bottle of antihistamine pills, held it in the air and shook it. "I'm ready. Plus, it's bullshit. One time my throat gets a little itchy and they tell me I can't eat peanuts anymore. Screw that. I like the honey-roasted ones."

Lu poured another glass of water. Larry continued to eat.

"I just left Kittredge's office," Larry said. "He told me they just sent you the official two-week notice. Did they at least lube it a little?"

"He was okay. Same as February when he first told me."

"How the hell is that asshole still employed?" Larry asked. "Blabbering all that online interweb shit. Guy can't even set the clock in his Range Rover."

"It seemed convincing. A few clicks, some unique eyes, many platformed something-throughs and what-the-ma-brands and *bada bing, bada boom*, ad revenue saves us all. Of course, to save this village, we have to burn a few villagers."

Larry grunted. "Yeah, and 'a few' means every single one."

"Yup," she said.

Larry went silent, and Lu didn't want quiet right now. She wanted to hear Potemkin complain about something—the poor state of high school sports, the length of major-league baseball games, grunting in women's tennis.

What she didn't want to think about was Eamon Conroy and that safe house. Eamon Conroy and his goons. For a year after Archer and his partner Moonie blew the whistle about the dead suspect, it had been all the city could talk about. People speculated.

Lu's sources on the other side of the legal system, junkies and pushers and thieves and scam artists, they all knew Conroy—at least the ones who would talk to him. They knew about the safe houses scattered throughout the city.

Other detectives used them to protect witnesses who couldn't be seen talking to cops. Conroy had his own uses for them and his own people to staff them.

Other cops avoided Conroy, so he hired contractors, Spanish-speaking former *agentes de policía* from South and Central America who'd emigrated to the city and pined for their old jobs while working in the bodegas or as taxi drivers or day laborers. Conroy had an eye for finding them, paid them with off-the-books money meant for confidential informants.

Things happened in those safe houses. Conroy's clearance rate as a detective was stellar, but his conviction rate for the eventual court cases was abysmal. It was hard to convict a criminal when most of the evidence was inadmissible, derived by bat-wielding School of the Americas graduates reliving their glory days.

Lu remembered one source, a car thief named Luis, who'd spent a day being questioned by Conroy and his inquisitors.

"I don't think he cares about the charges," Luis said. "I think he just likes to hurt people. The thing I remember most about my time in there? It was how much fun it seemed to the guy, the way they hurt me."

A low squeal from the seat next to her interrupted Lu's fugue. Larry grabbed his throat, eyes bugged out and lips going cyanotic. He slapped at her shoulder and then fell to the floor.

Mae yelled into the phone, begging for an ambulance. One of the men from Stony Forrester's table edged into the room and stood on tiptoe to take stock of the situation.

Jimmy's young nephew emerged from the kitchen. A busboy who'd come to America hoping to emulate his uncle, he carried the kitchen's large mop bucket, elbowed Jimmy aside, and stood over Larry. He raised his arms and dumped the cold, filthy water on the struggling man.

"Wha—wha—whatthefuckwasthat?" Larry squeaked.

Jimmy and the busboy screamed at each other in Vietnamese, each gesturing their hands and spitting their words in angry bursts. The busboy threw the bucket to the ground, tore off his soiled white apron, and threw it at Jimmy before storming off. Jimmy followed and the screaming duo disappeared into the kitchen.

The ambulance crew arrived and the paramedics drew up medicine into a thin syringe capped with a needle and plunged it into Larry's arm. Lu squeezed to the periphery of the action and a crowd filled in the gap, hiding Larry behind the assembled and curious.

Lu waved to Jimmy and headed for the door. On the sidewalk outside, another crowd in tuxedos and formal gowns glided into the lobby of the Odeon Theater for a performance by the city's orchestra. A police van rolled by with its blue lights on. A few bums and junkies sprawled on the benches across from the theater, occasionally hitting the passing crowd up for money. She looked downtown and started walking. It was going to be a busy night.

19

Knak hated hot dogs. All those parts of the pig, ground up and sealed in a tube. It was all they served at militia trainings. As much as he loved the training, he was done with hot dogs. They reminded him of family cookouts, his mother chain-smoking Winstons and beer-filled ashtrays filled with cigarette butts, brown and wet like a log flotilla on the Yukon ready to be ridden into town.

He lay prone underneath a water tower on the hill across from the Ray's Hot Dogs stand, scanning the scene through the Vortex Optics scope mounted on his Remington 700 rifle.

After shooting the bum earlier in the night, Knak considered possibilities. He considered simply walking up to Archer in one of the places the ambulance crews gathered between calls. There was the Bean Machine, over on Highland, or the Exxon in Kelley Square. He discounted both as too congested, escape routes limited by highways and vacant lots and trendy bars sure to be packed with beautiful people.

But Knak didn't want to simply put a pistol in Archer's face and pull the trigger. That was Ron Edson's preferred method. Edson ran the local feedstore that Avis Locke used to supply the hens on his egg farm and was the MMM's sergeant at arms. He'd pushed Knak to use the mission to avenge his dead wife as the group's first official strike against the system. At the last meeting in Locke's warehouse, after approval of the minutes and before new business, Edson's opinion had been voted into doctrine. Knak's mission of revenge had become the group's, and the group's mission had become Knak's.

*   *   *

Knak agreed, but he wasn't happy with his new partnership. For one, it was inelegant. He loved complication, the way even the simplest leaf was crisscrossed by veins and tendrils; loved highways that turned light into energy, that turned energy into oxygen, oxygen giving up its extra electron, turning the leaf into life itself. Complication was the mother of invention, Knak thought. Even Nature understood that.

There was complication in his lawsuits. It was one of the reasons he loved filing them. An old law was simply untapped power, and as much as the judges and other, righteous members of the bar might object, when Knak cited an ancient section of Massachusetts law that harkened back to the Puritans, he was releasing a kind of kinetic energy. He might not win, but Knak couldn't be ignored.

But the militia didn't believe in complication. In addition to Edson, unit president Rollie Underwood and his vice president, Mike Rolwes, demanded simplicity. They demanded action.

"If not you, Gerry, then who?" Rollie had asked at the last meeting. "We've waited a long time to bring our fight to the enemy, and the enemy has already exacted a tremendous price from you. Carry our standard into battle. Make your revenge our first glorious move."

Knak didn't know if he could do it. Put the cold of the pistol barrel to Archer's warm head, even as much as he hated Archer, felt he owed him as much pain as he could generate. Even with that, Knak knew deep down he lacked the guts. He might put the gun barrel to Archer's head. He'd never pull the trigger. It was one thing to shoot a man from a couple hundred yards away. The scope and the distance made it seem unreal, like an arcade game. Ever since the first killing, one thing had gnawed at him: he wasn't certain he could do it again. And now he carried the weight of the entire militia's mission on his shoulders. Where did that leave him?

Digression. Alternatives. Contingency planning. Knak had to adjust the odds. Locke had taught him that, among other things. You made your own luck. One of Locke's favorite aphorismic offerings. Shoot a cop, Knak reasoned, and every eager medic on every shitty ambulance in this entire city would show up. The medics and the cops had this bond, he knew. It was surefire. If Archer were on duty, he'd be there. Knak picked the spot, chose his targets, and waited. Archer would come. He would have to.

He knew Ray's would be heavy with bait tonight. Pretty girls behind the register, hot dogs for sale, a mostly male police force with little free time to eat anything on duty that wasn't quick, cheap, and guaranteed to release at least a little feel-good dopamine from the brain.

It was almost like placing a pile of apples in the woods and waiting for the deer to come, Knak thought. The small single-story takeout restaurant on the other side of the two-lane. The cops lining up single file, their backs to Knak as they ordered. Half a football field away. Knak across the street, on the hill above. He looked through the scope, put the small

red dot square on the back of the cop leaning in to order, flirt-
ing with the young college girl at the register. A soft breeze
circulated up from Knak's feet, puffed the shoulders of his
T-shirt, flitted the long wisps of hair on the back of his head.

Breathe.

Knak took in a deep breath, let it out. Paused. He was waiting
for that moment. That blink of a pause when everything stopped.
There was something about it, this brief interruption of time,
where life hung suspended, an instant of mortality, no breathing,
no heartbeat. That was the best time to kill, Knak had learned.
Hold your breath, wait for your heart's pause, so still, your aim
never better. Knak caught the connection. The best time to bring
death was when your body most closely mimicked it.

Relax.

He banished thoughts of Glen, his mother, the house,
Charlotte, the failed attempts at greatness. The greatness that
lay before him and within his grasp. The infinite realm of
data, the numbers telling Knak that this was now and this
was as it should be. He missed Charlotte. When he relaxed,
the chaos in his mind retreated behind a wall. He felt Charlotte's loss and saw clear as a brightest day the rightness of
this cause. Archer had to pay because without payment, by
someone, for something—without it Charlotte was just dead
and her being just dead was killing Knak.

Aim.

He followed the dot as it figure-eighted on the cop's
back. That's what the beating heart did, drifted the end of
the rifle barrel and sights in a lazy eight. He could see the
crease in the cop's shirt, telling him where the bulletproof
vest ended. His body was transported across the street. He
could smell the cop's sweat and aftershave and see the way his
smile filled with menace. Knak's dot patrolled the area.

Slowly squeeze . . .

The rifle leapt in the air with a crack that echoed down the row of taxpayers, row upon row of buildings with ground-floor businesses and warrens of apartments above, filled with families who had come here from somewhere else or people who'd never risen above here. Knak hadn't reattached the silencer when he assembled the rifle, felt that its weight had thrown off his shot at the bum. Not by much, but Knak was aware of millimeters.

The crack echoed over the city, pigeons scattered from city hall, a dozen police cruisers with gunfire detection units in them beeped to life and the arrows on their electronic displays all pointed at Knak, at his spot on the hill, but he heard only ringing after the rim of the rifle scope slammed into his forehead with the recoil he'd failed to contain. Blood ran in a river from his nose into his moustache and then his mouth, so that blood tasted of copper and iron and cheeseburger and tortilla chips.

He got up on his knees and shook the pain from his head and surveyed the scene below. The half-dozen cops in the parking lot, pistols drawn, leapt for cover and scanned. The gunshot echo made it seem as if a cannon had been fired at them from all directions. One cop rolled on the ground, screaming and grasping his left foot with both hands, and even from across the street Knak could see blood pouring through the cop's fingers. In all his training, Knak had never managed to stop jerking the trigger. So many of his shots ended as this one had, down and to the right. The pretty cashier was gone. The takeout window was a screen-fronted empty black square.

He'd missed his target, which had been center-mass on the cop's chest. He'd have to think it out, but he knew he'd jerked the rifle downward in anticipation of the recoil. Still, he'd shot a cop. He'd do better next time.

Knak grabbed his rifle and sprinted down the opposite side of the hill to the dirt access road and to his pickup truck, parked behind the squat brick pump house. He'd failed. Again. But this one felt closer. This didn't feel like failure. It felt like progress. He hadn't hit a civilian. He'd struck at the heart of the system—hit a *cop*! It wasn't Archer, but it was an important start. Archer would come. He knew it. This was huge. He'd broken his cherry. He was even more ready to kill. As he peeled away, Knak banged his fist against the roof and screamed in joy.

* * *

Eamon Conroy stood on the hill under the water tank and looked down toward Ray's. An old partner to whom Conroy regularly slipped Patriots tickets let him lurk, listen in to witness interviews, scour the crime scene like he was still on the job. The cashier girl told police that she'd seen a muzzle flash on the hill across the street, right in the middle of all the crabgrass, then had seen a man holding something that looked like a gun. She said he wore a white T-shirt.

"He was wicked old," she said. "Like fifty, probably. And balding, like, on top. He ran away before I could get a good look at him. That was so freaking scary."

She said he looked sad and lost, and maybe he waved at her before turning and sprinting away.

On the hill, Conroy found a single shell casing, took a look to make sure no one watched, then pocketed it. A small trail of blood led to the access road on the opposite side of the hill. Skid marks chattered up the hill toward the west. Conroy thought about the shooting, considered the possibility that an opportunity was presenting itself. There had been that thing downtown earlier tonight. He'd heard the chatter on the scanner, a dead bum by the turtle statue, shot through the chest. Nothing surprising there, except no one had seen the shooter. Twice in a night? Too much of a coincidence.

"The water department has a camera on the tower," said a voice behind Conroy. He turned and saw Pete Demonti, a mammoth detective who'd started on the force walking the same beat as Conroy in Jefferson Village. These days, Demonti was on Conroy's alternate payroll. He didn't want money, didn't seek power. Plied with sports tickets and bottles of Maker's Mark, Demonti reciprocated with information.

"You seen any video yet?" Conroy asked.

Demonti shook his head. "They're just cueing it up across the street," he said.

The tape was gray-toned.

"What, no digital?" one of the detectives asked.

"Too expensive," said another.

"This picture is for shit."

In the grainy footage, Conroy saw the man with the gun crawl up the hill from above, where the camera was perched in the lower spars of the water tower. A group of detectives and officers leaned closer to the screen.

"Anyone know this dipshit?" someone asked.

"Is that the best angle we've got?" asked another.

"Pause!" Conroy said. The footage stopped.

The man had arrived at the top and rolled over flat on his back to look up to the sky, or to the camera, or to something else none of them could apprehend. He looked right into the camera. He was wearing a white T-shirt with a slogan scrawled on the front in marker: *Fuck taxes. Don't pay the IRS.*

Something clicked. The Dinger, Murdock telling IRS stories. One about a lawsuit guy, a tax protestor and local nutjob, who had abandoned his dogs in a park, burned his house down, and disappeared after a simple interview about some internet threats and a yard sign. The sign had caught their attention first, and they'd followed him onto the gun show circuit. *Fuck taxes. Don't pay the IRS.*

Conroy smiled and walked out of the room. In the parking lot, police crime scene technicians continued taking measurements and painting yellow lines around the bloodstain where Officer Thomas Doran had taken his intended chest shot to the ankle instead. Conroy dialed his cell phone.

"Ira Murdock," a slurry voice answered. Either he'd awoken from a dream or was a couple Scotches into a Saturday night.

"It's Eamon."

"Fucker."

"Just your mother, 'cause your sister cost too much," Conroy said, laughing. "Question."

"What time is it?" A television in the background, a late-night TV band playing Dave or Leno off to commercial. "It's late. This must be good."

"Remember that crazy asshole you were telling me about the other night? The tax protestor in Monticello, the one with the pistol and the beer, left his dogs in a park and burned the house?"

"How could I forget?"

"Any chance you have a name?"

20

Neighborhood cookout, July 4, 1986

THE COOKOUT ALWAYS found its unspoken geometry. The women congregated in plastic chairs on the low patio behind the McCarthy house, which overlooked a small pond on the fifteenth fairway of Red Hill Country Club. A city course open to the public, it hugged the north side of the neighborhood of tidy ranch homes with their tidy lawns like a fox fur. Interstate traffic purred through a gully to the south, so far below that most residents quickly forgot about it. The women talked about their kids' sports teams, the hot summer, that thing with June Hargrove and the PE teacher. Olivia McCarthy refilled the group's glasses from a pitcher of Long Island iced tea.

"We're just so proud of Lu," she said, topping off several glasses. "She wants to be a journalist. Dave says it's a great move. Stable industry. The news, right? People will *always* need the news."

Olivia missed Martha Archer's glass in the rotation.

Twice.

"Where are my manners?" she said.

The men stood around the grill in the driveway out front, admired Davey McCarthy's new Harley, the recent seal coat job, the way he flipped burgers. They were most impressed by the burgundy Thunderbird with the half-leather roof, also colored a deeper shade of burgundy. The gold e-clef ornaments on the side windows were a nice touch, the men agreed.

It was the usual. Kabuki theater for the suburban crowd. The men knew where to stand, a semicircle around the grill as spontaneous and unplanned as a World War II beach landing. Sylvester Archer orbited close but didn't join the crowd. He leaned against a downspout next to the garage door and stared at the burgundy Ford sedan. Davey McCarthy smiled as he surveyed the crowd. Until he came to Sylvester Archer.

Everyone admired Davey McCarthy, and he basked in it. It was good to be the general manager at Topaz Ford-Lincoln-Mercury, he thought. His face rose on billboards high above Interstate 290. People trusted him. He was big and he was red-faced and he entered every room with a conqueror's assuredness. He *owned* wherever he was. And in the show-room, he returned customers' trust by making it seem like everyone there was getting the deal of a lifetime, even when he ripped them off—*especially* if he ripped them off. McCarthy loved separating people from their money, then letting them thank him for the privilege.

Davey McCarthy was as city as city got, was proud of it. He'd been born and raised in the same neighborhood where he now reigned supreme. He pounded beers at Salve Mater tailgates and sipped Christmas whiskey that came in bottles wrapped in blue silk bags. He was loud and slapped backs and cried at *Old Yeller* replays, just to let everyone know

Davey McCarthy was more than just a man's man, that he had a sensitive side.

"Burgundy is the hardest color to get the T-bird in," he said. He flipped burgers rapidly, enjoyed the sizzle that confirmed real work was being done here. "That one came all the way from Des Moines. Took me a month to find it. But Olivia loved the burgundy, and what Olivia wants, she gets."

The crowd of men laughed.

Sylvester Archer stared at McCarthy's back. "That seems to be a family policy of yours," he said.

The men around the grill found other things to look at. Into their cups. Across the yard. A couple took a sudden interest in the game of pig that McCarthy's daughter, Lu, played with young Tom Archer, using a basketball hoop nailed to a telephone pole out on the street.

Davey McCarthy looked back at Archer, then turned back to the grill.

"It is a family policy," McCarthy said. "Everyone gets what they want, especially if they can't get it somewhere else."

Sylvester Archer walked over to a wheelbarrow in the garage, filled with ice and beer and bottles of booze. He slowly picked up the bottles, inspected them, then returned them to the wheelbarrow one by one.

"All your beer," Archer said. "It's domestic."

"Who doesn't like Bud?"

"It's boring," Sylvester said.

"How about some whiskey?" Pete suggested.

Sylvester shook his head. Davey McCarthy bent more acutely over the grill.

"I'm just saying," Sylvester said. "It's lazy. I mean, you go to the packie, and there's all this beer in front of you. Beer from everywhere. Germany. Belgium. Fucking Japan.

Mexico. Whatever. And what does Davey McCarthy choose? Budweiser."

Archer laughed. Davey McCarthy stopped flipping burgers, kept his back to Archer.

"Budweiser," Archer said. "The most common beer there is. Beer that's, well, beer that's just a short walk away from wherever you are. You don't even have to go to the packie for it. How much Bud is in every refrigerator in all our houses? All he had to do was ask. Could have saved some bucks. But I bet Davey already had Bud in his own refrigerator. Right, Davey?"

The semicircle of men rotated, a kind of group mentation telling them it was best to keep Sylvester Archer at a distance.

"You know what I want?" he said.

McCarthy shrugged, continued to stare down at the grill.

"Come on now, Syl," a voice in the crowd cautioned.

"No, Pete, there's no problem," Archer said. "It just occurred to me, though, what I want. It's not in the garage here."

In the street, young Lu McCarthy grabbed a rebound and held on to the ball. She sensed storm clouds brewing over by the grill. She knew by the way her father hunched his shoulders, conserving energy before a fight. She'd seen it enough on softball fields, basketball courts, in the stands at high school field hockey games, soccer fields—all the places her father had started fights with other dads, usually the opponent's own version of Davey McCarthy, loudmouth provocateur.

Tom Archer called for the ball. No pass came. He followed Lu's gaze to the driveway, to the growing scene between their fathers.

"What's going on up there?" Tom wondered.

Lu shook her head. "Nothing good."

Down the street, someone lit off a roll of Black Cats, the staccato crackling followed by the whistle of a bottle rocket launched from a neighbor's back porch toward the highway. It was as if, Tom would later think, war had been declared.

In the driveway, Sylvester Archer had outmaneuvered the semicircle of nervous men. He wiped his hands on his white bowling shirt. His smile enervated the crowd. It was the smile of someone who knew everything and nothing, all at once.

"What I want," Sylvester said, "is a Long Island iced tea."

He poked Davey McCarthy's back three times.

Hard.

McCarthy turned.

Sylvester Archer leaned in close, their noses almost touching. Pete Miller slipped an arm between them.

"Come on, guys," he said. "I think everyone's just had a few too many."

Archer swatted Miller's arm away.

"You're fucking drunk," Davey McCarthy said. "Can't hold your liquor. How the hell do you sell power tools? Selling is for *men*."

"You think your wife would give me a drink?" Archer said. "I bet she would. I bet she'd give me a tall one. You been using *your* power tool all over the place, haven't you, Davey? Except your own home."

Davey McCarthy punched Archer in the nose, then jumped him. The rest of the men scrambled to pull McCarthy off Archer, whose bloody teeth appeared between scuffling legs and flailing arms while he laughed and called his wife's name. The women streamed into the driveway from the porch. Two men held Davey McCarthy back by his arms while Pete Miller pushed Archer across the lawn.

"Okay, okay, okay, it's all over," Miller said.

Blood soaked the front of Archer's shirt, covered his face. His nose was bent to the left. Davey McCarthy's shirt was torn, the buttons on the front missing.

"This ain't over!" McCarthy yelled.

Olivia McCarthy and Martha Archer found themselves together, on the patch of grass between their husbands. Neighbors came out onto their front lawns to watch.

"Why, Martha?" Archer said. "Just tell me why. Why with *this* piece of shit?"

"Piece of shit!" McCarthy yelled, then tried to break free. "I'll show you who's a piece of shit! Tool salesman who can't even use the tools he sells! You're a joke, Syl, a fucking joke!"

At the end of the driveway, Tom Archer looked up at Lu and wondered what he should do. Could he punch her? She was older. Bigger. Stronger. Did he have a duty to act? They weren't friends, but Tom liked her. All the boys in the neighborhood liked Lu. The fight between their fathers seemed under control. Tom was just thirteen, though. He wasn't sure about the problems of adults.

"We should get out of here," Lu said to Tom. "This is bad. Let's go up to the Tastee-Freez. I'll buy."

Tom nodded.

"Good fight, though," Lu said as they walked away. She smiled down at Tom. "Our fathers are such assholes, right? We'll be better when it's our time."

On the lawn, peace was restored.

"Can we just talk about this later?" Martha said. "Please?"

Davey McCarthy nodded.

"It's a holiday; we should be getting along," Olivia said. "This is about America, for God's sake."

She cut through the garage on her way back to the porch, her hands to her eyes.

Pete Miller let go of Sylvester Archer, patted his back, straightened out his shirt. He handed Archer a towel to clean off his face. Davey McCarthy went back to the grill.

"Fuck this," Archer said, then walked across the street to his own home.

For a few minutes, no one said a word. Conversation had become impossible. Cups were refilled. The remaining women returned to the backyard. The men surrounded the grill. The sizzling of food returned. Someone complained about the Red Sox. Careful laughs floated up into the summer haze.

"Who wants cheeseburgers?" Davey McCarthy said, some of the former levity returning to his voice. "Did I tell you guys the way I screwed those dipshits in Des Moines when I bought the T-bird?"

While McCarthy told the story, a mechanical rasp and cough shot from inside the Archer garage across the street. Then another. Then a third, and the sound of a two-stroke motor catching, like a chainsaw, but bigger somehow. Sylvester Archer emerged, holding a gas-powered saw with a huge spinning disk on the end. He crossed the road, revving the motor while the disk spun.

Archer walked onto McCarthy's driveway and the men backed away, except Davey McCarthy. He stood, defiant, a statue. Archer grinned like a Hatter. He brought the saw inches from McCarthy's belly and gunned the engine. The disk spun at several thousand RPMs.

"What the fuck is that?" McCarthy yelled. He held the spatula as if it offered some protection but leaned away from Archer.

"This is the X-200 with a diamond carbide, eighteen-inch blade," Archer said. "Toledo Power's best-selling heavy-duty saw. We sell this to fire departments. Cuts through

concrete. Metal support beams. Truss construction rooves."
His smile widened. "And cars!"

"No!" McCarthy said.

Archer shuffled toward the Thunderbird, keeping the
spinning blade between him and McCarthy. With his left
hand, he opened the driver's side door and placed the saw
blade on the hinge, opened the saw's throttle wide, and cut.
The door fell to the ground. Davey McCarthy let out a moan
and sat down on the grass.

Archer sidestepped to the passenger side of the car and
repeated the procedure on the other door. Then the pillars.
And the windshield. When he was done, he cut a line down
the car's roof, through the burgundy leather and through the
burgundy steel to the ugly brown metal below, then peeled
back the roof like the lid of a tuna can.

Sylvester Archer shut the saw down. He looked at the
crowd, then dropped to his knees and vomited all over the
nice new seal coat on the McCarthys' driveway. When he
stood, he no longer smiled.

"I'll understand if you want to call the cops," Archer
said. "If they're looking for me, I'll be over at my place. Getting drunk."

Then he hefted the saw onto his shoulder and staggered
back across the street, up the short spider-webbed driveway
with cracks riven by shoots of grass, into the garage, and out
of sight.

They canceled the annual neighborhood Labor Day
cookout two months later.

Olivia McCarthy and Sylvester Archer left soon after.
She joined her sister in Hollywood, Florida, where she got
her real estate license, made a nice living selling condos
where the pools overlooked the beautiful blue ocean just
yards away.

Archer got an apartment in Gardner and began drinking in earnest, which actually helped his career, closing most of his sales over Manhattans in the same booth at the back of the Stockhouse Restaurant. The booze destroyed his body, but he became New England sales manager for Toledo Power Tools.

Davey McCarthy never reported the destruction of his T-Bird to the police.

Martha Archer and Davey moved into the McCarthy house, sold the old ranch across the street, and eventually got married. When Topaz Ford-Lincoln-Mercury closed a year later, Davey McCarthy discovered he'd burned one too many bridges, wasn't welcomed at the big dealerships. He became a lot boy for South End Motors. He washed cars and charged batteries and made Registry runs for new customers. He sold the Harley. They needed the cash to keep Lu McCarthy in school.

Tom Archer moved into the spare bedroom in the McCarthy house. When Lu McCarthy returned home from college in later years, she and Tom found little to talk about. Soon, they had nothing at all.

21

A WEEK AFTER LD's death, a hundred more ambulance
calls in the book for Archer, and now the meeting. He
knew the news would be bad. Saturday night and the lawyers
wanted to interrupt the shift, interview him about the baby,
about his complaint against O'Toole. Nothing good coming.
No such thing as a Saturday night lawyer.

Archer parked next to the ambulance building on Booth
Street in a bowl-shaped parking lot hidden behind the empty
Nilsen Bread factory. Their quarters were cheap. Light industrial. A five-foot-high concrete base topped by gray corrugated metal walls and a peaked corrugated metal roof.

The building was a perfect reflection of life as a city
medic. It was too cold in the winter, suffocating in the summer. Diesel exhaust pooled in the bathrooms and tinged the
scallops in the cheap yellow soap clams a black-flecked smear
of brown. As he sat outside in his idling ambulance, Archer
considered what waited inside for him, bad omens accruing.

No Julio tonight; he'd called in sick. Archer's partner was
a new guy, Nate something. He'd learn it sometime. Not

anytime soon. They sat in silence by the side entrance door, the diesel burbling and the police radio already humming with the night's shenanigans.

Archer drew smiley faces in the stippled condensation on the passenger side window, near the vent where the air conditioning's cold air met humid, stifling late August night in mortal combat, only the thin window separating them.

"Are these things common?" Nate asked.

"What things?"

Nate shrugged. "Mysterious meetings in quarters in the middle of a shift. I mean, who's going to be in there?"

"A special meeting on a Saturday night? Maybe the Pope. Jesus Christ himself. Or, if it's a really big deal, maybe the mayor."

Archer looked out at the legion of cars in the lot, took stock of who was working tonight. A gaggle of small Accords and Camrys driven by the full-time medics with wives and small kids at home took up the nearest spots. Those medics got here earliest, claimed the best spaces. A handful of full-sized pickup trucks favored by the part-time staff, usually firefighters from local departments who moonlighted as paramedics, were farther away. Those folks were in no rush. They parked where they could. Sprinkled in among these two constituencies were the Harley-Davidsons and Subaru WRXs and other sports cars and motorcycles belonging either to young, single medics, older ones whose kids had moved on to college and beyond, or the newly divorced.

Archer stopped his observations by the Dumpster, where a black Lincoln Town Car sat, out of place. Its fresh wax glinted under a single yellow streetlight. A thin white trail of smoke drifted from its exhaust. Water dripped from under the engine. Archer figured the car was running, its air conditioner blowing.

He thought of Julio. Who'd called in sick tonight. Julio who never called in sick. Especially when he was sick.

"I wonder who belongs to that thing?" Archer said, pointing to the Lincoln.

Nate bent over, peered at the car, shrugged.

"My wife calls, come get me."

Nate nodded, leaned against the window, and was snoring before Archer stepped out to go inside the building.

They met in Prentice's small office. Archer smelled the disinfectant on the floor and the cigarette butts in Prentice's ashtray, made out of the hollow bottom of a Howitzer shell. Next to it sat a grenade with a red plastic tag bearing the numeral one and the message *Complaint Department. Please Take a Number.* A metal desk, a metal desk chair with dark-green cushioned armrests, a desk lamp with a silver aluminum cone for a shade, and a few chairs rounded out the room.

Archer took a step in, thought of escaping back to Nate and the ambulance, just saying fuck it, let's go, then picking up every call the dispatcher put out, so many that the other crews would get antsy from sitting around, wondering what the hell had gotten into P3 tonight. Archer started to turn. Prentice waved Archer over with a flick of two fingers.

"Secure that door," Prentice said.

Archer found two other men in the room, sitting in chairs blocked from view by the open office door. One he didn't recognize, a fat man, early fifties, black hair parted on the side, just a hint of gray at the temples. He wore a black suit and had a white plastic cast on his right leg, which he held out straight in front of him.

The other: Eamon Conroy. He eyeballed Archer through the cigarette smoke, jutting his chin toward the ceiling. Archer felt cold and alone.

"We need to talk about the call on Kansas Street from earlier this year," Prentice began. "You remember the one I mean?"

Archer nodded. The fat man leaned forward and extended his right hand.

"You'll have to pardon me for not getting up," the man said with a smile that turned up only the left corner of his mouth and never rose above his upper lip. "Little domestic injury. So. My name is Edward Lagrange, and I'm from the city solicitor's office. That means I'm the city's lawyer, but I just want you to know that, in a way, I'm your lawyer too. I don't know if you've had the pleasure of meeting my colleague here, Eamon Conroy. Mr. Conroy is a, well, a special assistant, working with Mayor O'Toole. You can assume anything that Mr. Conroy tells you is the same as having the mayor tell you."

Archer nodded.

"Mr. Conroy and I have a history," Archer said.

"Ancient history," Conroy said. "No hard feelings on this end."

"Not so ancient," Archer said.

"First off, thank you for taking the time to meet with me on what must surely be a busy night," Lagrange said.

"It wasn't like I had a choice," Archer said.

"Still, we appreciate it," Lagrange said. "Lord knows, I respect the hell out of what you guys do every day and every night out there, protecting the citizens of the city, making the rest of us look good. I couldn't do it." He pointed at his cast and chuckled. "See what happens when I even try to do a little light gardening?"

Archer remained quiet. He slouched, folded his hands on his stomach, and waited.

"As you know, there's the deposition on Monday in regards to your complaint regarding the mayor and his reputed relationship to a city file clerk named Daisy Fontana," Lagrange said. "There's this matter with Ms. Fontana's baby too. Unfortunate, of course, so sad, and the mayor has directed me to clear the decks and see how we can settle things without much in the way of press coverage. We think that would be in everyone's best interests. This meeting will be a very important part of that. Mayor O'Toole, as you know, is running for governor, and he needs to wrap up stuff like this before the campaign begins. He is very incentivized to find a solution."

Archer nodded.

"So, I thought we'd start by laying some groundwork. Since the core issue stems from what did or did not happen on Kansas Street last fall, why don't we go over your recollection of the call, start from there, okay?"

Lagrange clicked a ballpoint pen.

"That way, we have a foundational basis going forward," he said. "That's the thing with the law. It's like an aircraft carrier. Once it gets moving, it takes dozens of miles and incredible horsepower to alter its course. The sooner we lock into a trajectory, the better we can deflect anything that comes our way."

"I filed a lengthy report," Archer said. Prentice cleared his throat.

"Yes, you did," Lagrange replied. "Yes. You. Did. I have it right here. I was wondering if you could parse some of the more technical aspects of it?"

"It says we were sent to Kansas Street for a woman in labor, and on arrival we found a twenty-six-year-old female who'd just delivered a baby. The newborn was in serious distress and the mother was in extreme pain and had lost a lot of blood."

Lagrange turned back to the paper. "Perhaps, but if no one can understand it other than you, how can we hope to figure out what really happened?"

He handed over the report. "Why don't I just give this to you," he said, then turned to Conroy. "And I thought reading con law texts in school was tough."

"You ought to see police reports," Conroy said. "They're even harder to understand. Isn't that right, Mr. Archer?"

Archer glanced at Conroy, who was smiling. Archer read: "So we've gotten on scene, found the patient. 'Patient states she felt contractions beginning several hours ago and had husband contact emergency number provided by outside agency—' "

Lagrange interrupted. " 'Outside agency'? Who was that?"

"I have no idea," Archer said. "I think Mr. Conroy has a better grasp on that than I do."

Conroy smiled, leaned forward, and dropped his cigarette into a nearby coffee mug.

"Archer," Prentice said.

"Let's just continue for now," Lagrange said.

" 'Patient states that contractions became more intense, as did need to push. Unknown male parties arrived on scene approximately two hours prior to our arrival and performed in-home childbirth in patient's bedroom. Unknown skills or qualifications. Unknown respiratory, hemodynamic or neurological status of child, nor any APGAR score,' " Archer read.

"APGAR?" Lagrange asked.

"It's an acronym, measures how well the baby is doing in the first few minutes after birth," Archer said. "There's nothing easy about coming into the world."

Lagrange looked over at Conroy. Archer detected a faint shrug. He turned back to Archer.

"Continue, please," Lagrange said. More notes.

" 'Baby presented on patient's bed, cold, listless, poorly perfused centrally and distally'—which means his arms, legs, and chest were all blue, a sign of poor oxygenation—'and still wet, with no attempts made to warm nor dry newborn. The umbilical cord had been clamped with flexible handcuffs and cut at an appropriate length. The patient's placenta had already delivered and was resting in a glass bowl by the side of the bed. There appeared to have been significant hemorrhage.' "

Lagrange turned his yellow writing pad to a new sheet. He clicked his pen several times, chewed on his bottom lip.

"What do you mean when you say 'flexible handcuffs'?" Lagrange said.

"The white ones cops use at demonstrations to arrest lots of people all at once. You know the ones? One of those."

"Was it effective?"

"Sure."

Outside the window a commuter train rattled by in a flash. Archer wanted to reach out and touch it. He saw the passengers inside as in a flickering newsreel, glimpses of young couples sharing headphones and digital music players, a woman tapping away at her laptop. An old guy alone in the back of the car.

Lagrange pulled off his glasses and pinched them between two fingers and the bridge of his nose. He scratched the back of his neck, then pointed a finger at the ceiling.

"You say there was this outside agency involved? What makes you say that? The testimony of Ms. Fontana and her boyfriend"—Lagrange consulted his file—"Rigo Mejia, is that their first call of the night, to anyone, was to 911, and that you and your partner were the first ones on scene."

Archer heard a ringing in the back of his head. His temples throbbed. "That's a lie," he said.

"How do you know?" Lagrange asked.

Archer pointed to Conroy. "He was there when I got there."

Conroy shook his head almost imperceptibly.

"Mr. Conroy's testimony at deposition was that he arrived *after* you had delivered the baby, and that you threatened to beat him with a flashlight if he didn't leave."

"A lie."

"Who delivered the baby, Mr. Archer?" Lagrange asked.

"I don't know."

"Are you sure? Are you sure it was some phantom that no one else saw? How do you think it's going to look when the mother of the baby says you delivered the baby, and you deny it? Do you think that's going to be believable?"

"Mr. Conroy was there."

"He's already stipulated to that."

"*Before* me."

"He's denied that."

"Why don't you let him speak?"

"He's not here to testify to you, Mr. Archer. You know I'm trying to help you, right? You filed a complaint against a sitting mayor, the future governor of the Commonwealth, accusing him of covering up heinous things done to an infant—worse, insinuating that the mayor was having an affair with a city employee. Pretty heady stuff. Do you know what you've gotten yourself into?"

"I know this is ridiculous."

"Ridiculous is a possibility. But I don't think that's the word you're looking for here. I think the word you're looking for is *dangerous*. Are you really in a position to take such risks? Who's paying for your son's treatments in Boston? You? Or the city you're turning your back on?"

Archer looked at Prentice, who looked at Lagrange.

"You're between Scylla and Charybdis," Lagrange said.

"Between what and what?" Prentice asked.

"A rock and a hard place," Lagrange said. "I've helped lots of city employees out of a jam. But first rule? First rule is, you got to be honest with me."

"I am being honest with you," Archer said. He thought of the train. Of escape. He measured the distance in his head to the door, wondered if anyone would try to stop him if he got up and walked out.

"So, using your version of events, let's set the table," Lagrange said. "The whole world tells me you delivered a baby, even the mother herself, yet you say you didn't, that some other mysterious person with medical training who happened to know at three in the morning that particular day, this stranger divined that Ms. Daisy Fontana of 33½ Left Side Rear Kansas Street, Third Floor, was at that very minute in labor, and decided to simply walk into the apartment and deliver her child, and then left without saying a word to anyone? Is that what happened?"

"Jump in here anytime, asshole," Archer said to Conroy. Conroy exhaled a plume of smoke toward the ceiling.

"You can ask my partner," Archer said. "Julio Tavares. He was there. He'll tell you."

"We did talk to Mr. Tavares," Lagrange said. "This morning. Interested to hear what he said?"

"I know what he would have said," Archer said.

"You might be surprised," Lagrange said. Conroy nodded and smiled.

Lagrange flipped through some pages. "How's your son?" he asked.

"None of your business," Archer said.

"Cancer in a young child," Lagrange said. "Always a tragedy. Must be particularly hard on the family."

Archer said nothing.

"And how about you? How are you doing? Are you employing the many coping techniques they taught you in Westminster?" Lagrange said. "Or do I have it wrong here? The file seems to indicate you did a little time up at New Start Academy."

Archer felt a hot wave rise from his abdomen and behind his vertebrae. It wrapped around the back of his skull, eddied there, and roiled back down his spinal column. He couldn't blink. Lagrange looked up at him from the file.

"Wonderful work they do up there with you guys," Lagrange said. "All those broken souls."

Conroy chuckled.

"That's a sealed record," Archer said.

"You have nothing to be ashamed of," the lawyer said.

"Fuck you."

"One thing I'd like to know, though, is what drove you up there?"

"I don't really think—" Prentice said.

"Usually it's, what, stress?" Lagrange said. "Alcohol? Marital problems? Drugs, maybe?"

"Fuck you," Archer said.

"Of course, sometimes"—Lagrange was smiling now, caressing the open manila folder in his lap—"sometimes it's a little of everything, right? Life gets in the way and then you're out there doing this job, right there at the frayed edges of society, interacting every day and night with the places where things no longer work, where the social order breaks down, where people are no longer fit for society, and someone has to come in and clean the whole godforsaken mess up. Takes a toll, doesn't it?"

Archer stood up, fists clenched.

"Maybe you start drinking, maybe some of the drugs go missing, maybe you hit your wife one night and you get arrested, but she forgives you and the judge cuts you some slack because of some horrible fucking call with a little drowned girl, you go missing for a week afterward and they find you passed out stone drunk in the weeds by some abandoned rail siding, so you go to New Start and the records get sealed, except . . ."

Archer relaxed his hands and sat down. Lagrange was reaching, but he didn't really have anything. He was probing for weakness, gaps in the wire, didn't realize Archer hadn't even met Elaine when Evangeline fell in the pool, much less been married. They were testing him. So this was what a setup looked like, Archer thought.

"I wasn't married when I went to New Start. I hadn't even met my wife."

"Well, like you said, those records are sealed. Except perhaps they aren't sealed quite tightly enough," Lagrange said, jotting notes in his file. This ethics complaint you filed, this isn't the only time you've expressed your opinions about the mayor and his relationship to Ms. Fontana and her baby."

"I've only filed the one complaint," Archer said.

Lagrange pulled a sheet from the back of the manila folder.

"How about the last meeting of the paramedics' union?" Lagrange said, looking up at Archer over the top of his glasses. "Or do you deny accusing the mayor of fathering Ms. Fontana's baby, even making lewd jokes about his relationship with her?"

Archer shrugged. Prentice cleared his throat.

"How about this," Lagrange said, holding a new document from his oversized file, "the Ding Wa, multiple occasions over the last few months. Plenty of people have overheard your comments about Mr. Conroy, the incident with him a decade ago, your partner then, Mr. Moonandowski, issuing the complaint that ultimately led to Mr. Conroy's prior issues with the criminal justice system."

"He went to jail."

"As a technical matter, yes. But the court record is clear that Mr. Conroy was convicted only of obstruction of justice. A few phone calls, an ill-advised conversation or two with witnesses better left alone, all of which Mr. Conroy has taken responsibility for to a significant degree. He paid his debt. You, however, have gone out of your way to libel and slander both of these men, not to mention Ms. Fontana, whose baby you conveniently mistreated—"

"This fucking psycho mistreated!" Archer said, pointing at Conroy.

"Lots of people have heard you," Lagrange said. "No way to take back your comments now. A buzz has started, and it's starting to pick up a little steam. The mayor does not appreciate this. The mayor would like you to stop. He also would like you to know that there are very good reasons for you to stop. While it might be in the mayor's interest that you cease and desist this slandering of his name, he also wants you to realize it's in your interest, too."

Conroy was staring at him, nodding slightly.

"I didn't say anything about the mayor," Archer said.

"Well, you've had plenty to say about the Fontana baby, about Mr. Conroy here," Lagrange said.

"We have a history," Archer said. "Would you like to talk about that? About this psychotic, sociopathic—"

"I wouldn't," Conroy said simply. Quietly. The room filled with silence. Lagrange broke it with a laugh.

"Wow, that got intense pretty quickly," he said. "But it's good advice. Believe me. And if all roads once led to Rome, the mayor is afraid you're creating a road to him that he doesn't deserve. That he can't have. Not right now. There isn't much he wouldn't do to put a stop to it. Within the law, of course."

Lagrange let the threat sink in. He turned to Prentice.

"Would you step out for one moment?" Lagrange asked.

Another commuter train clacked and battered its way past Prentice's window. Prentice hesitated to stand, then walked to the door. He stopped next to Archer. "I'll be right outside."

Archer nodded.

Once they were alone, Lagrange put the file folders back into his briefcase and closed it. He straightened out his tie, then slid his chair next to Archer's and leaned in close enough for Archer to see the mole on Lagrange's cheek, scabbed over where he'd probably cut it while shaving.

"I think there's a deal to be made here," Lagrange said, almost whispering. "Now, if you were to, say, admit to a version of what you've done, retract the complaint, help make this go away, I think—and mind you, I can't speak for him, but I imagine the mayor would look quite favorably on that. He has many friends. Friends with the kind of deep pockets that can make medical bills just, you know, disappear. People that can make other money just . . . appear. You're a smart guy, Mr. Archer. Don't make me spell it out. This needs to go away. Someone needs to be held accountable for what happened to Ms. Fontana's son. We're too far along for this to end without someone paying something. We've already done you a big favor here. Most medics in your position would have been taken off the line without pay, pending the outcome of the investigation. Most people with the history you have with Eamon Conroy would fare even worse. Do the right thing here, and we'll take care of the rest."

Archer looked at Lagrange first, then over at Conroy. Conroy winked.

*   *   *

He slammed the ambulance door, awoke Nate from his slumber.

Nate put the ambulance in drive and rolled across the parking lot. Archer picked up the newspaper, then put it down. He felt the weight of a world that had turned on him. Surrender seemed his only escape. Admit to something he didn't do. Accept blame for a tragedy he didn't cause. Invisible men wielding invisible power, all of it focused on Archer, on someone who'd made the mistake long ago of choosing to serve.

He needed to find Julio. He needed to talk to McCarthy. The enemy was showing itself. Archer had been alone long enough.

22

CAVALRY ARMS WAS a swaybacked apartment complex off
Cohasset Street. The smell jabbed at Archer's nostrils
five steps from the apartment door. He was ready for it. In the
week since his meeting with Lagrange, relentless heat had
settled on the city, refused to budge or break. Around-the-
clock misery. Malodor was the de rigueur atmosphere for city
medics; heat made it more so. Warm ammonia with a hint of
almond butter—the smell of piss in a hot city apartment.

Archer was working his first shift with Julio since the
meeting. The silence between them confirmed his fears.
Silence always meant guilt. Archer couldn't imagine what his
friend had told the city lawyer. He pushed the thoughts away,
focused on the unpleasantness beyond the door. They came
here two, three times a week. Archer needed this. He needed
the mundane.

Archer knuckle-tapped the metal door a third time.

"Red," he called. "Open the door, Red. EMS."

Inside Archer heard feet scuffling on linoleum, glass bottles clanging off each other. Mumbling.

"Ripped already," Julio said.

Archer nodded. Tapped again on the door.

"Red, it's your favorite ambulance crew. Let us in."

More mumbling from inside, singing along to music that rasped in metallic flatness from a radio. Something fast, the lyrics impossible to decipher.

"We're not going away," Julio said. "You keep calling; now we got to come in. Next step, we get the fire department out here and break this thing down. Remember how long it took last time to get a new door."

Bottles rattled. Ceramic breaking.

"Shit!" from inside.

The music hit a crescendo and ended. Another song began, even faster, more indecipherable, like someone yelling over a million kazoos.

Archer tried the knob. It was unlocked. He pushed the door open. Red reclined on a couch, his long legs akimbo and pointing to opposite directions of the compass rose. A broken white plate was in pieces at his feet. Wetness covered his groin, ran halfway down each leg. A shock of white hair rose from the top of his head and over the back of the couch like Everest's peak. In one hand he held a near-empty bottle of Wild Turkey. The other tapped the air to the music.

"You ever listen to this new Albanian station?" Red asked. "Can't speak a word, but I love it."

Archer and Julio dropped their gear on the floor.

"Good song, Red," Archer said, smiling.

"Fucking A, young man," Red said. "Fucking A."

Archer surveyed the apartment. Cleaner than normal. One room with a couch and a television, the sole window dirt streaked and below street level, a constant procession of shoes the only indication of the weather outside. A small kitchen off that with a round wooden table covered in empty booze bottles. A short hallway led off toward the sole bedroom. Archer went to the refrigerator and opened it. Inside was only a case of Narragansett beer. The freezer was empty, no food in the cupboards. Mouse droppings littered the kitchen counter.

Archer joined Julio in front of the only decent piece of furniture in the place, a three-shelved display case full of trophies and ribbons and framed newspaper clippings of Red as a young man—tall, healthy, athletic—in the college's basketball uniform, driving to the hoop, held aloft on teammates' shoulders in one frame and by an adoring crowd in another, a rapturous smile, the remains of a basketball net around his neck.

There were pictures of an older Red, in a suit coat and turtleneck, gold chain around his neck, squatting in the middle of a huddle of teenage basketball players, diagramming a play, the clock behind him showing a tie score and thirty seconds remaining. He was focused, cool, not the kind of man to piss himself and spend a night on the phone mumbling to 911 operators.

Red Bowen was a legend, the greatest basketball player and coach in the city's history. His best friend was Johnny Wazchuck—*that* Johnny Wazchuck, NBA Hall of Famer, the son of the city who had risen beyond, to the sublime.

In the city, though, that kind of fame didn't matter. Provincial to the end—or maybe just protective of its own—this city would always see Wazchuck as playing second fiddle to Red Bowen, the best shooting guard in the history of Commerce High, the coach who had basked in high school basketball glory for almost three decades. Even today, drunk most days, drunk every night, even like this, when Red Bowen walked into a room, it was a happening. He hadn't paid for a meal in a city restaurant in years.

Archer had long ago lost any nostalgia he had for this broken vessel of a city, but he still held an affection for men like Red, an affection that wavered like a guttering candle flame, these old men who rumbled and groused through the city's diners and greasy spoons and coffee counters, men who'd been to war, made and lost fortunes, bought big houses and raised large, rowdy families in the city, and in the end, the only thing they really remembered and were remembered for was high school football or baseball or basketball games from sixty, seventy years ago. They clung to a prowess, a strength and skill that had hit its apex by their eighteenth birthdays, for the rest of their lives. Red was the alpha dog in this city. He was revered by men and women, boys and girls, most not old enough to even remember a time when Red Bowen's athletic exploits were a fresh memory. He had ascended into myth. It didn't seem to be enough.

Archer and Julio stood before this totem pole containing evidence of Red Bowen's place in the history of a city that had no history beyond the eight hills that ringed it. While they gazed, Red pulled himself off the couch and stood swaying behind the medics.

"That one there?" Red said, pointing. "That's me coaching the boys at States, 1971. Orofineo hit a fadeaway jumper with five seconds left, beat Newton South to win the whole fucking thing. Biggest deal in city history. Eddie O'Toole was mayor then, gave me a medal and the key to the city. Now *that* was a mayor. Not like that dipshit son of his."

Red rotated to his left and lurched a step back toward the couch.

"When's the last time you ate, Red?" Archer asked.

"I eat every day," he said, holding his hands out wide and spinning in a slow circle. "I eat all this. My existence is my sustenance. Eddie O'Toole. He never ran for governor. But his was a different time. People cared about each other. This place, we knew something about decorum back then."

Red stopped circling, staggered backward to the couch, and took a pull off the whiskey before dropping again.

"You've been on the phone a lot tonight," Julio said.

"I told them I didn't fucking need nobody."

"We know you get lonely," Julio said. "But you can't call 911 every ten minutes just for the hell of it, even if you are Johnny Wazchuck's close, personal friend."

"Fuck Wazchuck!" Red leapt up from the couch and pointed a finger at Julio. "He wasn't qualified to carry my jockstrap, and everyone in this city knew it! Red Bowen was the better man. Red Bowen was the *best* man. Anyone tells you different is an asshole." He looked at Archer. "What is it with you Irish guys?" he asked.

Archer shrugged. "I'm not Irish."

"Too bad, Archer. Maybe you'd see it coming."

"See what coming?" Archer said.

Red waved him off. He sighed. He scratched his groin, the stubble on his chin.

"I'm just a drunk," Red said. "I know that. But I still have friends. From what they tell me, and from what I read in the paper, we have one thing in common."

"What's that?"

"Not *what* but *who*," Red said. He yawned, closed his eyes. "*Who*."

Archer stepped closer to Red. The old man had a bad ear and trouble standing.

"Like who?" he asked.

"Don't you worry, young man. Do not worry. I'm still important to a lot of the idiots around here," Red said. "The name Red Bowen still means something, even if the man himself don't. You been good to me all these years. I'll make this disappear. I make magic all the time."

He collapsed onto the couch and stretched his arms over his head.

"We know," Archer said.

"That sneaky shit Conroy, your buddy, been around a lot lately, bringing me booze, checking was I okay. John O'Toole's errand boy. Wants me to hit the campaign trail for him around here. I said I'd think about it. Conroy said the mayor was taking his lumps in the paper for this baby that a city medic hurt. I seen the paper; I can add two and two. I go way back with Eamon Conroy."

"So you know him?" Archer asked. Conroy was now as much a part of his life as his limbs, only gangrenous, threatening to kill him. Archer knew Conroy wouldn't go away. He was everywhere, even in the living room of Red Bowen.

Red nodded.

"Can't prove it, but that fucker cost me my job at Commerce. Planted dope in my car because he beat up one of my players for driving while black and I wouldn't get the kid to drop the charges. Conroy was just a route cop back then, but you knew he was going places. All the other route cops hated him. That's how you know who the risers are, the up-and-comers. Most route cops just want to keep their sectors quiet, safe. Guys like Conroy, they want to stir shit up, make a name for themselves. Not a recipe for pop-u-lar-i-ty. But good for business."

"Why do you talk to him then?" Archer asked.

"What am I gonna do?" Red said. "You can't hold grudges in this city. There aren't enough alternatives. Rest of the world might as well not exist for guys like me. This city? It's all there is. I am bound to it, like a black hole. Nothing escapes. Enmity is short-lived here. It has to be. There's only so many of us. Only so many. A grudge is a luxury."

Red closed his eyes and was soon snoring. Archer wanted to wake him, draw it out of him. Conroy. What had Conroy said about him? Archer breathed deep and inhaled the mothballs coming from Red's closet, the stale liquor spilled on the yellow linoleum kitchen floor, the sweet, almost rotten-banana smell of Red's urine-stained pajama bottoms. A circle of hell—how far in or out from the center, he couldn't be sure. But he knew that was where he was and saw little reason to hope for escape.

Julio checked Red's blood sugar and took a set of vital signs. Archer looked closer at the shrine to Red Bowen, thought about his warning. Red's basketball heroics from Commerce High School, the years at the college, the decades back at Commerce, coaching. Was it a warning? The bottom shelf held a yellowing, framed clip from the *Courier* of Red shaking hands with a woman in a pantsuit. Neither was smiling. Red tilted away from the camera, bowed back as if to lean against the wall behind him. Headline: *City Legend and Beloved Coach Retires.*

"What the fuck happened to this guy?" Julio said.

"My father had him at Commerce back in the day, said he was as straight as they came," Archer said. "Great teacher. Everyone loved Coach Red."

"What was all that crazy shit he was talking?" Julio asked.

Archer scowled.

"I might ask you a similar question," Archer said.

"I was wondering how long it would take," Julio said.

"You can see why I'm worried."

"How long have we been friends?"

"You call out sick first time in who knows how long," Archer said. "Then I got to hear from the city lawyer that they brought you in. You couldn't tell me yourself? I'm starting to think we aren't on the same page."

Julio zipped up the equipment bag. He looked at Archer's feet while he talked.

"They made me come in last minute," Julio said. "And I've been sick. The kids brought something home from day care. Stomach's been a mess all week. I didn't tell them anything you and I haven't already discussed."

Archer believed Julio. He wasn't relieved, not exactly. But maybe this was Lagrange's strategy. Break the partners apart so that one surrendered, gave it all up, even if there was no *it* to give up. They'd given Lagrange the truth. The search for something else was bound to come up empty, but that didn't comfort Archer. Roll from the bottom and even the empty toothpaste tube delivered.

"Just saying," Archer said. "Seemed odd."

"Well, relax. You know what Maria would do to me if you got hurt?"

Archer shook his head. He looked closer at a large picture of Red driving to the hoop during a game at Commerce, the ball tucked down and to his left, away from a defender reaching, straining over his right shoulder, desperate for the ball. The defender's eyes were wide, feral, reaching. Red was as calm as the dead, except his eyes. Those were alive.

The hoop was three feet above Red, directly below one of the arena's bright, round ceiling lights. The camera faced into the hoop and a searing corona of white, and the more Archer stared at it, the more he convinced himself that Red wasn't seeking the hoop so much as he was ascending into the light.

Archer had the notion that the light wasn't going to cleanse Red, that there was no redemption at the end of some tunnel, no dead relatives to greet him, no great table set with an unending feast, nor songs, nor dancing angels nor a seat waiting for him at anyone's right hand. None of it awaited Red, or Archer, or the brain-dead baby or Evangeline or Charlotte Knak—none of the stuff the Brothers at St. John's had talked about during high school chapel. The light was the end. Beyond it was something, not a good something, but instead something that could bring the inattentive or unlucky to a place like this—urine soaked, alone, eking it out in a ratty basement apartment.

"What do you want to do?" Archer said.

Julio looked back at Red, asleep.

"About what?" Julio asked.

"About Red. We can't just leave him like this," Archer said.

"I know."

Julio went into the bedroom and came back with a pair of sweat pants and a T-shirt.

"I think these are clean," he said. "Sort of."

"No piss."

They donned purple medical gloves and undressed Red, piling the soiled clothes on the floor next to the couch. They moistened a towel Archer found in the kitchen and wiped Red down as best they could, then dressed him in the sweat pants and T-shirt. Julio reached under Red's arms and Archer picked up his legs and they carried him down to the bedroom and laid him in the bed. Red slumbered throughout. Archer returned to the living room and gathered the dirty clothes in a garbage bag, taped a note to the bag that said *Red*, and dropped it at the front door of the apartment across the hall.

When Archer returned, Julio was collecting the last of the booze bottles in a recycling bin.

"Did you give the clothes to Mrs. Konsciencszy?" he asked.

"It's late. I just put them in a bag outside her door with his name on it. She'll take care of it."

Julio nodded. "Every time we come here. Woman's a saint."

They gathered up their gear and prepared to head out the door. Archer was about to close it when he stopped, walked over to the couch, and picked up Red's phone, followed its cord back to the wall outlet. Archer wrapped the cord around his hand twice, then gave a fierce tug, as if starting a lawn mower. The wire tore from the wall, shattered the plastic guard, and left an ugly jagged square of empty drywall. He walked over to the window, pulled it open, and tossed the phone and cord into the bushes between the window and the sidewalk. He walked back to the door and took a last look at the place. He locked the knob on the front door, turned off the living room light, and walked out.

23

Years ago

ARCHER BREATHED DEEP and sucked as much oxygen into his lungs as the mask would allow. The liter bag of intravenous fluid running into his left arm was near empty, its sterile water-and-salt mix restoring him to a semblance of balance, making him feel like he could handle another summer night in the city.

It had been a hot one. A dozen old ladies had died in the Midwest in a weekend, and President Bush had ordered a nationwide emergency, opened cooling shelters in places like Chicago and Boston. Julio climbed into the back of the ambulance with a clear plastic trash bag full of supplies. He chuckled while he stocked the shelves.

"Why are you so fucking happy?" Archer asked.

"Maria's pissed at you, amigo," Julio said. "You skipped lunch."

"Your wife is not my mother," Archer said. If she were, Archer thought, she would have told him never to mix beer with the hard stuff. Especially if the beer was cheap and the hard stuff even cheaper.

"She made your favorite."

"I was busy," Archer said.

"I can smell that."

Archer pulled the oxygen mask away from his face and leaned over to the small trash barrel at the end of the ambulance bench on which he sat. Archer heaved three times, wiped his mouth, held the oxygen mask back to his face. Julio held out a small square gauze pad.

"Put this under your nose and breathe," Julio said. "It'll take care of the nausea."

"That's an alcohol prep."

"Trust me, there's nothing better for curing nausea than breathing in some of this. I read it in a journal, so it must be true."

Archer gave Julio the finger but took the prep and began breathing. He didn't want to tell Julio, but his stomach quieted and the nausea disappeared.

"You and your fucking journals," Archer said.

Julio laughed.

"I knew you'd feel better," he said.

The radio squelched to life.

"Medic three on the air?" the dispatcher said.

Julio keyed the radio microphone on his shoulder.

"Medic three's on, night crew, Tavares and Archer."

"Medic three, on a priority, one-forty-one South Florence Street, by the pool in the rear, for a child, possible drowning."

The drive seemed to take forever. No chitchat, no banter. Deadly serious. Inside, Archer prayed it was the usual, a kid who had struggled in the pool a little, panicked relatives calling it in as a drowning. Happened all the time. Archer pushed the other reality out of his head—a few times every summer, the call was exactly as advertised. He went over drug doses, tube and blade sizes, who he would tell to do what when he got there.

They found the girl supine on the concrete patio next to the pool. Firefighters from the station down the street and a couple route cops were there. The yard was sparse—clean, low-cut green grass, a small swing set over by a koi pond. Trees dotted a large lawn surrounded by low brick walls. As the firefighters and cops took turns compressing the girl's chest, water poured from her nose and mouth. Archer worked to suppress the bile that rose in his throat, the nausea at full swell now, knowing he had to focus.

"Four-year-old girl. Mom went inside to answer the phone for a minute, came back and found her in the pool," one of the firefighters said, panting as he pushed. "No pulse, no breathing."

Julio knelt on the ground next to the firefighter pushing air into the girl's lungs through a mask. He opened his jump kit, pulled out a rolled-up tube of canvas, and unfurled it on the ground, began assembling equipment. Archer stuck two large pads on the girl's chest, turned on the heart monitor, and watched a long flat line extend across the screen.

Archer nodded and the firefighters pumped on the girl's chest again while Archer started an intravenous line, pushed some epinephrine into her veins. Julio put a breathing tube into her trachea, began ventilating.

Two other firefighters arrived with the ambulance stretcher. A police officer tapped Archer on the shoulder and handed him the girl's name and date of birth that he'd gotten from the woman standing off to the side, wringing her hands in silence.

The cop nodded toward the woman. "That's mom."

Archer was a connoisseur of grief-stricken relatives. He knew the varieties of silence. Sometimes, if the patient had suffered long and intensely, Archer knew silence meant more than acceptance. It meant death was welcome, a release from pain. Archer had seen silence that came from guilt, as when a crying child had had his head bashed into a concrete wall and the boyfriend babysitter realized he was about to do some serious time.

And then there was the mother's pain. Archer knew this one best. He'd seen it at overdoses, at fatal car accidents near the victims' homes, at hangings and following gunshot wounds to the head so fresh that cordite still hung in the air.

And at drownings, usually one or two a summer. This was the silence of a pain so heavy that it precluded speech. It was the silence that accompanied a life that would never be, the loss of something that never was but had seemed not only attainable but assured.

Julio supervised moving the girl from the ground to a long fiberglass board and then onto the stretcher. Archer gave more epinephrine and walked over to the mother. She looked him in the eyes, neither beseeching nor angry, a new look, something Archer hadn't seen before. Archer had a dozen prepared speeches for these instances, but this was unexpected. He couldn't put a name to it, but he had the sense of speaking to a member of a new tribe, like first contact with an ancient civilization that had lived on a Pacific island, incommunicado, for a thousand years.

"Ma'am," Archer said.

"Ann," the woman said. Her eyes were rimmed in redness and tears.

Archer nodded. "Ann, Evangeline is critically ill. We're doing everything we can, but you need to know that, right now, she has no pulse and isn't breathing on her own."

"Don't give up," Ann said, her calm unsettling to Archer. Bits and pieces of traditional grief and terror were there, and the calm denial he'd encountered with people of strong religious faith. But Ann was different. She was both of those things—scared and sure of some kind of supernatural order guiding the moment—and yet neither of them.

"We're doing absolutely everything we can; she's getting the best care possible. I just wanted you to know that she's very sick, that she may not survive—"

Ann straightened. Held something out for Archer to see, her arms shaking, as if she lifted something of great weight. Rosary beads.

"I just found them," she said. Her eyes widened, and when she turned to Archer, it seemed she had to force each cell in her body to cooperate. When she spoke, it was from somewhere a thousand miles away. "I haven't thought about these in years. Why did I find them right now?"

"Archer, we've got pulses back," Julio said.

Archer turned, nodded, returned to the mother. He felt his own heart rate jump.

"We've got a pressure," Julio said. "She's biting on the tube."

"I really need to get back," Archer said.

Ann nodded, held the beads up to Archer like a child holding up a seashell found on the beach. "These must mean something," she said.

Julio and the firefighters raised the stretcher, began rolling to the ambulance. They stopped by Archer; they knew his thing. He always stopped sick kids long enough for their parents to give a kiss, a pat on the hand. He looked at the heart monitor, felt a strong pulse in the girl's elbow and wrist.

"I had to give her a little sedation," Julio said.

"She's still very sick," Archer said to Ann. "Why don't you give her a kiss on the cheek, talk to her for a second."

Ann leaned forward, rubbed the back of Evangeline's right hand, whispered something into her ear.

Archer told Julio to go ahead to the ambulance, that he was right behind them.

"Things have improved," he said to Ann, "but Evangeline is still very, very sick."

"She'll live," Ann said. "I know it."

Ann hugged Archer, squeezed Evangeline's hand, then sank to her knees and sobbed.

"Can you watch her?" Archer asked the nearest cop, who nodded.

Nothing changed on the trip to the hospital. Evangeline's heart kept beating. Her blood pressure stabilized. Archer squeezed the oxygen bag and Julio waved a penlight into each of the girl's eyes. He shook his head.

"Right pupil blown, left unreactive," Julio said.

Archer looked down at the little girl's face. No injury, no sign of the destruction behind her eyes, the way a part of her brain had already died from lack of oxygen. He squeezed again. No battles were ever truly won, he thought. Inside him, the weakened dam broke. The things he had told himself night after night when the system failed, when medicine failed, when Archer failed—all of it now drowned him. There was nothing special about the drowned girl, and something horrifying about that. All this tragedy, big and small, and Archer could do nothing about any of it. The moment passed in a blink, and no one who saw it would have noticed a thing. Outside, Archer going through the motions. Inside, Archer done. Finished with all of it.

*   *   *

Five days later, they found him. Julio and Knuckles had been looking in their off hours. The entire service had scoured the city during shifts. They'd asked around. They'd poked and prodded and the cops had braced every homeless guy and street tough they could find. Archer had gone missing.

They found him in the bushes between the abandoned Healy Machine Works factory and Dooley Pond, lying across a rail siding that hadn't borne a train in a hundred years. Knuckles got there first, on a Thursday morning. They'd had a tip from a frequent flier that Archer was down there, that he'd been drunk for days, getting into scrapes with the regulars, might have been tuned up by some guys from the Posse. Knuckles laid him on a sleeping bag in the back of his pickup and drove to Julio's duplex.

The two of them dragged him into Julio's bathroom and cut away his clothes. Maria bathed him. Archer woke up. Maria handed him a towel and left the bathroom. A few minutes later Archer emerged and Maria pointed to a hope chest at the end of the bed. He sat and she handed him a pile of Julio's clothes.

"You're going to that place," she said.

"New Start? No fucking way."

"I wasn't asking. You're going."

She knelt in front of him, cupped his knees in her warm hands.

"My kids love you. Julio loves you. I love you. You're going."

"I was doing okay, had some bad calls, just something about that girl's mother," Archer said.

"This job gets to people," Maria said. "I beg Julio to go back to school, do something with computers. This job, it's not good for you, any of you. Someday you'll meet someone and get married, maybe have some kids. You want to be like us? You want to work a hundred hours a week just to keep your kids in braces and food on the table?"

"You know that feeling in the summer where it rains all week and you get to a point where you think it's never going to stop, it's going to be like this forever and ever and the sun's never going to come up, nothing's ever going to be dry again?" Archer asked. "I feel like that every day."

"Get dressed," Maria said. "After we eat, Julio is taking you up there. I already packed for you."

She stood, kissed the top of his head, and walked out of the room.

Later, while they drove, Julio said this was for the best, that this had been coming for a while and none of them could stand to watch Archer kill himself. Archer didn't say anything. Julio told him it would only be a month, that he'd heard lots of great things about New Start, that Archer would come back ready to hit the streets with a clean head and sound heart.

Archer turned to Julio.

"Moonie and I, one time, before you were even on, we had this guy, got stuck to the wall by a machete," he said. "Dude in a hockey mask, like Jason, did it to him. Right through the chest. Nothing to do for him, right? Dead right there. Asked me not to let him die, then died. I feel like maybe all the new starts in the world won't make me any better."

"Just need a little time away," Julio said. "From all of it. From the shit and from the shit you do to make the shit go away. You'll see."

They pulled into the parking lot of a wide single-story house in the middle of the woods. They hadn't seen another car in half an hour. A huge lake rippled dark purple in the fading daylight, disappeared into the distance behind the house. A side door opened and a tall, heavyset man with gray hair and a gray beard waved at Julio and Archer.

"Thanks for the ride," Archer said.

"Want me to get your things?"

"I got it."

"You sure?"

"I've got to go in alone," Archer said. "I'll give you a call when I get a chance."

"Get better, bro."

They shook hands, then hugged. Archer got out and never looked back. He was there on the porch, and then he was gone.

24

S HE TOOK THE booth with her name carved onto the
wooden tabletop. Lu cloaked anxiety in nonchalance. She
knew Conroy thought they were meeting to talk about
Archer, to talk about tomorrow's story. That had been her
plan originally, and still was, in a way. They'd talk. But
things might not go the way Conroy expected.

Lu looked at her name. A lifetime ago, she thought.
Commerce High, thirty years ago and then some. Lu had
carved an ornate *L.M.* in this booth using Susie Windmere's
cuticle scissors. She'd put it in a prized spot, over by the corner with the napkin dispenser—Red Bowen's simple, block
R.B. was there too.

The Riverside was living history. Eighty years now, the
sons and daughters of the city had come to its musty hall and
dinged-up wooden booths for two dogs with the secret Riverside sauce (the secret, she had since learned: canned, bean-
less chili from Barker's deli) and a soda, carved their initials
on the wooden tables, along the wooden walls separating

booths, even on the wood paneling in the bathrooms. The joint itself was a roll call of the last century, a roster from an ersatz Ellis Island chronicling the tide of humanity that had washed up here.

Lu ate two dogs, drank a Polar cola, and waited.

She couldn't think of a better place than the Riverside. No one here on a weekend night but drunks and teens and families from the suburbs looking to do something daring, take part in one of the Worcester's most famous unofficial institutions. Power brokers went to the Dinger or the Sole or even Rosetta's Steakhouse or a dozen other places. The Riverside was as out of the way as it got. They were hiding in plain sight.

Conroy slid into the bench across from Lu and looked around the room.

"Aren't you going to get a couple dogs?" she asked.

Conroy shook his head. "I haven't mythologized this place. Not enough so that I'd actually eat here, anyways."

"You really ought to put on some pounds," Lu said.

"Haven't you read the studies? Every extra pound you carry is like a year off your life-span, or something like that."

"You trying to be immortal?"

"When I was a cop, you know how many vegans I pulled out from under buses?" Conroy said. "All these people living in denial. Waste of time. We can't spend one extra second alive that wasn't given to us the day we were born. That being said, I'm not looking to exit any faster than preordained."

A police car flashed by on the street outside, its sirens wailing for an instant and then gone. Lu spun her empty white ceramic plate around on a finger and watched a busboy struggle with, then drop, a plastic tray of plates and silverware. The crash stunned the conversations in the room, and a teenage girl in a back booth screeched in surprise. Conroy barely noticed. He slid a large manila folder across the table.

"It's interesting reading," Conroy said. "Tells you a lot about your boy Archer."

She noticed the city seal embossed on the cover, saw Archer's name in uneven letters typed manually on one of the old IBM typewriters on which the city bureaucracy still depended.

"Impressive," McCarthy said.

Conroy smiled. "People want John O'Toole to owe them favors. Better than savings bonds."

McCarthy flipped open the folder, read Archer's demographic sheet. Saw his pay rate and the pages of commendations and awards. No military service. A degree in electrical engineering from the Tech. A wife, Elaine. One child, Michael. Four. Lots of memorandums from the city's health insurer about "catastrophic health claims" for the boy. Hospitalizations in Boston. Chemotherapy, surgeries, millions in bills, broken down between what the insurer would pay and what Archer had to cover. Fucking guy must be broke, Lu thought as she examined the statements.

"Look in the back," Conroy said, peeking over his shoulder. "Behind the red sheet."

The red sheet was marked *Confidential*. She flipped it over and read.

One entry stuck out to her. It was from ten years ago. Archer had begun showing up for work drunk. He'd punched a partner. Said he was having dreams about men with holes in their chests who begged him to live but whom he could never save. Insomnia. Sick calls. Then no-call, no-shows for shifts at work, suspended for a week without pay, threatened with termination. Enough was enough, and they'd sent him to something called New Start Academy for a month.

"What's New Start Academy?" Lu asked.

"It's where you go when you're soft," Conroy said. "Drug addiction, alcoholism, bad dreams, that sort of crap. You only get sent there if you can't hack it, if your mind isn't tough, if you're not up to the stresses of doing a job like that."

She shrugged.

"So what?" she said. "This was a long time ago. Lots of people have trouble at work. These guys—cops, paramedics, firefighters—I mean, those are tough jobs. So what if they need a break once in a while?"

"You're missing the point," Conroy said. "This fellow Archer has already proven he can't handle the stress. He has a habit of hitting the bottle when he's against it. He had problems long before this latest, with the baby."

Lu ate a french fry, considered Conroy's point.

"Daisy Fontana doesn't seem to hold any grudge against him."

"You've been around," Conroy said. "You know the things people won't just come out and say."

"That's true, I've been around," she said.

She thought of her car burning in the middle of the crowd on her last night at the paper, a sacrifice. She was certain they'd have burned her, too, if things had gone differently.

"You know what I did when I got done talking to her?"

"Presumably called the police about your car," Conroy said.

"Nope. I went back and read all my stories about your trial, the one that cost you your job," Lu said. "Interesting tidbits in there I'd forgotten about."

"Why would you do that?"

"It's a rule I have. 'If your mother says she loves you, check it out.' I was reading it, pretty hard-core stuff. I'd forgotten about your freelancers. Who knew so many School of the Americas grads lived in Worcester?"

Conroy sat straight up, dipped the corner of a napkin in Lu's water glass, and dabbed at a spot of ketchup hardened on the table between them.

"Archer was the main witness against you, wasn't he?" she asked.

"You know he was."

Lu nodded, tapped the point of her index finger on the table for emphasis.

"And here we are now, you come here, you say the mayor wants to get rid of Archer, clean the books, avoid future uncomfortable questions, and I figure it's on the up-and-up. I mean, that's as good a motivation as a guy like John O'Toole needs, right? Now, though, I'm starting to wonder. I'm starting to wonder if this is even about the mayor at all. Like, does he even know we're having this conversation?"

Conroy stared at Lu. The silence was meant to unnerve. She saw Conroy's features shift even while outwardly still. His cheeks became hollower, his eyes a paler shade of light blue. His brows furrowed and the redness of the cowlick in the middle of his forehead brightened.

"What do you want me to say?" Conroy asked. "This is a small city. Coincidences are bound to happen."

"Maybe," she said. "But some coincidences seem mighty coincidental, if you know what I mean."

"Is there a question in the offing soon? I have somewhere to be."

Lu shrugged, looked down at the personnel file. "Can I keep this?" she asked.

"Ten minutes for notes, that's it. I have to get it back tonight or I turn into something worse than a pumpkin."

"How about a photo?"

"No. Photos have a way of wandering, and the fewer crumbs leading back to us, the better. Pen and paper or nothing at all."

Lu bent to the work. She felt monastic, like a forebear copying pages of the Bible before the Vikings arrived to burn it all. She filled half the pages in her notebook with a sideways shorthand, the words smudged where her left hand crossed over wet ink. When she finished, Conroy scooped up the file and dropped it in his lap. She tucked her notebook in the inside pocket of her coat. Her hand ached, clenched like a claw, and she massaged it to relieve the strain.

"What do you think?" Conroy asked.

"It's doable. There's definitely stuff to go to print with in there. 'Sources close to the mayor'?"

"Too close. 'City Hall sources,' perhaps?"

"Fine."

"We need to work out the next payment," Conroy said.

"Cash."

"That's what we were thinking. Why make a trail?"

"One question, though," Lu said.

"Of course."

"Why just Archer? Why not go after his partner too? They were both on the call. It seems like a loophole needlessly left open."

"I have no idea," Conroy said. "I fix things. I make things go away. When the mayor says he needs something done, I'm the guy going to do it. It's a simple life. I work fifty weeks a year, spend a couple weeks down in Dennis Port each summer with the wife, no problem. I try not to think too deeply about any of it. Guys like the mayor, they lose sleep every night playing chess in their heads. Me? I sleep like the dead."

"So Archer is the mayor's problem, not yours?"

"Why are you worrying about it now? You didn't have so many questions when we first asked you to write about this guy. You took our money, no questions."

Lu nodded.

"I did. But you know one thing I've never seen in all my time as a reporter? A city personnel file. And that's some serious shit. I didn't see it in '99 when the school superintendent got caught in that hotel with that girl. I didn't see it in '05 with the police lieutenant and the poker machine thing. Never seen one on any other story. Suddenly, here I am in a hot dog shack on a Saturday night with the mayor's go-to guy reading the Holy of Holies about some paramedic John O'Toole seems to have a tremendous hard-on for."

Conroy tapped the edges of the file and looked around the room. He licked his lips.

"This is a big deal. John wants this thing finished. The Commonwealth cannot be denied the greatness of a man like John O'Toole, future governor, simply because a minor city employee lodges a complaint. This Archer kid screwed up, but he's been making a lot of noise about this brain-damaged ghetto mutt and he's been trying to drag the mayor into it. Ethics complaints. *Please.* Who's he kidding? Primary season begins in a month, and the feeling amongst the party leadership is that a successful mayor from the state's second-biggest city might make a good horse to bet on. John O'Toole is asking for your help, and he's going to make it worth your while."

"So who's got my back?" Lu asked. "What is his excellency offering me exactly?"

"You know the deal," Conroy said.

"I'm starting to think maybe I'm far out on a very lonely limb."

"You are," Conroy said. "It's why we chose you. We knew you could handle it."

Conroy stood up and slid the file folder under the arm of his suit coat. He tapped the table with his index finger.

"Just do the job we're paying you to do and make sure you put the last nail in Thomas Archer's coffin. John O'Toole is a man of his word, and there are people with deep pockets behind him. Who do you think pays my salary? You won't find me on any city payrolls. When he's governor and you're pulling down a hundred grand a year writing press releases, this"—Conroy waved his arms in a circle, took in the sweep of the neon-lit crowd—"this will all seem like a dream, a mediocre dream from which you've awoken, your wallet fat, this whole thing a detour, your conscience clear."

Lu nodded, took a last drag off her can of cola, then tossed it into the nearby recycling bin. She'd wanted to hear it. She'd wanted to hear Conroy say it was ironclad.

He couldn't do it.

Lu admitted what she'd known since that day in Kittredge's office, what she'd wanted to deny, wanted to believe wasn't true: there were no plans for her. Never had been. Not here, not now, not ever, not for her whole life. She'd always been on her own, no matter who promised to stand by her. The understanding hurt less than the other truth, that she'd let herself believe in salvation. It had been a long time since she went to church, and now she remembered why she'd stopped in the first place. She laid her hands flat on the table, felt the cool linoleum.

"I don't know, Eamon. I think I'm out."

Conroy sat back down. "A little late for that, don't you think?"

"There's nothing next for me, is there?"

"Everything is sitting just fine," Conroy said.

"So how does it happen? Does the phone just stop ringing? No more chats at the Ding Wa? Everyone refuses to take my calls? Maybe you show up at my door, middle of some night. I go away too. Something like that?"

Conroy leaned back. "Lu, if you can't trust a crooked ex-cop, who can you trust?"

"Just tell me there's a job."

Conroy hesitated. "Almost certainly."

"How much did you pay Kittredge? Was there even really a layoff?"

"Your job is gone. That part is true. Kittredge didn't drive much of a bargain on that front."

She wanted to choke on it. All of it. Decades of shit-eating, of being received by every two-bit, wrinkled-suit hack in this city as if in audience with a sitting Pope. Having to bow and curtsy to ensure a quote for the final edition, then chucking the resentment back in endless bull sessions over cheap booze at the Ding Wa, as if any of it made a difference, and all the while knowing what was in store for these assholes, all of them: a new condo with granite in the kitchen and granite in the bathrooms and granite-gilded plaques from the Kiwanis on the wall, a moderate coastal Florida palace where these thieves went to bed every night in their senescent years under soft winds and pink dusks, laid their heads next to sleeping wives who ran errands all day in cheap, floral-patterned track suits like it was a uniform requirement, slept with their curlers in, all of it financed by careers spent ripping off taxpayers, the common man, the rabble, anyone with money there to be had, robbing them blind like it was the family business, people like Lu letting it happen—*making* it happen, and for what? So in the end she could be coerced by thirty pieces of silver into throwing away the one thing she actually owned in this whole mess, her *name*—so that a degenerate sociopath like Eamon Conroy could settle a couple debts on the way to bigger and better.

She stood, dropped a roll of cash in front of Conroy, a weight on her chest lifting, floating away. "We're square," she said, "and I'm out."

25

Summer 2004

WHEN MARIA MADE the pairings for the wedding party, there was a happy coincidence: Most of them married or otherwise attached. Except two. Archer, the best man. Elaine Trifolo, the maid of honor. Both single. Both claimed not to be looking. Maria was thrilled. Archer balked.

"Elaine is perfect for you," Maria said.

"I can't date another nurse," he said. "There aren't any left in the city who don't hate my guts."

"Whose fault is that?"

"I've been on a dry spell."

"She's not a nurse," Maria said.

"Respiratory therapist? Physical therapist? Please, for God's sake, not another paramedic?"

She swatted his shoulder.

"She's a paralegal, actually. Works at Bowman and Something. I can't remember. You two would be perfect. She's a huge Red Sox fan."

Maria arranged a get-together.

"It's not a date," she said. "So don't get squirrely on me."

They met for dinner at Cactus Jack's, along with Julio and Maria. Elaine matched Archer word for unspoken word. Archer thought she was pretty, in the way so many women her age were pretty. Loose brown hair tied in a ponytail, green eyes, freckles on the bridge of her nose. An honest face. Maria and Julio tried to carry the conversation, eventually gave up and retreated to their own cocoon. They fed each other fried calamari and interlocked arms as they drank their beer.

"Maria says you're a paralegal," Archer said. "That must be interesting."

"You're kidding, right?" Elaine asked.

"What?"

"Someone says 'paralegal,' and word association brings you to 'interesting'?"

Archer sipped his beer. Cast a glance over at the bar. Empty. He ate a calamari. "I don't know. I figured working in the law must be interesting."

"It's boring as shit," she said, "but I'd be lying if I didn't say I enjoyed it. It's not exactly *in* the law, but I get to see the inside of how things work around here. How about being a paramedic? That must be *interesting.*"

Archer shrugged. Normal move was to play fake cool with the women. Turn on the world-weary-life-saver act to full volume. Something about Elaine, though. He couldn't bring himself to tell her anything but the truth.

"It has its moments," he said. "But most of the time, it's bullshit. Lots of drunks and psychs and people with minor problems. Ninety percent of the people we bring to the hospital don't need it. Once in a while, though, you get a good one. And it keeps you going for weeks. Which is good, because sometimes it's weeks before you get a call that was even worth the effort of showing up for work."

Elaine scratched her forehead. Squinted across the small round table at Archer. Laughed.

"What's funny?" Archer asked.

"Tell me that's not your usual pickup line?" she said.

Archer liked her laugh, the way it made her green eyes greener.

"No, I usually make up some BS," he said.

"I hope so. That's pathetic."

"It's a good job, just not as exciting as people think."

She pointed at the television over the bar. Archer turned.

"Sox game," she said.

Archer slid his chair next to hers. They watched the game, barely spoke, split a pitcher of Sam Adams, ate bowl after bowl of popcorn and didn't notice when Julio and Maria left. Red Sox designated hitter David Ortiz ended the game with a walk-off home run in the bottom of the ninth. Archer and Elaine screamed in joy, hugged each other in the excitement of the moment, then lingered a bit before separating.

In the parking lot later, after the restaurant closed, they talked about the game. When it came time to leave, neither could figure out how to do it.

"So, I guess I'll see you at the wedding," Archer said.

"I guess so."

They waved at each other. Elaine got in her car, and as Archer walked back to his, he heard her car clicking instead of the usual sound of the engine turning over. He stopped. Elaine thumped the steering wheel, got out of the car.

"You have any cables?" she asked.

"Dead battery?"

"No, I just want to test your road safety preparation," she said, smiling.

Archer nosed his car to hers, popped the hood. He removed a set of jumper cables from his trunk. Elaine took them from him.

"Start your car when I give you the word," she said.

He sat behind the steering wheel and watched Elaine hook the cables to her battery, then his. She gave him the thumbs-up. He started his car, revved the engine, then heard Elaine's Impala come to life. She stepped out, removed the cables, and dropped them into Archer's trunk.

"I don't want to be too forward here, but if you wanted, I'd love to take you out to dinner sometime."

"You got something to write on?" she asked.

Archer picked up a McDonald's receipt, handed it to her. She wrote on it, handed it back.

"That's my number. You should call sometime. Maybe we could go to a Sox game or something."

"I'd like that," Archer said.

She kissed him on the cheek and was gone. Archer sat behind the wheel of his car for twenty minutes in the empty parking lot of Cactus Pete's, feeling the weight of the world dissolving into the stars above.

26

ARCHER AND JULIO didn't believe in coincidences. Kansas Street. Tonight. No coincidence.

Fire tore through the roof of the triple decker, another torched building on Kansas Street shedding bright orange embers like lightning bugs. Not just any triple decker, not just any street. Archer watched through a window of the burning building as a handful of firefighters poked at the third-floor ceiling.

The place had taken off. More and more firefighters bent against the heat and the smoke to enter. They sought the seat of the fire—Archer remembered the term from a class. It meant where the fire reigned, where it had begun and where the firefighters needed to go to put the thing out. It seemed an anachronistic name, as if the fire held court on a throne, waiting to do battle with streams of water thrust at it by mere mortals.

They'd arrived twenty minutes earlier and set up across the street, at the command post where district chief Walter Loman reigned. Archer and Julio rolled their equipment-laden stretcher over to the chief's Suburban.

Loman, in white turnout gear smudged black by so many fires that he looked like a Victorian chimney sweep, nodded to the crew, his eyes lingering on Archer an extra moment. Archer turned his back to Loman, watched the fire.

"Tough week for you," Loman said to Archer, yelling to be heard over the din.

"Another subscriber to the *Courier*, I see," Archer said.

Loman was about speak, then stopped. His left eyelid twitched. He'd heard something. Or someone. Archer knew the look, cast a sideways glance to see the source of Loman's irritation.

It was Reading. Loman's driver.

Reading stood by the door to the Suburban, his job being to recover those electronic missives lost in the logjam of radio confusion and conjecture and relay them to Loman—things like firefighters asking for more water, less smoke, where to park late-arriving apparatuses. Reading listened to all this on a portable radio held in front of him like he was Frank Sinatra with a mic stand, but mostly he was listening to the Red Sox on the Chevy's radio through the open door.

Loman was distracted by his disgust with his driver. He didn't hear the fuzzy urgency over the net at first, the voices yelling about the body.

"I wonder, what about the canteen truck?" Reading asked.

"What?" Loman asked. A vein popped up on the side of his neck.

Archer thought Loman looked at Reading the way the assembled servants must have watched Nero as he fiddled while tortured Rome burned. Instead of violin music, though, Reading exulted to the hum of a Red Sox–Tampa Bay game.

"Fancy meeting you here," said a female voice next to Archer.

Lu.

"Fires draw the worst crowds," Archer said.

Somewhere in the crashing and the swooshing of high-pressure water jets and the rasping chainsaws, a voice came over the airwaves. A body. Something about a body, Archer thought. Not a body—a victim. Still alive, maybe. He looked at Julio, who was already unloading the equipment from the stretcher, then lowering it and unclasping the straps.

"If you're still looking for a conversation, I'm down."

"Things have changed," she said. "I don't want quotes. Just give me five minutes." She nodded toward Julio, who continued readying his gear. "Alone."

"The canteen truck," Reading said. "Guys could use some coffee. Maybe doughnuts. You know, after all this hard work."

Loman dropped his dry-erase marker to the ground, stomped over to where Reading stood, ripped the radio out of his hands, and threw it as far into the darkness as he could.

"Why'd you do that?" Reading asked.

"Because in your hands, a radio is an insult."

"What did I say?" Reading asked.

"The canteen truck?" Loman said. "I got fifty guys in there busting their asses, and you want fucking doughnuts?"

"I just need a minute," Lu said to Archer. "How about right now?"

"I don't have a minute," Archer said. "They're pulling someone out of there."

"How about the Bully?" she asked. "Midnight-ish. Whenever you get a chance. I'm buying."

"Keep your money," Archer said. "If we're not busy, we'll be there."

Lu walked away, chatted up a cop working crowd control across the street. Archer and Julio wheeled the stretcher around the argument to the side of the truck nearest the burning building. A buzz had gone through the crowd, the handful of fire buffs with their scanners having relayed to onlookers the emergency call sent over the radios. *They found someone. A victim. Someone was alive in there.*

Silhouetted in the flickering and raging gloom behind them, three firefighters sprinted toward Loman's command post. They were in full gear, the hissing sound of air being sucked from the bottles on their backs and into their face masks coming in deep rushes and clicks. The tallest ran in front of the group and carried something over his right shoulder. They headed straight for Julio and Archer, then dumped their cargo in a pile at the medics' feet.

"We found this one on the third-floor kitchen!" yelled the tallest firefighter, his voice muffled behind his face mask. "She was stuffed in a refrigerator! Jonesie bumped into it and the door opened and this rolled out!"

As Archer looked down, he recognized the form as a woman. Her clothes were blackened from heat and smoke. Her hair was a wilderness of brown and soot. Black streaks jutted down from each nostril. Her face was swollen and glistening. She wasn't breathing. Archer felt a strong *bump-bump-bump* in her neck.

Archer placed a mask on the woman's face and began squeezing oxygen into her lungs. Julio scissored away her clothes, looking for injuries. Archer thought the contours of the woman's face were off, disjointed. It took a moment for him to appreciate the swelling, the left ear torn half off, her eye sockets blackened by bruises instead of fire smoke.

"Someone kicked the shit out of her," Archer said.

Julio nodded. "Not burned too much. Lots of broken stuff."

"Holy shit," said Reading.

Archer inserted a straight metal blade along the right side of the woman's tongue, then lifted, up and to the left. He saw a field of angry red swollenness. Black sooty streaks dashed here and there. Nothing looked the way it was supposed to. Her airway was swelling shut. She couldn't breathe and he couldn't breathe for her.

Archer cursed under his breath, reached into his equipment bag and pulled out a scalpel.

"What are you going to do with that?" Reading asked. His voice warbled. The circle of men around them quieted. Even Loman seemed to forget about the fire for the moment, stood wide-eyed and silent. Archer bit his lower lip, located a spot on the woman's neck, and cut.

A pale, pearl-colored film appeared beneath all the severed skin and fat. Blood oozed throughout the site and down the sides of the woman's neck. This was the worst time for Archer. The point of no return long gone, success yet unsure. He fought the urge to panic, to drop the scalpel and raise his hands in surrender. Instead he pierced the pearl tissue, removed the scalpel, spun it end over end before poking the handle of the scalpel through the hole and twisting, making the gaping wound larger.

"Holy shit," Reading said again, then collapsed unconscious, banging his head with a dull thud against the Suburban's black plastic bumper on his way down.

Archer placed the flexible breathing tube through the hole, attached the oxygen bag, and noted with relief the rise and fall of the woman's chest each time he squeezed air into her lungs.

"I'm retiring next week," Loman said to no one in particular. "Maine. Wells Beach. Thank fucking God."

Reading moaned, and Loman gave him a soft kick in the ribs.

On the ride to the hospital, a firefighter drove while Julio and Archer took care of the woman. The crisis over, Archer looked closer while he took care of loose ends—started another intravenous line, gave sedatives to make sure she wasn't feeling any of this, rechecked vital signs. He cleaned off the soot and looked for injuries while Julio squeezed air into her lungs.

Archer began to see features, realized quickly that it was a young Hispanic woman. It was hard to tell where the bruises began and the burns ended, but Archer knew one thing. This woman had been hit hard and repeatedly. A small butterfly pendant on a chain had melted into her skin on her left shoulder, leaving a swollen impression that Archer thought looked like a brand.

Archer looked closely, found broken arms, legs, ribs. Eyes swollen shut. Nose bent to the side, partially torn off. Teeth missing. In her front jeans pocket Archer found a plastic card. An employee identification card. It was melted on the edges, but the front of it was legible. The woman worked in city hall. City clerk's office. *Administrative Assistant I.* Archer read the name.

Daisy Fontana.

Archer handed the card to Julio. He read it, handed it back to Archer.

"I don't want this," Julio said. "Keep this shit far, far away from me."

At the hospital, the ambulance backed into the bay, and waiting hospital staff yanked open the doors. When they rolled by, Archer saw Lu standing in the crowd. She was pale, stood on tiptoe to see the patient.

When they were done and had left Daisy with the trauma team, Archer came out onto the ambulance dock to find Lu still standing there.

"It was her, wasn't it?" she asked. Archer said nothing, squirted hand sanitizer into his palm.

Archer rubbed his hands together. One thought rumbled through his head. One name, over and over. He'd seen this before. Archer looked up at Lu.

"You know who did it to her," Archer said. "It's what he's always done."

"I know," Lu said. "Meet me at the Bully in an hour. Come without your partner."

27

Eamon Conroy circled the heavy bag at the Ionic, the metronomic punching a soundtrack to his thoughts of the past two weeks. Midnight was his favorite time to work out, the cavernous gym empty, nothing but the hum of fluorescent floodlights and the dull smack of glove on heavy bag. He used the sessions to think, to review how things were coming together. How they might yet fall apart.

Jab. Jab. Slide. Duck. Repeat.

He was close. The final act in a play. Sunlight at the end of a long storm. He had the loose ends tied up, the problem children right where he wanted them, the coup de grace inevitable. He just had to get everyone to show up.

When Daisy first broke the news of her pregnancy to O'Toole, Conroy had lobbied for the home birth as a way to keep things quiet. O'Toole was a family-values guy, after all. She wouldn't go for it, insisted on scheduling a C-section at Memorial, but Conroy knew the junk she couldn't stop putting in her arms played a part. The baby came three weeks early, before anyone was ready.

At least she'd called him first, when her water broke. He'd done his best, but he was in over his head, and when the baby arrived limp and blue skinned and barely breathing, he punted. Daisy begged for an ambulance. Conroy told her to wait, paced the kitchen, putting his plan together. Easiest thing, put a bullet in everyone in the room. Worry later about the details. It would buy him time.

Then Rigo muddied the works by calling 911, Conroy barely out of the room. It had all been business to Rigo, so cool with everything—*all* of it, the thing between Daisy and O'Toole just another piece of business to him—until he saw the baby.

When he heard Archer's voice on the radio, signing on as the ambulance en route to Kansas Street, the same voice Conroy remembered from his own trial all those years ago, sealing the deal with the jury, ending his career, taking his freedom, he smiled.

A new plan. Satisfying. Today's problem solved while settling an old score.

It was so easy to isolate the guy. A phone call to an old number at the PD, pretending to be the district boss, ordering dispatch to call off the route cops and the firefighters at that medical call on Kansas Street. Ambulance to handle alone.

Conroy planned to be gone before the ambulance got there. Leave Archer to pay the price, try to explain what had gone wrong with the delivery of Miguel Fontana. But then Rigo wouldn't go, handed the paperwork to the guy. It was a complication, but that soon would end too.

McCarthy might no longer be on board, but with the press coverage she'd already given, Archer would soon be history and, the cherry on top, he only had to pay that snake Kittredge for the honor. He smiled at the best unintended consequence of the newspaper stories, the way they'd flushed that nut Knak from the bushes. He might let Knak do some shooting, but all he was really there for was to take the fall if things fell apart.

He still couldn't believe Lu had returned the final payment he'd made.. Last guy who'd given the money back out of guilt was Judas. And how had that worked out?

Jab. Jab. Slide. Duck.

The Tavares kid being muscled into trading his partner for a house in the suburbs—that was a real miracle. The logic was sound, but he hadn't been sure he could get the kid to sign on until he'd showed up at the house showing. Tavares was a tough one to crack, but guys like him, they wanted to believe so much in a better life. Wanted to believe it was possible in this America, despite all the proof to the contrary, that hard work paid off. That a better life was there for the taking, not realizing that someone else had to give you the permission first. That was the secret no one talked about. But Conroy understood the desire, counted on it.

He prided himself that he'd never been foolish enough to hope for anything.

There was no better life coming, unless you made it, unless you were willing to be as ruthless as the forces holding you back.

It wasn't enough to *take* it. You had to ruin the land you'd just occupied, just to make sure no one came looking to get it back.

He punched and slid, jabbed left and right, the heavy bag pendulating in opposite orbits, waltzing a box step to Conroy's advance. *One-two. Slide. One-two. Slide.*

He knew that improving his life was a zero-sum game. For him to win, someone else had to lose. Guilt was a luxury, and luxuries only made you soft, he believed. No one had ever accused him of being soft.

Tonight's dilemma was like putting together a thousand-piece jigsaw puzzle scattered by a toddler just a couple pieces short of completion. O'Toole wanted the thing with the baby to go away. He'd never been in favor of offering an answer if you could make the question disappear. If things went as planned, O'Toole would give him the one thing he really wanted—beyond the money, of course.

Mayors made promises.

Governors made shit happen.

A pardon from Governor O'Toole would get Conroy back where he belonged, as a detective on the police department. Back where the juice was, where the power kept itself covert. A detective who knew that the grass grew greener in some parts of the city because of what lay buried below—that was a man with power. Better than elected office. Better than anything you could buy.

His mother would have approved. She'd spent a career in the city tax collector's office, eventually retiring as assistant collector. Margaret Conroy had told her son that the human condition bared itself most baldly when it came to taxes. Taxes bought nothing and yet paid for everything, and people acted in all sorts of ways when the stakes were so high.

She'd taught him that obeying the rules wasn't enough. The rules were fluid. The rules could trip you up. Rules, she said, were for people without imagination. The risk averse.

"Sheep," she said. "They have no one to blame but themselves when the auctioneers show up on their doorsteps."

Eamon had learned the lessons well, used them to further his career in the police department. From his first day in the academy and into the first few years on the job, he'd alienated himself from his colleagues, made no friends with his loose and aggressive approach to the job.

That was fine with Conroy.

His colleagues were family men and women. They patrolled their routes and stood their details and bred large, rowdy families they took to the Cape or Disney World or Hampton Beach. They bought houses in Uxbridge or Grafton, forsook the city for the quiet countryside and its gated housing developments, lived boring, effective lives as good citizens who went to church on Saturday evenings, coached Little League, joined the PTA, waited for their pensions and dreamed of retiring to West Yarmouth or maybe Maine.

Conroy wanted none of it. He'd been raised in the city, couldn't stand the thought of leaving. He'd never known his father. Margaret Conroy had refused to discuss the issue, even up until her death. Instead, the city had reared Conroy, taught him the lessons he'd needed to learn about survival, about getting ahead, about power.

He was sweating now, working the bag and remembering the way it all began, his journey to the beating heart of the living creature that was this city. It had started with a shakedown. Hector Alizondo. The Woodland Lane Bodega. Conroy four years walking a beat, itching to get onto the detective bureau but needing to prove he had the chops. Hector was a regular on his route. Conroy had stopped in for free bottles of water in the summer, free coffee when it was cooler.

One day, Alizondo said there were some kids around the corner stealing cars. Selling them for parts to garages in the East End. Alizondo said he didn't really care about the cars, or the kids, but he thought Conroy should know. It was bad for business, the thefts.

"It scares away my customers."

"Do you have a name?"

"Benny Tomaiolo," Hector said. "Runs with a bunch of Orion Street kids out of East Park."

"I'll look into it," Conroy said.

"I could help," Hector said. The bodega was empty. Hector leaned over the register as he whispered. "I have some . . . knowledge . . . in this arena."

"I don't need help."

Hector held his hands up.

"Okay, I understand. But a few of us, some of the other guys I work with here and over at the cab stand, we share a common, what would you call it? *Lineage*. We have talents to offer, and we know about you. We watch you work. We're *simpatico*. I think we could do a good business together. You're not like the other cops. You understand things in ways they do not."

A teenage boy walked into the bodega. Hector and Conroy stopped talking but regarded each other while the boy went to the freezer and selected an Italian ice. Hector broke away only long enough to cash the boy out. When he left, Hector locked the front door, put up the CLOSED sign. He motioned for Conroy to follow him to a small back office, where the pair sat across from each other at a dented green metal desk.

"There is untapped potential in this place," Hector began. "If we partnered with a police officer? Let me tell you a little bit about who we are and what we can offer."

Three nights later, three AM, Benny Tomaiolo was duct-taped to a chair in the storeroom of Hector's bodega. Hector and two others—Raul, a driver from Orange Cab, and Luis, a roofer Conroy recognized from the dominoes games Hector always seemed to have going—worked Tomaiolo over with rubber hoses and buckets of water.

"Who pays you for the cars you steal?" Hector asked.

"Fuck you."

A smack to the face with a length of rubber hose. A kick to the crotch. The chair kicked back, a bucket of water poured into Tomaiolo's face.

"We can do this all night, Benny," Hector said. "Can you?"

The sun peeked over the hillcrests around the city before Benny Tomaiolo came to his senses and agreed to the plan Hector laid out. Conroy would allow Benny and his crew to continue their car operation, but twenty percent of the proceeds came to them. And Benny would forward to Conroy anything he heard about who was stealing what from whom in the city.

It hadn't been an easy pill for Benny Tomaiolo to swallow, Conroy remembered, but a few volts from a car battery to his testicles had sealed the deal.

Soon, Conroy had a stable of talent, a score of guys from Honduras and El Salvador and Panama, all of whom had trained at some shadowy school at Fort Benning, then ended up in the city when conditions in their home countries turned unfavorable in later years. They weren't polished. Their methods were unsophisticated. But in the application of pain, his guys were fearless and eager, and Conroy respected them. That's the one thing few understood—causing pain was in itself painful. To do it, he knew one had to be willing to turn into something else, something less than human, a force stripped of morals and principled thought, a slave to the mission. How could you turn on the juice otherwise?

His team in place and the last of his compunctions erased, Eamon Conroy's rise began in earnest.

The thing they avoided at all cost was greed. The money they shook out of the petty criminals in just the East Side was enough. He declined to expand or bring others into their cabal. More people meant more attention. He decided that power was best accrued invisibly.

Conroy used his new crew on legitimate investigations too, clearing case after case, the most on the department, making him a star. He didn't flash a lot of the money they made, his only big purchase a small house in Dennis Port that he bought with cash and in his wife's name. The house was a refuge, a place for Conroy to escape the city, although often also a place to conduct business far from prying city eyes.

The money crashed against Conroy's shore in waves. He made detective. His estrangement from his colleagues meant he worked alone. This suited him fine. No one watching meant no one to report him to Internal Affairs. No one to see the tens of thousands of dollars he made every month on the side. No one to tell him to stop.

He was the king of an invisible kingdom, and it was all he'd ever wanted.

If only Raul hadn't panicked when they'd taken that safe house interrogation too far. It wasn't the first time a subject had died during their ministrations. They had a procedure in place. No need to panic. But Raul lost his composure, called for the ambulance. Even the discovery of Raul's body in the city landfill a few months later couldn't make up for the fact that one errant phone call had ended Conroy's career and sent him to jail. The DA hadn't batted an eyelash, asked for thirty years, seemed disappointed when Conroy only got the ten.

Jab. Jab. Slide. Duck.

He'd taken care of Raul, first making sure he hadn't talked with anyone else—that part of the job Conroy did himself to spare Hector and the boys the trouble before they fled the country. They knew they'd be deported if they waited for the police to arrest them.

"Better to make our own arrangements than have the State Department hand us over to our enemies," Hector said the night he left.

Conroy lost it all. The money. The career. The power and influence. It had seemed like a death knell at the time. But enough of that. He was within striking distance of getting it all back. Just like he knew he would.

Jab. Jab. Slide. Du—

"Must be nice, having the whole place to yourself."

He pulled his punch in midair. He hugged the heavy bag to stop its motion. John O'Toole slid between the ropes and into the ring.

"I like my privacy," Conroy said.

O'Toole nodded. "It's your best attribute," he said.

Conroy drank water, wiped his forehead with a towel.

"Did we have a meeting scheduled?" he asked.

"I couldn't sleep," O'Toole said.

"My mother always used to say, you can sleep all you want when you're dead," Conroy said.

"Summer's almost over."

Conroy let that hang in the air.

"Remember when we talked in February?" O'Toole said.

"We're almost there," Conroy said.

"Where's McCarthy stand on all this? It just seems like maybe she's not part of the team anymore."

"McCarthy won't be a problem."

"She already is," O'Toole said. "Isn't she on our payroll? Why's she asking all over city hall about Daisy?"

"She definitely isn't a problem."

"But she is! I don't want to know what really happened in that fire. How you handle your business is your business. But McCarthy's asking lots of questions. I've got people pulling me aside all the time, telling me about it."

Conroy dropped the towel to the mat. He took a deep breath.

"There has been a setback on the McCarthy front," Conroy said.

"I knew it!"

"I didn't want to bother you with it. She's already given us everything we need. The paper trail is clear. Whatever happened with the Fontana baby, that sticks to Archer, no matter what complaints he files with whoever."

"DNA tests?"

Conroy shook his head. "We've got people in every DA's office, a few judges in the right places, and some well-placed friends in the state police ensuring that'll never happen. I've spent your money wisely."

O'Toole gripped the top rope on the ring, stretched his arms out straight as if pushing it away. "This is bad," he said.

"It's under control."

"Is it?"

Neither man spoke. O'Toole let go of the rope.

"We need to rethink some of this," he said. "We need a clearer path. You know where I was tonight? I was at a school athletics department fund raiser. A few thousand of my closest friends. And donors. Red Bowen was the guest of honor. You know what Red asked me about? Up on the dais, just between us chums?"

Conroy lifted his left leg and pulled a piece of white sports tape from the sole of his boxing shoe. He crumpled the tape and tossed it out of the ring.

"He wanted to know if I'd heard that Eamon Conroy was back in town, and that lots of crazy stories were going around about 'that crazy fucker' delivering a baby," O'Toole said.

"Red Bowen is an inconsequential drunk," Conroy said.

"In this city, Red Bowen sits at the right hand of God. In this city, no matter how your life turns out, if you were once a winner, people will listen to you, no matter how many fifths you've had or what crazy shit comes out of your mouth!"

Conroy knew what O'Toole sought. "I could handle Red too," he said. "But remember, the messier things get, the more likely someone will figure it out."

O'Toole looked around the darkened gym. He scraped a patch of chalk on the ring floor with the toe of his shoe.

"Remember when you came to me, right after you got out—after *we* got you out? Remember what you promised me?"

Conroy bent his head to the floor. He nodded.

"You promised me I'd never regret a penny of what I paid you," O'Toole said. "Remember that? You said you were willing to make things happen, you said it was all about being willing to do what the others wouldn't."

He stepped back, bent down so he looked into Conroy's eyes.

"I think it's time to put that to the test," O'Toole said. "No more diversions. No more plotting and manipulating. You know what you need to do. McCarthy. Archer. Red Bowen. You've put people on the shelf for less. Every moment you don't take care of these things is another moment we, you and I, come closer to losing everything. You ready for the circus again? Ready to go to prison again? Ready to start from scratch for a third time? Because I'll tell you one thing. I'm not ready to do it at all."

CHAPTER

28

Envelopes and people, Julio thought. The important stuff was always on the inside. He turned the manila envelope over in his hands. A rectangular lump in the middle of it. It looked like any other manila envelope, except for the lump. The lump made this one different from any other he'd ever held.

Conroy had been waiting in the driveway an hour ago when Julio returned from the night shift, leaning against the door of his Crown Vic, wrinkled black suit, cigarette smoke haloing his head like fog. Julio opened the door of his old Hyundai slowly so the squeaky hinge wouldn't wake Maria. He didn't want her to see him with Conroy or ask questions he didn't want to answer.

"We can't do this while I'm at work?" Julio said.

"I figured it would be better not to be seen."

He stubbed out his cigarette, held out the fat manila envelope.

"Your testimony was well received," Conroy said. Julio reached out for the envelope. Conroy pulled it back. "That should make you happy."

"You know it doesn't."

"It's always good to have the next governor as a friend."

"I don't want a friend," Julio said.

Conroy tossed the envelope to Julio. "You shouldn't waste energy worrying about Archer. He had this coming, with or without you. Why shouldn't you benefit? Beautiful house in Northborough? On your salary as a paramedic? This is better than the lottery."

Sitting on his couch, Conroy long gone but the kids and Maria asleep upstairs, Julio hefted the cash. He'd cashed out his 401k and borrowed money for every relative he could find in order to pay the downpayment on the house. This money would repay those favors and cover next month's closing. The house was so close he could taste it. He imagined his kids playing on a flat green lawn in a neighborhood where no one locked their doors at night, going to schools without metal detectors at the door, where no cops patrolled the halls.

Still.

Even while the money could buy a better life for his family, he couldn't shake the beacon blinking in the dark recesses of his mind, that cavern of rooms and passageways where he hid the job from the rest of his life. He never brought the gargoyles home. The worst of them shouted loud reminders of what Conroy's money might also buy. He'd betrayed his best friend, and it had come at a cheaper cost than he'd ever imagined.

He'd thought he'd gotten beyond the doubt, but this felt like a Rubicon he no longer wanted to cross. The heft of the envelope weighed light against the burden he'd carry forever. He'd thought he was willing to do anything for his family, but a chorus of doubt was finding its key somewhere deep inside him. He had it here in his hands, the future, a better life for Maria, for the kids, and yet it now seemed so cheap and unsuitable for the task of being a husband, a father, a partner.

Outside, the sun rose higher. Birds awoke. A garbage truck began its route, the banging of the Dumpster lids a klaxon breaching the peace. The neighbors in the next apartment yelled at each other. The first jet of the day took off and banked over their building and began its climb, bound for Orlando, Julio knew. Always Orlando. He wanted to be on the plane.

Maria padded into the room, pulled her bathrobe tighter around her waist, and sat down next to Julio. She looked at the envelope.

"What's that?"

He'd planned to hide the envelope before Maria awoke. He'd never told her about Conroy's offer, about what he had to do to get the money.

"It's nothing," he said. He tucked the envelope beside him, away from Maria. "How'd everybody sleep?"

"Don't change the subject. What's in the envelope?"

"A hundred thousand dollars."

Maria laughed.

"Don't joke about that."

"I'm not joking."

He handed her the envelope. She opened it, pulled out the stack of bills, all hundreds. He rubbed his cheeks. The windows of the condo shook to the bass beat rumbling from the speakers of a passing car. Someone yelled. A neighbor dragged a trash barrel to the corner, the plastic scraping on the cracked concrete driveway.

"It's for the house," he said.

"Where did you get this?"

He put his face in his hands, rubbed his eyes.

"I don't think I can keep it," he said.

"Did you steal it?"

"Come on."

"Explain."

"I talked to these guys, these lawyers for the mayor. They wanted me to say that the baby we delivered in January, the one they keep talking about in the paper, they wanted me to bend the truth, say that Tom delivered the baby, that he screwed up. They want Archer gone or quiet or just—I'm not sure, but all I have to do is sign some statement and they said they'd give us enough for the down payment."

He went to the kitchen, poured a glass of orange juice.

"I told him, no, *begged* him, not to file that fucking complaint," he said. Outside the kitchen window, he saw two junkies rooting through the trash. Everyone had their own version of survival, and he'd chosen his. Or so he'd thought. He watched the pair dump trash bins and scavenge through the detritus and he felt sick to his stomach. Not because what they did disgusted him, but because he was disgusted by himself. Unable to provide for his family, he'd sacrificed his closest friend.

Then the words poured from him. "He should have listened to me. But he wanted to be a hero, like he felt guilty for the years he'd wasted drinking, or for her son being sick. I told him it wouldn't work. Now they want him gone, and they need me to seal the deal, and I thought I was okay with it and I thought I could handle what it meant to do it, the trade-off I'd have to make, and Archer can burn his own damn bridges, he doesn't have to include me, but dammit we're partners and that used to mean something. That envelope you're holding, that's the trade-off. That's our ticket out of this dump. That's the only way we can scrounge up the down payment on the Northborough house. I just don't know one thing. I don't know what kind of man I'll be when we get there."

Maria looked at the envelope. He watched and imagined she was thinking of the things it contained. A bright future for her kids. Life in the suburbs. Quiet. Green. This close, the weight of it all almost too much for her to hold, and the indecision on her face was definitely too much for him to stand.

"I think you're right," she said.

"About what?"

Maria shook her head. Caught her breath.

"We can't keep it," she said.

"But we can't get that house without it."

"Could you live with yourself if that's how we got the house? Could you look the kids in their eyes ever again? We'd always regret it. We'd always know where the money came from. I'd rather stay here for a thousand years than live one day in a mansion bought that way."

He shook his head. "It might be too late."

"I don't want the house," Maria said. "Not if so much as a doorknob of it is paid for by this money. Give it back. Then call that reporter who's been writing the stories. Tell her what you did. Tell her the truth. We'll figure out the rest."

He finished the orange juice in one gulp, then sat down next to Maria.

She grasped Julio's hands. She could feel the tendons between his fingers quiver. She'd told him once that most men betrayed their nerves with their faces. Not him. The window to his soul, she'd said, was in his hands. They splayed with pleasure, were sure when they made love, touched the kids' heads with a softness, as if he were handling eggs.

"This Conroy," she said, "he was the one who used to be a policeman?"

He nodded.

"They fired him?" she asked.

"He's a bad guy," he said. "Legit crazy. He was mixed up with those guys on the East Side. Hector Alizondo and them. He's killed people. He's had people killed. He knows where we live. He showed up at the Northborough house while you and Jacob were inside looking at it. I'm scared. I took his money, which was stupid, but the only thing that scares me more is the idea of what he'll do when I try to give it back."

"You said he works with Hector Alizondo?"

"All those guys."

"Then he knows my Uncle Timo."

"Timo?"

"Uncle Timo, well, he wasn't really my uncle, but close enough," Maria said. "He came to our wedding. Remember the lavender soap set? That was from Timo. He was working mall security back then."

"What about him?"

"He used to be part of that crew. When the cop, this Conroy, got arrested, they all took off. I'm not sure where he ended up, but my father will know how to find him. Uncle Timo will know how to deal with this guy."

"I'm not sure I like this," he said.

"A couple phone calls."

"I'm already in way over my head."

"Three phone calls, tops. If I can't find him, if he says no, fine. We stop."

"Should it really be this hard to have a decent life for a family?"

29

Locke answered on the second ring. Knak exultant from the shooting at the hot dog stand.

"Don't call me anymore," Locke said. "Not tonight. Somehow they know it's you. Your name is all over the scanner."

Knak tucked the phone under his ear, spread out the topo map of the city on the open tailgate of his pickup truck. He was down by the river in the Dunedin Street parking garage, and fog rolled in from the banks of black mud and abandoned tires. The fluorescents in the parking garage light fixtures bathed everything in the place in a patina of chalky gray, as if the light absorbed all colors. The nonlight pleased Knak, hid him well.

"I need your opinion," Knak said.

"You've been identified," Locke said. "The entire apparatus is looking for you."

Knak was stunned at first, then scared. Then aroused. "They know my name?" he said.

"They know everything," Locke said. "I heard them talking about the houseDid you shoot a cop from a water tower?"

"I hit his foot."

"That was a bad spot," Locke said. "Since 9/11 there's cameras all over those things. The system knows to protect its water. They saw you, identified you somehow."

Knak thought about it. He didn't like the idea of his cover being blown, but now that his name was out there—Knak felt elated. He felt cleared, as if given permission to avenge Charlotte's death. Her name would be known. No faceless judge could hide behind a marble statue of Solomon. They knew Gerry Knak was out there; they were afraid of him. Charlotte would have been proud, Knak thought.

"I need your advice," Knak said.

"You've gotten all the advice I have to offer, Gerry. I'm sorry you weren't able to be more effective. We can't talk anymore."

"Wait, wait," Knak said. "Please! Don't give up on me now! I just want to run a couple shooting spots by you."

Locke exhaled deeply. "You've put something into motion here that you can't stop, and I applaud you for that, but we—my interests and I—we agree. If I keep helping you, the movement could be endangered. The system is thorough. They'll get you and then they'll get us, and then there won't be anyone left to defend what is right. We can't have that. You won't survive tonight, but do your duty and remember that you will always hold a special place in the hearts of all of us in the movement."

The line went dead.

Knak lowered the phone, stared at it for a minute.

"Shit," he said.

Knak threw the phone into the river. Banged his fists down on top of the truck hood. He saw everything clear as day now. Betrayed, but not just tonight. Locke had seen him coming from a mile away. Knak should have known. Locke hadn't had time for Knak when Knak was married to Charlotte. Not until Knak came to him, lost without Charlotte, angry, a loaded weapon ready to be pointed.

"Fuck it," Knak said.

He returned to the map. Distance, he decided. Locke had trained him to seek height and distance from his targets, all the better to escape.

Targets of opportunity, he thought. He'd hit the system, and through those hits Archer would present himself, would be present at some unknown future moment when Knak would be waiting. But if he wasn't careful, it would end up as a random, rogue string of chaos let loose in the city, with no purpose, no outcome he could call his own. It was dangerous, he knew. Infinite amounts of data, all about prediction, surety. Chaos was the devil to data's angel. Still, Knak didn't see another way. And he couldn't stop now.

He drove around the city. A passing rainstorm drenched the streets, making them look flat and clean for a time. Knak knew it was a mirage, an oasis in a desert nomad's heat dream. There were no oases here. Only thirst without shade. He saw police cruisers on Main Street, lit up and speeding. The firehouses were buttoned up against the rain and the night.

Ambulances. He found the city ambulance dispatch frequency on his scanner, started shadowing calls.

Man down on Front Street. Knak arrived in time to see two medics loading a drunk onto their stretcher. No cops in sight. Knak was curious.

Seizure on Richmond Place. The ambulance beat Knak by two minutes. He arrived in time to watch two medics walk a teenage girl down the front steps of a large Victorian mansion and into the back of the ambulance. One cop showed up, never got out of the cruiser, left before the ambulance. Knak took note.

Then came a tapping at his driver's side window. Knak looked up, saw an emaciated redhead with a scarred face rapping on the glass with a Salve Mater class ring. The man pointed for Knak to roll down the window, as if to ask a question.

Halfway down, the man slid an arm across the steering wheel, close enough for Knak to smell the Aqua Velva and tobacco and, in one swift motion, to twist and pull the keys out of the ignition before Knak had a chance to protest. The man pulled the door open. Knak saw a pistol under the man's left shoulder.

"Don't make a scene, Gerry," he said. "Let's just go for a ride, talk about some things."

"Are you a cop?" Knak asked, stunned.

The man smiled. "If I were a cop, do you think I'd be so polite?"

"I don't go anywhere with just anyone," Knak said.

"Call me Mr. Conroy."

They drove in Conroy's Crown Vic to a brick-box four-story apartment complex on Freeland Street, overlooking the long-dormant slaughterhouses and cold-storage buildings. The broken elevator made it easier for the residents to avoid looking each other in the eyes, and Knak wished he had managed to at least bring a pistol with him, but Conroy hadn't given him the chance. Knak thought at first that he'd been busted, that they'd figured him out, but the longer he remained with Conroy, the more he doubted.

The apartment was spare. There was a kitchen with a small, round, linoleum-topped table and a handful of mismatched chairs. An old Electrolux refrigerator hummed in the corner, and the gas oven was covered in old food stains, hardened circles of dried spaghetti sauce and burned pan marks. There was a television on a tray in the living room, the kind with the old ear antennae that no longer pulled signals from the air. The two tiny bedrooms were empty.

Knak sat at the kitchen table and Conroy opened the refrigerator and pulled out two cans of Guinness. He handed one to Knak.

"Canned Guinness," Conroy said. "Can you believe it? Of course, canned Guinness is better than no Guinness, right?"

Knak nodded, popped the tab on the can, and took a sip. Conroy sat across from him. Knak felt himself being evaluated. He was used to it. He was one of those guys that people just couldn't seem to take on face value, always had to inspect for something else, an entirely new order of human. Worse than the norm, he thought. At least, that was the way such inspection always left him feeling.

"You were close," Conroy said.

Knak sipped his beer, wiped his mouth with the back of a hand. "About?"

"I used to be a cop," Conroy said. "No more. Gave it up—well, truth be told, I was encouraged to give it up in the strongest of ways. With prejudice. Give it up or get fired, maybe go to jail. Not much of a choice, really."

"You do a pretty good imitation of a cop," Knak said.

"Think so?"

"I'm here, right? No way that happens if I don't think you're a cop."

"You only fear the police?" Conroy asked.

"Am I supposed to be afraid of you?"

"You don't need to be, but it would strike me as perfectly reasonable, all things considered."

Knak bowed out his chest, stretched his shoulders back. "So who are you?"

Conroy held out his hand. "Eamon Conroy. I work for John O'Toole. Executive security, officially, but also in an off-the-books way."

"Are you a kneebreaker or something?" Knak didn't reach out to shake Conroy's extended hand.

Conroy laughed. Knak couldn't help but stare at Conroy's teeth. It was like he had a mouth full of incisors, each pointed in a random direction, holes where his canines should have been. It was a terrible mouth, a mouth of neglect and anger. Merciless. Knak thought Conroy was capable of chewing through all sorts of things. Through all sorts of people.

"*Kneebreaker* is not exactly how I would characterize my duties," Conroy said. "But you're not too far off there, either. When push comes to shove."

It had started raining again. Knak could hear it thrashing against the window beyond the drawn blinds. Gusts of wind, the rain tinkling like the icicles that fell from Knak's gutters every winter. Had fallen.

"It's amazing, isn't it?" Conroy said. "This meeting of ours. The thing we share."

"You must know something I don't," Knak said.

Conroy nodded. He drank from the can, burped. "You never asked how I know your name," he said.

"It never occurred to me."

"Really? Random guy taps on your window and you just, what? Figure what the hell? Happens all the time?"

Knak shifted in his seat. Conroy sat back, cracked the knuckles on his left hand one at a time.

"I'm not in a position to make a fuss in public," Knak said.

"No, you are not," Conroy said. "I went to college with this guy, works for the IRS these days. I believe you know him. Ira Murdock?"

Knak's eyes went wide. He looked at the door, calculated the odds of making a break for it. Part of him beginning to comprehend his place in the universe as immensely small, insignificant. If they could pluck him from thin air, what else could they do?

"Don't worry about it," Conroy said. "They're looking for you, but you're one of a hundred. Once they connect you to that poor cop who got his toes shot off tonight, though, you're going to go to the top of the list."

Knak shrugged.

"I also know about the guns, about the shooting," Conroy said. "I know about Charlotte. I know about a shared . . . friend . . . we have."

Knak took a long drag from his beer.

Ten years ago, Conroy said, he'd been a night shift detective. Great job. The greatest job. He was untouchable. Who was going to fuck with him, right? He'd spent years building it, this little empire of his, first for Eddie O'Toole and then his successor, John O'Toole, the Boy Mayor. Conroy said he'd carried water for Eddie, done things, taken care of problems, kept John O'Toole's youthful indiscretions out of the official logs and, by extension, out of the pages of the *Courier*.

So one night they'd caught a guy, a kid really, this Honduran in the city making a deal to sell a few million in cocaine. He talked long and loud in Main South about wanting to set up a franchise here, said he had a pipeline to good stuff at a reasonable price and was in a position to negotiate.

John O'Toole got wind of it, worried. That much money destabilized things. The locals would get squeezed out, and since John O'Toole had his boots firmly on the necks of all the local players, extracted bucketfuls of money from them—for his campaigns, for other off-the-books uses—this wasn't a tenable development.

"I have this crew of guys, freelancers, El Salvadorians, a couple Hondurans, ex-army types, really skilled, work cheap—which is important, since it's all coming out of my pocket." Conroy chuckled. "But they're good. Effective. So one night, we grab the kid coming out of this club, Tropigalactica, throw him in an unmarked, and head to an apartment we kept for sensitive conversations. This apartment here, in fact. Same room we're in now."

Things didn't go well, Conroy said. This kid was tough, unbreakable. None of the usual tricks worked, Conroy said. Kidney punches. Beatings with rubber hoses filled with sand. Waterboarding. At one point, he even tried the oldest trick in the book—the old car battery to the testicles.

Conroy laughed at the memory. "When *that* didn't work? Well. Then we got intense."

Knak felt his hand on the cold glass bottle go hot. Conroy was cool, unwavering. Banal evil, Knak thought. Here with him, within arm's reach.

"Then things went south," Conroy said. "A couple of my guys got carried away. Beat the guy unconscious. One of them gets nervous—worried about his green card, it turns out—called 911 without telling anyone. I was able to cancel the police response to the apartment, but the ambulance crew, no joy. They never got word. Two of them showed up. Best I could do was clean up the place while they stood outside."

Knak coughed.

"It was *almost* enough time," Conroy said. "Almost. But I didn't get a chance to uncuff the kid from the chair. He must have stopped breathing right before I let the medics in. The kid ended up dying. One of the medics filed a complaint. There was an investigation. I lost my job. Lost my pension. Charged me with manslaughter."

Conroy finished his beer, crushed the can and tossed it into the trash. Knak was surprised by the power in Conroy's slender frame, the way he smashed the can flat by flicking his wrist and pounding his palm straight down in a movement too fast to see.

"At the trial, this medic laid it all out for the court," Conroy said. "I was fucked. I was going away for a long time, and this asshole medic was sending me there. Thankfully, though, there was some divine intervention—wink, wink—and I skated on the serious charges. Got a couple years for obstruction only."

Conroy smiled at Knak. "We threw around a lot of cash for that."

Knak had stopped drinking. It wasn't the story itself that terrified Knak; it was the way Conroy told it. Like he was describing a big fish story. Detached. Amused by things that ought to make a human tremble. Knak saw the hypocrisy, he a man on a mission to kill—had pulled it off, once—disturbed by the story of another man who had killed plenty. But you ought to feel something about the act, even if you were ready to perform it. This man Conroy, though, Knak thought. He was ready, and he felt nothing.

"I know what you're thinking," Conroy said. "You're thinking, jeez, why is he telling me this whole story?"

Knak nodded. Tried not to look Conroy in the eyes.

"Well, here's the thing," Conroy said. "I think we can help each other. You shot a cop, Gerry. They're not going to let that slide. Best guess, within an hour of leaving this apartment, you'll be dead. Less than that if I make a call and tell them where to find you. Hell, maybe I'll just save them the effort and tell them where to find the body. Maybe. Except I think we have a shared goal. I need you to take care of that goal, and one other. Do these two things, and I'll make the rest of your problems disappear."

Knak cleared his throat. Scratched the side of his nose. "What do you need me to do?"

"I need to you to take care of Thomas Archer the way you're planning."

Knak opened his mouth to speak, too shocked to say anything.

"You think I couldn't figure that out? Believe me, I get it. I've waited a long time to take care of Thomas Archer properly. I watch him every day. I know you do, too."

Conroy pulled out two new cans of Guinness from the refrigerator, handed one to Knak.

"Don't worry, I won't stop you," Conroy said. "I'll even get you close enough to do it. But I also need you to tie up one loose end for me in a similar fashion. Do you read the *Courier* at all? Do you know who Lu McCarthy is?"

30

"THEY SAY THE pond is like three hundred feet deep."
Lu scratched her forehead and looked closer at
the calm black waters. Gong Pond was on top of the city's
smallest hill, which meant, if Rigo was right, that all the
houses and apartment buildings bending over this eastern
enclave scratching the edge of downtown were built on a thin
piece of crust on top of nothing but a water-filled void.

"I hadn't heard that before," she said.

Three o'clock in the morning. Her deal with Conroy
long dead. Daisy Fontana dead. But she still worked the
story, unsure where it would lead or if anyone would read
whatever she wrote about it, but certain that she couldn't just
walk away, even if there was no certain place to walk *toward*.
They huddled behind the graffiti-covered blockhouse on the
far side of the pond, away from passing traffic on Landover
Street. Away from prying eyes in the Holmgren Estates next
door, the massive city housing complex circling the back half
of the pond like a breakwater, protecting the small patch of
tranquility from the city below the hills.

When Rigo reached out, Lu had worried it might be a
setup. She knew Rigo's connections to the Grand Street
Posse. Daisy's too. She couldn't divine a reason they'd be
mad at her, but maybe the word had gotten out that she and
Archer were related. Maybe they blamed her for Daisy's
death. The phone call last night had been specific. Gong
Pond. Three AM. The blockhouse. Be alone.

"Lot of problems end up at the bottom of that pond,"
Rigo said.

She nodded. She blew warm air into her hands. Despite
the summer heat, she was cold. She was cold because she was
scared, and also because this was the time of night when the
body was programmed to check out, slow down, find some
warm sheets and a dark room, sleep away bad dreams like this.

"I've covered a few of them," Lu said.

"I bet."

"Rigo, I have to ask—"

"When we first found out Daisy was pregnant, it was, I
mean, I felt like it made me whole," Rigo said. "I would have
raised Miguel like my own. Me and Daisy, together. I didn't
even care how he came to be. I didn't care about O'Toole.
Daisy said it was over before it began. We were getting off
Kansas Street. Had a house in Southbridge all lined up. We
were going to be like a family."

Lu tried to think ahead of Rigo. Old survival trick. Beat
your opponent to the punch. She figured it was a valid idea,
even if she wasn't entirely sure Rigo was her opponent. The
more the man spoke, the less she understood.

"There's nothing better than family," Lu said. "You can't
count on anyone else."

"Exactly!"

Rigo stuffed his hands in the army fatigue jacket he
wore, kicked at some dirt. He had yet to look Lu in the eye.

"Family," Rigo said. "I don't have any now. They took Miguel away, told me I can't see him."

"Daisy said you took off." She said it before she could stop herself. She didn't know Rigo, but she knew lots of guys like him. She knew if she set Rigo off, there'd be no undoing it. Whatever reason he had for calling her, so far it hadn't gone off the rails.

Rigo didn't seem mad at the comment, Lu noticed, so much as hurt.

"She been saying that to *everybody*, man," Rigo said. "It hurts. I love Miguel, even if he isn't mine, at least by blood. It's like the second they took him away in that ambulance, they stole him from me."

Lu wished she hadn't left her notebook in the car. She steeled herself to remember all of it, everything Rigo had said and would say.

"So, you didn't take off?"

Rigo spit on the ground, scowled.

"Hell no! I've been in Pigtown, staying low, keeping out of sight. But I never left Worcester. Once that asshole started coming around, offering Daisy things to keep her mouth shut. You in the Posse, you know all about Conroy. You know what he's all about. When Daisy turned up dead? I knew it was him."

Lu tried to control her pulse. But it was the same thing as when a hunch at the paper panned out. She was nauseous, heart beating faster and faster so that even the act of trying to calm down only made things worse.

"The night Miguel was born, who actually delivered him?"

"Who do you think?"

"What's going to happen to him, now that Daisy's . . . gone?"

"That's why I called you," Rigo said. "I seen all them stories you been writing. I figured we can make a trade."

"Depends what you're offering."

"Simple. I'll tell you anything you want to know, you can use my name. Put it in the paper. I don't care. I'll tell the world who that baby's father really is and who really hurt Miguel. I can handle any beef from that. I only want one thing from you."

Lu waited.

"Me and the Posse, we want to pay back the debt. You're part of the system; you know where shot callers like Conroy are."

"Not as well as you think," she said.

"Maybe, maybe not. But here's the trade. I'll tell you everything, but next time you see Eamon Conroy? You give me a call. We want to have a talk with the man."

31

Yesterday morning

A N INTERNATIONAL CALL appeared on Conroy's cheap burner phone. He thought about ignoring the message, but Hector Alizondo wanted to speak with him. And Hector Alizondo couldn't be ignored, no matter how far away he was. Above all, Conroy figured this was no social call.

"Long time, Eamon," Hector said, his voice rising and falling like the tide, like he was at the distal end of a long cardboard tube.

"Great to hear your voice," Conroy said.

Alizondo laughed.

"We both know that's not true," he said.

Conroy stood in the lobby of the Fleetwood Hotel. Inside the Grand Ballroom, John O'Toole was stumbling his way through a fund raiser. The candidate's inability to hold a crowd was worrisome to Conroy. He remembered the elder O'Toole, the father—now *that* was a politician. His son hadn't inherited the gift. Conroy knew the handlers were on it, a half-dozen national party types, flown into town to brush up the wunderkind's poor visuals and charmless demeanor. Thus far, the money hadn't been worth it.

"How could you say that? After all we went through?" Eamon said.

"I know you. I know men like you. You know what's in my head. You'd prefer it if I were near you, close enough to control, or whatever else needed to be done."

"All this time away, and we're going to be like this together?"

One of the handlers exited the ballroom. Tall, early thirties. The same fucking beard they all wore these days, Conroy noted, as if the backup plan to whatever soft job they had—so many of them in marketing, selling shit to each other in circles, cheap ideas masked as inspired revelation, not selling but *content marketing*, everyone attempting to convince the rest of them of their own sincerity, all of them full of shit and highly aware of it—might be lumberjacking, or welding. The old economy was a backup to the electronic dissonance, the false emotion, the maudlin crap that passed as sentiment these days.

Conroy knew the bearded guy was a specialist in manipulating in the new regime. Conroy was old-school. The thing the bearded guy needed, Conroy thought, was a quick punch to the face.

The bearded guy rubbed his eyes, went out into the parking lot for a smoke.

"We do have a problem," Hector said.

"All problems have a resolution."

"I don't think you'll like this."

"Depends on what the solution is. Problems are a dime a dozen."

"You have something going on with a medic up there?"

"You heard about that?"

"Maybe. One of them, Tavares. Julio Tavares. That name ring a bell?"

Conroy waited a beat. Hector spoke first.

"So we don't need to waste time. Good. International calls are still expensive, even on my plan."

"Let me guess, Tavares is related to you somehow," Conroy said.

"Not exactly. Timo Tejeda."

Conroy swore under his breath. "What about fucking Timo fucking Tejeda?"

"Don't get mad at me!" Hector said. "I told you what we should have done about this."

"You weren't in Honduras anymore," Conroy said. "We couldn't just go around dropping bodies every time we had a disagreement in the organization."

Hector drew a deep breath.

"Timo ended up in Costa Rica. Runs a charter fishing boat out of Jacó. We talk from time to time."

"Oh yeah, well send him a big fuck-you from me."

Hector laughed. "I will. And I'll just go ahead and return the salutations, Eamon. You know how he feels."

"I should have listened to you. Cost me a lot of money, too. And headaches."

"And worries," Hector said. "A half-million dollars of your money *and* a bunch of your secrets. Timo Tejada could be a nightmare for you. It gets worse."

Conroy walked outside to the hotel's circular driveway. Bearded guy stood over by O'Toole's Lincoln Town Car, smoking. Conroy sat down on the edge of the marble fountain in the middle of the roundabout.

"Worse?"

"So your friend Tavares. You gave him some money?"

"Maybe."

"Well, Tavares's wife, Maria. Timo is her mother's cousin. Or uncle. Some shit. I forget. Whatever it is, they're close enough that she called Timo, Timo called me, and now here you and I are."

"Why would Timo still care about anything up here?"

"Timo doesn't, but when Maria Tavares called and he heard your name, it became the most important thing in his life."

Conroy rubbed his temples. He spit into the white rocks between his feet. The burbling water in the fountain behind him, meant to resonate peace and tranquility, reminded Conroy instead that he was in a small oasis, and that even here, the dirt of the world could get him.

"What does Tejada want?" Conroy asked.

"He says you gave Maria's husband a hundred thousand dollars in exchange for some testimony."

"Maybe."

"Timo says the husband is going to recant. And that you're going to let the Tavares family keep the hundred grand. Timo says, if you do this, he'll be willing to stay down in Costa Rica and keep certain things to himself."

"And if I tell him to go fuck himself?"

"Why do we have to dance so? Pathetic. You know what Timo will do. That's how this shit goes. I can only be poetic for so long. It's simple. They keep the money. You leave them alone. You find another way to screw over whoever you were going to screw over with Julio Tavares's help, only now, no Julio. Otherwise, Timo makes a phone call. The FBI hires a charter jet to go to Jacó. And you go back to jail. About as plain as I can make it."

"Why are you telling me this?"

"Timo hates you too much to make the call himself."

"And you're doing it out of the kindness of your heart?"

"Hell no. His price is good. I don't really want to talk to you either. Truth be told."

Eamon stood up. The bearded guy over by the door was talking into the air. He waved his arms around. He sneered and rolled his eyes. Conroy noticed the earpiece in his left ear, the cell phone in his right.

"I suppose you're going to tell me to do the right thing," he said.

"I wouldn't dream of it. I knew who you were when we worked together. Timo, too. I'd never ask you to do the right thing, because you'd have no idea what I was talking about. Instead, I'd say, do the smart thing. Eat the hundred grand. Move on. Forget about Julio Tavares."

On his way back into the lobby, Conroy passed the bearded party hack. The man had his back to Conroy. He waved his hands in fury. He yelled, but Conroy couldn't understand him, as if he spoke a foreign language. He despaired of understanding any of them. He punched the man once on the back of the head. The man fell to the ground unconscious. Conroy straightened his tie and passed through the automatic doors.

32

THE BOAT RAMP was quiet. Archer had the spot to himself. Julio catnapped in the ambulance parked farther back in the lot. A beaten Toyota sedan with steamed-up windows rocked in a far corner, over by the closed concession stands. Small waves lapped against the rock-dotted concrete ramp that led down into Lake Pakachoag, and the lights of the luxury condo complex on the nearby hillside looked like a vast fleet, set to sail.

"He's sleeping, sort of," Elaine whispered.

Archer thought his wife sounded distant tonight. He hoped it was the cell coverage. He was sure it wasn't. Archer worked nights because he couldn't bear all that sleeping. Whenever he laid his head down on the pillow, he faced the truth. He and Elaine had maybe crossed two separate bridges, one heading north, the other south. They talked, but they might as well have been listening to the wind.

"Did he get his shots?" Archer asked.

"Why don't you trust me?"

"Been a shit night."

"How's that different from any other night?"

"Not at all. Just more of it."

"Things aren't all that great here either," Elaine said.

Archer walked to the water's edge. It seemed so easy to just walk in. The lake was spring fed and deep.

"The mother of the baby, the deposition I have to give on Monday."

"You're still worried about that?"

"Might be coincidence, but I just feel like someone's following us, you know? You learn to feel when someone's on your bumper, or when the same car keeps turning up," he said. Fear breaching the levee, Archer unable to stop himself. "This black Crown Vic. Everywhere we go tonight, there it is. It feels dangerous. Like a predator. I've . . . never mind."

Elaine let out a sigh. "You were close to it?"

"I've been talking to Lu McCarthy."

"You trust her? You're not in a position right now to get into fights with people who might be on your side."

"Are you on my side?"

Elaine paused. Archer's heart stopped.

"Yes," she said.

They'd warned them, the people at the hospital, when Michael was first diagnosed. Sick kids could split marriages, extending the damage. It was counterintuitive. Archer believed in bonding in a crisis, all hands on deck, everyone pulling in the same direction. But it turned out that parents of sick kids could get pulled in opposite directions, fear being a poor torch to light your path.

"How do we do this?" he asked.

"You're a good man," she said.

He crouched down, a baseball catcher ready for a pitch, and massaged the back of his neck while a tinnitus emerged from the deep, a needle probing, drowning out his thoughts.

"When is it too much? I keep waiting for it to get easier, but it doesn't seem to, and I haven't seen you in weeks and we're so far apart, and now I've got this psycho guy from that thing with Moonie way back, he's back, it's like he's after me, and I don't know what to do. If I can't talk to you, who can I—"

"I don't have the energy to fight with you," Elaine said. "I want to help you. I want to make all these things better, but I can't. Anything I've got in me, it just goes into making it through days here."

Archer understood. He agreed. If they were choosing between losing their son and losing their marriage, Archer knew the choice they'd each make.

"I want to be there," Archer said.

"You're doing your job."

"I just wish we could have the small problems again. Can't we worry about paying the mortgage, paying for braces, going to Disney World, little problems like everyone else?"

Elaine wept. Archer heard it in the receiver. He felt ashamed. The same conversation twice, three times a week. Little problems. Big problems. None of it unique to them, a dozen other families on the same floor of the hospital having the same conversations, Archer knew. Only somehow, even in *that* world, he felt like a failure. Even the land of the duressed—was that even a word?—escaped him.

"It's not—" she said.

Her voice was choppy, the cell phone signal breaking up.

"Elaine, what—"

"Never mind," she said.

"Never mind *what*?"

"Someday you'll understand. I've got to go. The NP just came in."

The connection died.

Archer redialed a few times. Each call went straight to voice mail. Archer wanted to scream, but there was no breath in his lungs, no fire in his breast. He pocketed the phone and stalked back to the ambulance. Life was new. Life was old. The things he held on to so dear were slipping through his hands. Worse, he was slipping with them.

They drove up the hill to the Bully, an old dining car perched in what had once been the city's Italian section. These days it was home to whoever could afford the rent. The old bottling plant next door that employed thousands had been converted to upscale lofts, and while remnants of the wiseguy clutches who used to make deals in the Bully's scarred wooden booths still appeared from time to time, they came now with canes and walkers, complained about the price of hearing aid batteries, pinched each other's cheeks. Yuppies from Oliver's Tavern next door stumbled in, usually on weekend nights, sailor-legged and slurring their orders, asking for eggs and hash browns to add ballast to the Patron and Grey Goose and whatever else they'd ingested.

They found Lu in a rear booth. The diner was empty otherwise. Archer and Julio sat down. A waitress brought two mugs of coffee. Archer ordered a ham-and-cheese omelet, hash browns. Julio asked for a plate of scrambled eggs. Lu drank coffee.

"Can we have a moment?" she said to Julio. "No offense."

Julio looked at Archer, who said nothing. Julio picked up his silverware, retreated to a booth at the far end of the diner.

Lu and Archer stared at each other for a moment, prize-fighters circling, but neither seemed charged for a brawl.

"I needed the money," she said. "They took my job. The money they gave me. Too much to turn down, but I did. Or, half of it, anyway."

Archer stirred cream and sugar into his coffee.

"I don't care," Archer said.

"Meaning?" she asked.

"I don't care," Archer said. "I don't care, and for the first time in months, I feel good. It's amazing how great the world looks when you don't worry about anything in it. For so long, everything worried me. Am I a good husband, father, para-medic, human being? No more. I can't fight everything and everyone all the time. You write what you want. I don't care anymore."

Lu sipped her coffee. The Bully smelled of fried potatoes and pancakes and coffee percolating in tall stainless-steel urns next to the grill. The spare rectangular windows of the old diner fogged up in the winter, the steamy warmth of the narrow dining room holding the harsh Massachusetts winter at bay. Even on cool Fall nights they opened the windows, the thick glass panes arcing out on hinges and letting the chill city breeze in through gray metal screens.

"The fuck of it all is, that's exactly how I've operated for the last, I don't know, ten, fifteen years," she said. "So easy. Like water off a duck, just come in, detach, disconnect. Guy ripping off his elderly neighbor? Write about it, move on. House painter rapes the old lady who hired him as a handy-man, beats her near to death and sets her house on fire? Write about it, move on. The shit I've written about and seen. I didn't care. How the hell could you? How could you see that stuff, report on it, touch it, smell it, roll around in it, and—what? Turn it off at the end of the day so that you can have some semblance of a normal fucking life? I couldn't do it. I couldn't turn that switch off, so I just . . . I just decided not to turn it on."

"It's survival instinct."

"I never liked you," she said. "I want to be up-front about that. Not when we were kids, not now. That thing with our parents. I always blamed your mother. Wasn't fair, but I had to blame someone. I was too scared of my father to hate him. I chose your mother for her weakness, and you for being related to her."

Blue lights from a passing cruiser strobed across the diner. No siren. Wet tires on pavement in a high-speed hum. A bell tinkled and three old men entered the diner. Lu stirred her coffee, dropped the spoon to the table. Shrugged.

"Especially after they got married and my mother moved to Florida," she said. "I hated you, but really it wasn't you. Once you started working as a medic, I thought you were kind of a cowboy. When every story we ever wrote about Evangeline Vacca included your name as the hero who saved her, I never believed it. I even pressed my editors to let me go deeper into it at the time. I wanted to tear you down, and my bosses wouldn't let me. I want you to know that too. I think I blamed your mother for splitting up my family. But really—really, I think it was because I always thought you reminded me of my father. You were more like him than I ever was. And I couldn't stand it. At least, until I realized what a prick he was. Which is kind of like the prick I've become."

Archer unfolded a napkin on his lap. The waitress placed his food in front of him. He peppered his eggs, mashed them up, swirled in a squirt of ketchup.

"Another thing about which I have no feelings," Archer said. "When my dad chopped up that fucking Thunderbird,

I was scared shitless. I mean, I was a kid. Didn't take me long, though. You and your father can both go to hell, all I care."

Lu leaned back while their waitress brought a refill.

"So you'll understand that, when I say I'm here on a mission of truth, it's costing me. In all sorts of ways. But I've thought a lot about this. The mayor's the one pushed for coverage on the baby thing, but that never made sense to me. And why just you? The name Julio Tavares has never once been mentioned, even though he was with you the whole time."

"I'll go you one better," Archer said. "The city lawyer says Julio may have actually testified against me."

"What?"

"That's what he told me when I met with them. Conroy was even there. , They basically told me to rescind my complaint against the mayor or else."

"You got to ask yourself, why would the mayor care about some low-level city employee's baby?" she asked.

"The baby's his," Archer said.

McCarthy nodded.

"Conroy running your show, too?" Archer said.

She nodded. "He was. Until I quit."

Archer shook his head. "I should have known that. He's everywhere. I expect my wife to call, tell me he visited the hospital room. The guy wants to kill me. Maybe something worse. He didn't tell me, but we both know. It's what he does. I'm thinking of bringing a gun to work. The forty-five's already under the driver's seat of my car."

"I'm out of a job. Conroy paid me to go after you, said the mayor was going to hire me for a city job after. None of it's true. They've used me. Worse, I knew what was happening and went through with it anyway. No more. I'm burning this shit to the ground. I gave half the money back."

"What? Never give the money back. First rule."

"I bought an old Saab with part of it."

He thought about his son, struggling to breathe in a hospital room in Boston, his heart pumping in a parakeet's cage of a chest, transparent, his skin like onion paper. Archer could actually see his heart beating.

Breathing. Hearts beating. This city beating, a sickness in it, in the air around them.

And for what? For another rung, so some people could get forward in a city going nowhere. Everyone protecting themselves, furtive conversations in dark-wooded bars and concrete-block strip clubs and hockey games at the War Memorial designed to nail someone, someone from another tribe in this crumbling industrial village that no one would ever want but was worth almost any price to those who did.

"You know what meconium is?"

"No," Lu said.

"It's shit," Archer said. "It's fetal shit, and once in a while, newborns get that stuff in their mouths during childbirth. No big deal unless you don't do anything about it. Unless you sit there and don't suction the baby, don't get it breathing. In that case, the baby never starts breathing, or if it does, it inhales this meconium and develops pneumonia. After that baby was delivered but before Daisy's boyfriend called 911, Conroy delivered the placenta. It was in a baking dish by the side of the bed, filled with blood and amniotic fluid. And the most meconium I've ever seen. Ask the boyfriend. He'll tell you. He was scared to death."

"I found him," Lu said. "He's willing to go on the record with the same story. He's only willing to help if I promise to tell him when I find Conroy."

She let that sink in.

"Then you know what that means," Archer said. "You're in the same deep shit as the rest of us."

"The crazy thing is that, when this all started? Only one who had anything to worry about was you."

"And now?" he asked around a mouthful of hash browns and eggs he could no longer taste.

She shrugged. "And now I'm not sure who's in deeper shit: you . . . or me."

CHAPTER

33

THE HOUSE ON South Florence was surrounded by cars, but Archer didn't see any lights on, not even the Christmas bulbs surrounding Evangeline's viewing window. Except during the weeks when Evangeline was on tour, Archer had never seen the place dark.

His visits had slowed lately, especially now that Evangeline had attracted the attention of the Vatican itself. There was talk of making her a saint, and lots of strange priests with foreign accents had appeared, looking for the same confirmation that the thousands of pilgrims who came to see her at her appearances sought. Same as Archer.

If you lived long enough in a world in which god seemed silent, he reasoned, you either dived into the silence or looked for signs of communication, for any possibility.

He scanned the front lot for cars, saw a few. In the driveway, the massive coach bus the family used to transport Evangeline sat like a toppled obelisk, black against the black night.

Archer and Julio walked to the front door. Archer rang the bell. No one came. He rang again. Still nothing. They walked over to the viewing window. The blinds were drawn. Archer couldn't see any lights inside. At one point he thought he heard low murmurs from inside Evangeline's room, but when he tapped the glass, no one came. They circled the house.

"Did someone else take Evangeline out earlier tonight and we just missed it?" Julio asked.

Archer stood on the slate patio next to the pool. He shook his head.

"No."

"You ever feel small, next to these statues?" Julio asked. "They aren't big, but they represent big ideas. People willing to die for faith. All those martyrs. I don't know whether I admire or pity that kind of commitment."

Archer dipped his toe in a small water fountain surrounded by cherubim.

"I was raised Catholic," he said. "Catechism, altar boy, youth league basketball. They lost me with the mystery. I never found the robes impressive, or the gold. I always hated the smell of incense. But Evangeline? Almost enough to believe again."

They returned to the ambulance. Archer didn't want to admit what he knew. She'd been so sick last time he came. But if Evangeline could die, if someone with a direct line to whatever God might or might not be out there could die, what hope did anyone else have? Why couldn't she heal herself?

Archer pulled his cell phone from his pocket, dialed his wife's number. Straight to voice mail. He redialed, choosing the direct extension to his son's room. Archer hung up after fifteen rings and no answer. He dialed the nurse's station. The unit clerk said everyone was too busy with an on-floor emergency to talk to him at the moment.

Julio pulled the ambulance into traffic.

"Storm coming," he said.

"That's the forecast," Archer said.

Archer looked out the window, quiet.

"You were right," Julio said. "About Conroy. What they'd want me to do."

Archer nodded.

"You wouldn't believe the money they gave me, just to sign a piece of paper," Julio said. "I just wanted to move Maria, the kids, get out of the city. Then Conroy showed up, offered enough money to make it happen. He made it easy. He wasn't asking me to do anything so much as he was daring me *not* to."

"It doesn't matter. They'll come and get me with or without you."

"It's going to have to be without me."

"You didn't give it back, did you?"

Julio scratched his chin.

"I recanted, but we haven't done anything with the money yet. Told the lawyers I'd made the whole thing up. I said our original statement would have to be enough. Maria made me. She said she couldn't live in a house bought on your blood. If I'm being honest? I was ready."

Archer shook his head.

"I would have understood," Archer said. He remembered Julio and Maria, there for him during the collapse, during the drinking all those years ago. Part of him felt he owed them. Another part was just too tired to be angry, too exhausted to feel betrayed.

Julio bent his neck to check traffic in the rearview while he changed lanes, his knuckles white on the steering wheel.

"It's not like I didn't warn you," he said.

"I know," Archer said.

"You put us in the cross hairs, man. Conroy, guys like him. They been doing this shit since the beginning of the beginning. Who the hell are we? He made it clear what might happen if I didn't play ball. I was scared, man. I was scared this psycho might take everything from me that I'd worked so hard for or, worse, everything that *might be* in my family's future. To be honest, I wasn't happy with you either. I begged you not to say anything."

"I know."

"I begged you not to make waves. Maybe I was being a coward, but I'm tired, man. I'm tired. Hundred hours a week, everything hurts all the time. I need some sleep, I need a decent meal, I need some sense that the future holds more than just a hundred ambulance calls every weekend for the next forty years. I won't make it. We won't make it."

"Just a couple sorry-ass medics," Archer said.

"We're janitors," Julio said. "Got our mops. Slopping this place up, move the misery from one place to another."

They drove in silence. Archer broke first.

"What do we do now?"

Julio shrugged.

"Just keep doing what we've been doing. Shift. Sleep. Eat. Repeat. Maria and I still have the money. I was going to bring it back to Conroy last weekend, but she told me to hold off. She's worried giving it back would be more dangerous than keeping it. She's working to see if we can give the money back safely."

"I'm thinking of bringing my gun to work."

Julio scowled. "Are you crazy?"

"On my way."

"You get caught with that? Plus, I've seen you shoot. Probably hit me before you'd ever get a shot at Conroy."

Archer saw a black sedan in the side mirror as it glided onto the road behind them, followed at a distance. A shark, tracking its prey in some warm ocean current. *Still alone and still hunted.* Archer told himself the cold came from the air conditioner. He closed the vent, but the chill remained.

"You see that car?" he asked.

Julio looked in the rearview. He gripped the steering wheel tighter. Turned off the radio.

"Yeah," he said. "I know that car. You do too."

"He must be getting desperate," Archer said. "Third time I've seen him tonight."

"Conroy desperate? No way. I'd say, more like, he's looking."

"For us?"

Julio shook his head.

"For you."

34

CONROY FOLLOWED ARCHER'S ambulance, shadowing far enough behind that he didn't think the medic would notice. Knak sat in the passenger seat, his Kimber in a holster inside his right elbow. He ran his left thumb over the notches in the pistol's hammer. It calmed him. He justified his predicament, swallowed the bitterness of it, by reminding himself of one simple fact: he would still kill Thomas Archer.

Surrendering to Conroy increased his odds, he thought. No matter the malice behind it, Conroy's pitch made sense. Kill Archer, kill this reporter, McCarthy. It was all the same thing, in service of the higher good. Conroy was like Charlotte in that respect. Pragmatic. Subsurface thinker. Knak was always learning lessons from someone.

Still, there was a disturbing thought he couldn't escape. Charlotte, Avis, Conroy. One commonality. Even if he'd wanted to, Knak couldn't hide himself from them.

Conroy dangled his right wrist over the steering wheel as he drove, a cigarette in his left hand, hanging out the open window. The Crown Vic softened the streets, glided over bumps and swayed through potholes. Conroy had the heat on as high as it would go. Ashes speckled the chest of his suit coat. Knak was certain he saw spots of dried blood on the white cuffs of Conroy's shirt, *EC* in ornate script on each.

The late-night talk radio station droned in the background, a nationally syndicated show reporting conspiracy theories from the lunatic fringe, every thought transmitted as unadulterated fact. It was Knak's favorite.

"Can I turn up the radio?" he asked.

Conroy waved his hand. Knak cranked the volume.

"This is Hank Dembrel, and you're listening to the Black Helicopter Hour, broadcast to you live from the base of Mount Hurricane, somewhere in the American Midwest," the announcer said.

Conroy lit a cigarette off the nub of the last one, tossed the other one out the window in a comet tail of sparks. They'd left South Flagg Street, followed Archer's ambulance down Pine Lane and back into downtown proper. They'd watched the ambulance stop in front of the Bean Machine, seen Archer get out and go inside. A police radio mounted under the dash crackled with minor traffic, details and questions, and the occasional joke.

"Hank, Hank, listen to me, the eurozone is going to be a war zone before the end of the year," an excited male caller said. "The euro is broken, and we need to move all our money into gold *yesterday*, Hank. Yes. Ter. Day."

Knak laughed. "The euro is so last year," he said. "The euro is fine. Goddamn politicians watering down the U.S. dollar? Now *that's* a problem."

Conroy rubbed his forehead, sat up straighter in his seat.

"You sure you're up for this?" Conroy asked. "You need to focus. When the time comes. You need to jump when I give the word."

He nodded.

Conroy followed the ambulance through an intersection by the downtown medical center, then took the on-ramp for the interstate.

"They were hovering over my house all night," a radio caller said. A meek, female voice, young, perhaps a girl, even. Wobbly. Maybe half-asleep. "These black helicopters, and they dropped pamphlets in our yards, thousands of them."

"And what did those pamphlets say?" Dembrel asked.

"They said, 'Their foot shall slide in due time,' " the girl said.

Knak leaned forward and turned the radio all the way up.

"What does that mean?" Dembrel asked the caller.

"I don't know," she said. "I mean, I'm on a lot of Xanax these days. A *lot*."

" 'Surely thou didst set them in slippery places,' " Knak said.

"What?" Conroy said.

"This girl. The thing she's talking about. My mother was real religious; I had a lot of churching. It's from the psalms. 'Thou castest them down into destruction. How are they brought into desolation as in a moment.' "

Conroy turned off the radio. "Enough," he said. "Focus."

Knak pulled the pistol out from his jacket pocket again, dropped the magazine, made sure there were enough rounds, slid the action on the pistol back and forth, then popped the magazine back in the weapon.

"I'm ready."

Knak could see: Conroy, in full fight-or-flight, lit electric. He'd complained earlier that his sciatic nerve boiled, the pain shooting down his left ass cheek and into his leg—telling him, he'd said, that all was ready. He jabbed out cigarettes, stomped on the brake pedal, turned the radio on and then off.

The ambush was a moving one, Conroy explained. "Everything is in place. The only thing we need is a good piece of terrain. Just like Panama."

The radio under the dash scratched to life. Ambulance call. Well-being check, Cavalry Arms.

"The usual," the dispatcher said.

In front of the Crown Vic, Archer's emergency lights strobed to life.

Conroy smiled.

"Perfect," he said.

"You know where they're going?" Knak asked.

Conroy nodded.

"Same place they've been going for years," Conroy said. "Let's go meet them."

35

R ED WAS AT it again. Even the dispatcher sounded exas-
perated with the call. Sick person. Cavalry Arms. Archer
was relieved. He and Julio still weren't right. That balance
they'd always had, the effortless partnership, the way they'd
needed to talk less on the bad calls because they knew each
other, better than spouses, better than siblings—it was gone.
They'd need time to get it back. Simple call like this, clean
up Red and clear out—perfect.

"Sound like a route car going on this?" Archer asked.
He'd been listening to the police radio, knew the ambulance
was going alone.

"Cops and fire are at a big fire on the other side of the
city," Julio said. "We're going solo."

"Crown Vic still there?"

Julio checked, nodded.

"Ever since we left Evangeline's," he said.

Julio floored the gas pedal. Streetlights haloed by rings of
humidity made a soft clunking noise as the ambulance
rushed along empty streets. The city had gone to sleep. Julio

stopped in front of the Cavalry Arms and signed off with dispatch. Archer grabbed the first-in bag, slung it over his shoulder. He struggled up the small hill from the road to Red's door.

Red answered on the third knock. White T-shirt, white underwear, the crotch wet and yellowed. Mad-scientist hair. Bleary eyes, the basketball player's frame in decay, hunched and bent like an old nursery rhyme hag's. The smell of cheap booze and urine wafted over Archer and Julio.

"Goddamn you, Red," Archer said.

Red blinked. He started to speak, stopped, nodded, and walked back into the apartment. Archer and Julio followed, closing the door behind them.

*   *   *

Conroy pulled up to the curb just behind the ambulance. He nodded toward Red's. Knak got out, walked to the red metal door. He looked back at the Crown Vic but couldn't see past the streetlight glare on the windshield. Conroy had said he'd get Knak close. He was feet away now. He sensed the closeness of Archer, a proximity to the thing he hated.

The toothache, that could be ignored. It was a sharp pain, a lower right wisdom tooth. It began as soon as Knak realized the time had come. No more planning. No more prep. Knak racked a round into the pistol chamber.

He rang the doorbell.

"Did you just ring the fucking doorbell?" Conroy called out from the car. He didn't trust Knak's abilities in the heat of the moment, had wanted to do the job himself, with Knak there only to take the blame.

Knak shrugged, nodded to the ringer. "You want them to let us in, right?"

A light went on in a third-floor apartment.

"At least you didn't ring the right one," Conroy said, looking up at the lit window, relieved when he didn't see a face. "Kick in the fucking door. Hurry up."

The longer Knak stood on the cement steps and waited to exact his revenge, to close the loop on the defining rationale for everything he'd done the past few years, the guns and the plans and the Super Oxygen Factor, the house he'd burnt and his dogs, his poor dogs, the less excited he was to shoot. A weakness took hold. He'd been driven forward by a vexing hate that had stripped away the rest of his life. His was a scalded soul, Knak knew, and the only cure was beyond this door. He raised his foot to kick, lost his balance, fell against the wall to his left.

Conroy grew impatient. He got out of the car, climbed the small hill.

"What are you waiting for?" Conroy asked. "They're in there. Kick in the goddamn door."

Knak raised his hands and rubbed the pistol barrel against his cheek. Faces appeared in the yellow-squared windows above, saw the gun and the Crown Vic and disappeared. Here and there, blinds in other apartments descended behind dirt-smeared windows. No one had seen anything. No one wanted to know anything. People in the Cavalry Arms understood those two rules better than scripture.

"Give me a sec," Knak said. "Just give me a minute here. I can't feel my hands."

"All you're really good for is dreaming," Conroy said. "It's a big difference, killing a man and planning to kill a man."

Conroy pushed Knak against the building, drew his own pistol.

*   *   *

Inside, Red sat on the couch, head bobbing up and down in time to his breathing. Archer sat before him on a frayed ottoman. In the kitchen, Julio dropped old takeout containers into the trash.

"Why do you keep doing this, Red?" Archer asked.

Red shrugged.

"You get as old as me, you realize there aren't as many of you as you think," he said. "When you're young, you compartmentalize. You're a basketball coach, a player, a husband, a father. You're all of these things. Eventually, though, you become none of them. You realize you're only yourself. And that's the thing you've got to live with."

"We need more towels," Julio said. "I'll get some from the ambulance."

"You can either live with yourself, or you can't," Red said.

Julio opened the apartment door and stepped out into the night.

"Some of us just can't," Red said.

* * *

On the steps outside the apartment, Julio bumped into Knak, saw the gun in his hands, turned back toward the building. Conroy stepped between Julio and the door. He raised the .45.

"Tell Timo," Conroy said, "I said hello."

Julio stood straight.

Conroy pulled the trigger.

The bullet smashed into Julio's forehead. He hung for a moment in the air, suspended like the wisp of smoke curling from the barrel of Conroy's pistol. Then he sank to the ground.

Conroy turned back toward Knak.

"See?" Conroy asked. "Was that so hard?"

Conroy pushed through the door, saw Red on the couch across the room. A small window behind the couch was opened wide, a curtain drifting lazily in the breeze. Through it, Conroy saw a lone form sprinting down the street beneath yellow cones of electric streetlight. Archer. He disappeared down a sidewalk behind a small stand of trees and out of sight. Conroy pointed his pistol to Red's chest.

"You were always a lousy kid," Red said. "That's why you never played varsity."

Conroy shot twice, both rounds striking in the center of the chest. Red coughed once, then slumped over on the couch.

Back in the Crown Vic with Knak, who'd fled to the car at the first shot, Conroy drove around the neighborhood, hoping for a glimpse of Archer. He listened to the police radio. Nothing yet, but that would change once someone checked out the empty ambulance and found the two bodies. Time was short. Conroy drove fast.

*   *   *

Archer ran. Three blocks away, no pursuer in sight, he stopped, vomited into an alley behind a Vietnamese laundry. He wiped tears and puke from his face. In Red's apartment he'd looked out the front window after the shot, seen Julio lying on the ground. A paramedic's reflex—never go into a room you can't get out of: Archer had leapt through the window behind Red's couch and taken off down the sidewalk. The thing that had hounded him for months, the thing looking for him, it had found him, but Julio had paid the price.

He thought about keying his radio, making the distress call, a hundred cops descending on the scene and Eamon Conroy arrested. That was no solution. Conroy had gotten out of jail once. He'd do it again. Archer left his radio turned off, stopped running at St. Patrick's. He found a tool shed behind it, slid inside, and dialed.

She answered on the second ring.

"I'm in some shit, Lu. Come get me."

*   *   *

"Why didn't you call the cops?" McCarthy asked. She and Archer huddled in the shed, Archer soaked in sweat and shivering now in the chill, still catching his breath. He shook his head.

"It's got to end," Archer said. "If he gets arrested, it'll never end. It'll just keep going and going. He's a ghost. It's only been ten minutes. I've got another twenty before the dispatcher checks on us. She knows we're usually at Red's for an hour. We don't have much time."

"What do you want me to do?"

"I don't know," Archer said, panic rising. "I thought maybe you'd know someone. Aren't there people for stuff like this?"

"Stuff like what?" she asked.

"I don't know!" He kicked a wheelbarrow. "Isn't this your thing? Isn't this what you've been doing all these years?"

McCarthy shook her head.

"I'm not—"

Then a light went on, right there in the musty shed, redolent of lawn mowers and oil. "I know a guy," she said.

McCarthy pulled out her cell phone, scrolled through the contacts, chose one. "This might work," she said.

*   *   *

Thirty minutes later. Radio silence, Conroy was pleased to note. No one from Cavalry Arms had worked up the courage to check out the scene at Red's. And this new development. Tonight could still end up as planned. Messier, perhaps, but goals achieved. The phone call from Lu McCarthy had been a surprise, but in the big picture, Conroy realized he needn't have worried. McCarthy was no fan of Thomas Archer.

"I don't like it," Knak said. "Out of the blue, and this reporter, she offers to bring us Archer, like, on a platter?"

Conroy smiled.

"Lu McCarthy is not a strong woman," Conroy said. "Bend her at the most breakable point, she'll do anything."

When she called, he'd been suspicious at first. But then it made some sense. Archer had fled Red Bowen's apartment, probably called her. She'd seen an opportunity. The money was starting to loom large, her job just about at an end. Morals were morals, but bills were bills. Had to be paid; otherwise the card house fell.

He'd come to like Lu and was almost sad he'd have to kill her along with Archer. But Conroy was against witnesses. Conroy was all done with witnesses.

The Crown Vic was pulled into the shattered remains of a processing plant in Pigtown, the city's abandoned meat-packing district. Blocks and blocks of empty red-brick hulks looming over the dark streets, filled now with squatters and junkies. The car faced out onto a large courtyard bounded on all four sides by decrepit buildings connected by narrow cobblestone alleys.

"How's she getting him here?" Knak said.

"She told him she knew some people who could help," Conroy said. He had to respect the subterfuge.

The night was lost, Knak thought. He'd screwed up. If he got a shot at Archer, he knew he'd have to kill this reporter and Conroy too. Silence. The organization wouldn't abide so many loose ends.

"Money is thicker than family, even when there's no blood involved," Conroy said. "You don't need love or sex as much as money, because money can buy you those things too. We'll complete the job and then we'll get out of here. Figure out next steps. She said she'd get Archer to meet us here in half an hour."

"What if he runs? He sees us and bolts?"

Conroy shrugged.

"People will believe what they most want to believe. Archer wants to think McCarthy will take care of him. Oldest confusion in the book. Look at Rwanda. I was there as an election observer in '94 all those people butchered in voting lines. Someone had promised them safety. Promised democracy, they got the blade instead. Hundreds of thousands of them."

A pale light flickered against the wall of a building across the courtyard. Conroy and Knak got out of the Crown Vic and walked out into the edge of the courtyard. More flickering lights appeared in the surrounding alleys4. Knak paced in circles, stamping his feet to keep warm and blowing into cupped hands.

"You'll get the medic," Conroy said.

"I just want this to be done," Knak said. This wasn't bugging out. This wasn't freedom. There was no system being attacked, just another system waiting to assimilate. Being around Conroy—prison in all but name. They hadn't attacked the system tonight, Knak knew. He wasn't even sure if killing Archer would make Charlotte's death right. And he didn't care.

The alleys of Pigtown glowed with a pale-orange light that grew as the scuffle of boots on gravel came closer.

It took a moment for him to see it. Too many lights. Flashlights and a handful of torches. Dozens of them, clogging up every alley. Into the courtyard they streamed, young men in flannel shirts and sleeveless T-shirts, bandanas on their heads and around their necks, serious faces. And they were looking at him.

Knak circled back toward the Crown Vic, bumped into Conroy, stayed a beat too long. Conroy pushed him away, then turned back toward the advancing mob.

"I don't like the looks of this," Knak said. He walked a few steps closer to the car. Conroy advanced toward the crowd, squinted into the flickering lights, searching for recognizable faces.

It was like the city coming for him. Every perp he'd beaten, every witness he'd intimidated, every vow he'd broken, all coming now.

"Do you know who I am?" Conroy shouted.

There was no sound except the guttering of torch flames in the wind gusts from the reservoir.

One man stepped from the crowd.

"A better question," Rigo said. "Do you know who we are?"

Conroy remembered that the last thing drowning victims felt was euphoria. Death better than any drug's high. First, though, terror. Conroy started there.

"Who are these guys?" Knak asked. He'd opened the driver's side door to the sedan. Slowly. Quietly.

Gerry Knak floated above the car on a newfound fear and saw himself.

Small.

Scared.

Alone.

He'd never been a hero.

He'd never been misunderstood.

Life had been clear all along, and now he saw it like a map to his own destruction. He looked at Conroy and saw someone from another unknowable species. Conroy was dark and fearless, no need for Svengalis or elixirs to give him courage.

Knak's mission flew from his chest, a wounded sparrow over the ruins of Pigtown, invisible and fleeting.

"This is the Posse," Conroy said, his back to Knak and the car. "Rigo here, Rigo and I have business together."

"We do," Rigo said.

Behind Conroy, the Crown Vic engine roared to life. He patted his pockets for keys that were no longer there. Knak revved the engine, dropped the car into gear, and stepped on the gas, disappearing down an alley in a rooster tail of dirt and pebbles and crushed cobblestone. As he passed, Knak tossed the police scanner out the window. It landed in front of Conroy.

The rush and skidding growl of the Crown Vic gone, the courtyard descended back into silence.

Conroy shuffled his feet. Put his hands on his hips. Dropped them to his side, then back to the hips. He smacked his lips, a carpenter examining a troubling trellis.

"I'm sorry it came to this, Eamon," said a voice from the darkness outside the ring of Posse members.

A gap opened in the line. John O'Toole stepped into the circle.

"I thought it would work out, but Rigo here tells me everything's gone off the rails."

Conroy shuffled from foot to foot. "That so?" he said.

O'Toole nodded. "I tried to be patient, Eamon. I really tried. I think I asked you to be too many things."

"I'm working this out," Conroy said.

"Not what I hear. I was already on the fence about you. I spent a lot of money getting you out of prison, used up a bunch of favors. I'm thinking you're an investment that's not paying off."

Conroy pointed at Rigo. "You tell him what you ordered me to do to his girlfriend?"

O'Toole nodded. "Rigo and I have an understanding."

"I wonder, Mrs. O'Toole have any idea your view of the sanctity of the marital vows?"

O'Toole rubbed his hands together, washing them in the air. "I'm done," he said. "Rigo, at least, will get me what I was promised."

O'Toole looked at Rigo, saluted, then disappeared back through the hole in the line, back into the darkness of Pigtown.

Conroy felt it. Joy. Elation. A drowning man, far from shore.

"Fuck it," he said, reaching for the pistol tucked in the small of his back. Rigo saw the move and chopped down with his machete as Conroy's hand came forward with the pistol. A shot rang out, upward, harmless, toward the stars.

Rigo was on him with the machete. Swing after swing. In the flickering light, Rigo was elemental as the wind, a force of nature that revealed what hate really looked like because, Conroy knew, it was a mirror flawless in its reflection. His own version lacked, he realized too late. Tepid and half-formed, it had led Conroy to this dead and forgotten corner of Pigtown. He knew it would lead no further.

The Posse worked over Conroy's body, dragged it to the center of the courtyard, and set it ablaze. When they left, the buildings in the Pigtown square shifted and pulsed while the flame glow flickered against them like a pale-yellow tide. The Posse tossed their weapons in the reservoir and dispersed, a band of spirits conjured by the dead factories themselves.

Rigo got a few blocks away, then dialed a number on his cell phone.

* * *

"Understood," McCarthy said, then ended the call.

She turned to Archer.

"It's over."

Archer doubted he'd ever breathe easier again.

"Can you drive me back to my car?" Archer asked. "I need to get into Boston."

36

IT WAS THE best night of sleep Gerry Knak had had in years. No nightmares. No waking and prowling the house, looking for things he couldn't name, certain only that *something* stalked the halls, or staring out the back window across the small yard, using the sides of his eyes to seek movement in the long shadows cast by the moonlight beaming through the trees, over the shed, washing up against tractors and lawn mowers scattered around the yard. Charlotte would raise the covers when he returned to bed, still half-asleep when she asked him if everything was okay.

Turning on Conroy had been a natural extension of his every instinct in life. He'd seen the desperation on the steps of the apartment. Killing for a cause was one thing, but he refused to think of himself as a murderer. A patriot, yes. A widower. A man with a mission worthy of some operatic resolution, but Conroy had proven himself a small man, unworthy of the kind of immense gesture the ghost of Charlotte Knak deserved and demanded.

He knew he ought to be wired. He knew there would be trouble for leaving Conroy to the Posse like that. His mind raced and he expected insomnia. But sleep had come moments after his head hit the pillow. Avis Locke's egg farm did that to him. Probably the New Hampshire air, being in the hills. The smell of chicken shit never bothered him.

He'd gotten to the farm shortly after one AM, climbed into the old bed he'd once shared with Charlotte by two. The strip of light appeared under the door at 3:48 AM. The light woke him, its thin beam directly in his eyes. Knak knew the exact time because he'd checked his watch. The foot shadows pacing back and forth in the light under the door began five minutes later. He knew he should get up, check things out. He pulled the blankets over his head instead, relived the earlier triumph of the night and tried to shake off the nagging thought that the light outside the door announced bad ides catching up to him.

Snatching the Crown Vic keys had been perhaps the greatest moment of professional satisfaction he'd ever experienced. He'd waited years to try it, ever since he'd bought *Pickpocketing, Dumpster Diving and Life Off the Grid* at a gun show in Tilton years ago. Books were his favorite purchases at prepper conventions and survivalist shows. Anyone could own a gun or a knife or whatever. But for real subversion, Knak knew nothing compared to a book.

That's what a lot of these guys didn't understand. At the end of the day, a bullet or a bomb disrupted for only a short time. Bullets that missed their targets followed the curvature of the earth, eventually falling to the ground from loss of momentum and gravity's pull. Bomb waves petered out; the shrapnel spread only so far. Words, books—they hit everything, and they lasted forever.

Knak had met the author, a grizzled, rail-thin man with straight white hair down to his ass and a white goatee who autographed books with his head bent to the text and no chance of eye contact. Knak stood in line for an hour. The author took the book from Knak's hand, signed, and handed it back without raising his head.

Knak looked at what he'd written: *Sic semper evello mortem tyrannis.*

"What's it mean?" Knak asked.

The writer looked up, disgust contorting his face.

"I don't mean to be rude," Knak said.

"If you have to ask," the writer said finally, "then maybe you aren't ready for what's inside."

He'd read the book a dozen times, memorized its chapters on composting and siphoning gas the same way he'd once memorized the Bible at one of his mother's churches.

Last night with Conroy was the first time he'd tried out his favorite chapter, the one on pickpocketing, on a real target. It was all about distraction, sleight of hand—or, in this case, sleight of body. Bump someone's hip with your own, touch their shoulder with your left hand while the right reaches in for the wallet. Simple. He'd taken too long reaching in for the keys, fumbled over a pleat he hadn't accounted for, but Conroy hadn't noticed. He'd never forget Conroy's expression, first when he realized the keys were gone, then when Knak drove away in the only means Conroy had of escaping his judgment.

After leaving Pigtown, Knak's destination was clear. He needed to get far from the city, far from the people who'd be looking for him, if they weren't already. He wanted to go back to the egg farm, site of his second birth, the real conversion, the one that stuck. Where he'd learned the hard rules of natural order, in a place where the memory of Charlotte was something he could smell and taste. Avis Locke would know what to do. Avis Locke would help him.

Knak had sent Locke a text explaining he was on his way. The drive to New Hampshire had taken almost two hours, and when he'd arrived, Locke had met him at the metal gate to the property. The midnight moon was full and round and turned the hills around the farm silvery, with deepening shadows washing up against the compound.

"You can't bring that car here," Locke said.

"No one's looking for it."

"Yet."

"It'll be a while. We could store it in the tractor shed for a while, crush it later over at the salvage yard."

Locke rested his arms on the top of the gate, spat at his feet, and moved the gob around with the toe of his boot. "Things didn't go quite as planned tonight, did they?"

"No, they didn't. I learned a lot. Next time, no way I can fail."

"You could have hurt our movement tonight," Locke said. "A lot of good people are cleaning house tonight. They worry you've exposed us to the light before we're ready. Now there's a line from you to all of them. Good patriots. It's all over the news. The feds, the staties, the system itself, ain't going to let up until they get you. Folks in the organization are worried the search for you will lead the system to *them*."

"I'm the best hope you've got. I've been inside the belly of the beast. I've got a lot of good intel to provide. The group needs to hear what I have to say. Avis, please. You can't turn me away now. Not when we're so close to the things we've talked about all these years."

Knak could hear the night wailing of foxes down by the train tracks on the far end of Locke's property. He'd never gotten used to the nocturnal shrieks and growls.

"You got ghosts out here, Avis."

Locke cocked his head toward the sound.

"You think so?"

"When I try to imagine what the rebel yell sounded like, like Pickett's charge at Gettysburg or whatever, that's what I hear. It's like you got rebel ghosts, wandering spirits too far north."

Locke's phone buzzed in his pocket. He pulled it close to his face, then held it out. "Forgot my damn glasses," he said.

Locke tapped a few times on the keyboard and put the phone away. He pressed his left nostril shut with a thumb and blew a plug of snot onto the ground behind him.

"They say the exact sound has been lost to time," Knak said.

He imagined a few thousand empty-bellied, shoeless Confederates tapping in to some force deep in their souls as they surged across fields where the hot metal washed over them like sheets of rain. The southerners he'd met in their circle had their Lost Cause. Knak had his, too.

"You get distracted sometimes, Gerry. All I'm saying. You need to focus, worry less about ghosts."

"Can I come in?" Knak asked. "Let me get a little shut-eye. I can explain it all in the morning."

Locke hesitated, then nodded.

"Probably for the best," he said. "Get that car off the road before the feds come in here and roll us all up."

They hid the Crown Vic in the large shed along with Locke's tractors, a backhoe, a front-end loader, a small flatbed pickup. Locke covered it with a soiled canvas tarp. Knak felt a distance between them.

"I feel like you're disappointed in me," Knak said as they walked back to the main house.

Locke scratched his back with a stick as they walked, then tossed the stick away.

"It's not that I'm disappointed," he said. "I'm just . . . confused. You had a chance to make a statement, take some important action, so many counting on you, so many there with you, if only in spirit, and, what? You fled. Ran away."

Knak stopped, put a hand on Locke's chest.

"I didn't run away. It was a tactical retreat. No, wait, not a retreat. An advance in another direction. What happened last night, that wasn't what we wanted. It wouldn't have forwarded our cause. We're patriots, not murderers."

"You had the enemy in front of you, and you left. That's not going to look great to some of the group. That's all I'm saying." Locke's face softened. He dropped his shoulders, put a hand on Knak's arm.

"We should save this for tomorrow, you're right," Locke said. "Let's get you back to the house. You can sleep in the room you and Charlotte used to stay in."

At 4:02 AM, Knak noticed more footsteps pacing outside the door. He heard men's voices, talking low. He sat up in bed.

"Who's out there?" he said.

A set of feet stopped in the middle of the light strip.

"I said, who's out there?"

Louder.

Knak looked at his watch.

4:03 AM.

The door flew open. The light from the hallway blinded Knak. He raised his arm to block it. A tall figure in a black hood stepped into the room, pointed a yellow pistol at Knak's chest. More hooded figures gathered around. Knak felt two beestings in his chest.

"Tasing!" a man called out.

Then the world exploded.

His eyes wouldn't focus. He knew he was sitting, but he couldn't move his arms or legs. There were people in the room, but he couldn't make any of them out. One of them approached from the right, the blurry form carrying a box he raised over Knak's head. The water was an ice-cold punch to the face.

"Private Knak," said a man's voice. "Are you awake?"

The chamber came into focus. Knak recognized it as the tool room, a cavernous warehouse of corrugated metal and concrete set apart from the rest of Locke's compound, on the far side of a rolling ridge that hid it from the rural highway beyond Locke's front gate.

Knak sat in a metal chair in the center of the open work bay. High-intensity halogen work lights on stands had been set up around him. The heat burned the top of his head and shoulders. His wrists were bound together with zip ties, as were his ankles. They'd tied his arms behind him and had used thick nylon rope to bind his chest and legs to the chair.

His chair was placed before a folding table, the flag with a mountain herald and the letters *MMM* draped over the top. Three hooded figures sat at the table facing Knak. There was a thin figure in a dark suit in the middle. On the right, a corpulent man in coveralls and a dirty gray sweater. The one to the left was broad chested, head-to-toe black military fatigues, at least six inches taller than the others at the table, the sleeves of his fatigue blouse taut against his biceps.

"Edson, Mike, Rollie, take off those fucking hoods," Knak said. "I know it's you."

None spoke.

To the right of the table was a lectern. Knak didn't recognize the man standing behind it. He wore blue jeans, dark leather boots, a white button-down shirt, and a brown sport coat. Knak thought he looked like a professor.

"I'm sorry, Private Knak, but as you know, we conduct these matters with a certain amount of privacy, so that the jury can render its decision in true anonymity," the man said.

"Anonymity? Jury?"

The man nodded.

"Otherwise, personal feeling—ill or otherwise—might color the true, objective meting out of justice. And justice, after all, is really what every man in this room seeks."

Knak looked around the room. In the darkness he could see dozens of shapes watching from the shadows.

"I know all of you!" Knak said. "Untie me. I'm one of you, goddammit. I can explain."

The man at the lectern opened a manila folder and read from a piece of yellowed parchment.

"In accordance with Mount Marne Militia guidelines and regulations per the free and sovereign rights of same, be all advised that this court is gathered to hear the case of triple M versus Private Gerald Knak, who stands accused and subsequently indicted before this tribunal of cowardice in the face of the enemy, actions detrimental to the good order of the Mount Marne Militia, willful dereliction of duty in the face of the enemy, and treason of thought, word, or deed. I am Sovereign Judge Milton Q. Talmedge, presiding. All who will bear witness, please approach the bench."

Knak tugged and pulled at the ropes. Struggling only made the bindings tighter. Avis Locke emerged from the shadows and stood to Knak's right, facing the three men at the table.

"Please state your name to the jury," Talmedge said.

"Avis Locke."

"And what is your rank and duties, please?"

"I am a colonel in the First Front Battalion, planning and logistics bureau."

"And how long have you been a member of the Mount Marne Militia?"

"Since it started back in '86. I'm one of the founders."

Talmedge leafed through a stack of folders. Knak looked over at Locke, who stared straight ahead. The judge lifted a piece of paper. He walked from the lectern and handed it to Locke.

"Can you tell me what that is?" Talmedge asked.

"It's a militia marriage license for the wedding of my daughter and the defendant."

"And is that your signature on there as a witness?"

"It is."

"Colonel Locke, you are aware of the seriousness of the charges against the defendant?"

"I am."

"Could you tell this court, please, what sentences might be handed down?"

Locke shifted on his feet. Knak stopped struggling. He couldn't catch his breath.

"I want a lawyer," Knak said. "Don't I get a lawyer?"

Talmedge tapped the lectern.

"Colonel, please?" Talmedge said. "What sentences are possible in this case?"

"Normally, a simple reprimand, loss of rank, maybe expulsion if it was serious enough."

Talmedge leaned his elbows on the lectern. His voice echoed throughout the chamber.

"Colonel, this organization has never seen such betrayal as evinced by Private Knak's cowardice. Every man and woman in the movement is now at risk. Decades of work is being dismantled as we speak because of the defendant. I ask you again, sir. What sentences are possible for such a despicable failure?"

"You weren't there! The movement wasn't being served! I preserved our good name for the bigger mission!"

"You shouldn't have come here," Locke whispered, before turning back to Talmedge.

"Death," Locke said. "Automatic sentence."

Talmedge crossed the room again and retrieved the marriage license from Locke. He placed it on the table in front of the hooded jury.

"I'm entering this license as Prosecution Evidence One. Now, Colonel Locke, when you signed that license, you accepted Private Knak into the organization, correct?"

Locke nodded. Knak knew he should be fighting whatever was going on, but he'd never seen Locke like this. Never thought he would. He hadn't thought Locke capable of fear. And yet here he was.

"I was his sponsor, yes," Locke said.

"And are you familiar with the bylaws regarding capital punishment involving sponsorees?"

Locke bowed his head. He breathed deep, as if at the top of a long mountain climb. Diesel and sawdust fumes filled the room. He nodded.

"I am responsible," Locke said.

"Responsible for what?" Talmedge asked.

"This is fucked up!" Knak yelled. "This isn't how a court works. Where's the evidence? Why are we talking about sentences? You have to prove I done something wrong first. I'm no coward. I'm no coward!"

"For carrying out the sentence," Locke said.

"What sentence? I didn't do anything wrong! The ex-cop, Conroy, that's the guy that screwed this all up. I didn't do nothing wrong!"

Talmedge turned to the jury.

"In accordance with Mount Marne Militia General Order one-point-naught-point-five, subsection four, paragraph one, revised 2014, I hereby ask this jury to render a judgment on the charges outlined in the indictment and writ of findings against Private Gerald Knak."

"This isn't how it works!" Knak exclaimed. "This isn't justice. This is murder!"

The three hooded jurors conferred at the table, and then the one in the suit stood and read from a single sheet of paper.

"In the case of the Mount Marne Militia versus Private Gerald Knak, we, the Sanctified Jury of Covert Justice—"

"You're a fucking accountant, Rollie!" Knak jabbed a finger in the air.

"—do hereby affirm the defendant's guilt as applicable to the charges under the indictment and writ of findings."

"Is the jury unanimous in its findings?" Talmedge asked.

The three men in hoods nodded.

His life had minutes left, but Knak didn't think of dying. Nothing flashed before his eyes. Instead he watched the tears flow down Avis Locke's cheeks, and a horrible thought came to him. How wrong he had been.

Locke pulled a Beretta nine-millimeter pistol from the holster at his waist.

"Don't I get an appeal?" Knak asked, panic setting in.

Locke racked a round into the chamber.

"That seems fair," Talmedge said. "Tell me you want to appeal this verdict."

"I appeal!" Knak said. "Please. Have mercy."

Locke placed the barrel against Knak's temple.

"Appeal—" Talmedge said.

"I'm so sorry, Gerry," Locke said.

"—denied."

CHAPTER

37

So many things they wanted her to talk about these days. It wasn't an easy trick for a woman who'd spent her whole life writing. They wanted to talk to her about Conroy, about the baby, about rumors that there was some connection to the governor-elect and the dead ex-cop. They asked if she was writing a book. A few asked about screenplays. Someone always asked about Archer, about whether the two of them remained in touch.

Lu told the story so often that she was almost able to forget she'd been there. She could tell the story while thinking about her grocery list, or how long it would take her to get to the airport, or where she was going next, or the way a certain television personality had slipped her his number after an appearance and should she call him? She didn't need to think at all to tell the story.

Most often, though, Lu thought about Archer. When they talked, it was usually late at night when an insomniac Lu, working as a freelancer for a national news service, dialed from some third-rate hotel on the road and an insomniac

Archer answered while the walls closed in at home. Archer sounded relieved, light, told her his life was a financial disaster, he was out of work, but they'd never been happier. She offered to help. Archer declined.

"It's your story," he said. "We've been through worse."

Tonight was a big night for Lu. Her first talk scheduled in the city itself. After her final articles had come out in the city's alternative paper—the *Courier* was too busy dealing with fallout from the Kittredge mess, its lawyers advising the paper to cut Lu and her former boss loose as liabilities—lines in the city were drawn. You were either for or against John O'Toole. The mayor himself remained silent, even after forensic auditors got hold of his campaign books and a grand jury was seated even before he could be sworn in.

Lu was a celebrity now, at least in Worcester. Tonight's crowd was mostly against O'Toole, but not all of it. When Lu leaned into the microphone to speak, a lone voice called out from the back of the auditorium:

"Rat!"

The man was shouted down and escorted out of the room. She shrugged it off with a smile. "Everyone's a critic," she said.

Lu looked down at her notes, then back up at the crowd. All those faces. Looking at her, expectant, ready to devour the sordid details like junk food, looking for something to release all that dopamine in their brains, to make them feel better, no matter who had paid what to suffer, to survive the experience whose telling would brighten the days of a thousand strangers who couldn't give a shit otherwise.

That's the deal, Lu thought.

That's the deal you make with the devils all around you.

She leaned into the microphone.

"I live by one rule," she said. "If your mother says she loves you . . ."

Lu sipped from a glass of water on the lectern.

"If your mother says she loves you? Check it out."

*   *   *

Archer wasn't sure what saved his son, science or faith. Some gifts were like that, he thought. Nature unknowable, grace in its many forms. He couldn't wrap his head around it and settled ultimately on an acceptance, thankful for a gift that came unwrapped, no names attached, so many possibilities.

They'd taken Michael through radiation and chemotherapy and surgery after surgery, step by step, sure in something. The scans showed improvement. Tumors shrinking, then gone. Easy connection—medicine to cure, straight-line sure.

But Archer also faithfully applied Evangeline's oil to Michael's head every night. After Cavalry Arms, his supervisors had taken Archer off the ambulance while things sorted themselves out. After a while, he decided he didn't want to go back. It was his first extended break from work since his teenage years.

Without Julio, it didn't seem worth it. He still didn't understand Julio's betrayal, thought they could have used more time to work that one out. Julio had been the one partner who helped the job make sense. He was principled in a profession that made it up as it went along. He had kept Archer on track, reminded him that there was worth in moving all this grief around from one part of the city to another. Any sense to be made of this job, that had died with Julio on the steps of the Cavalry Arms. Archer couldn't go back without him.

Instead he slept in his own bed at night, ate dinner at the kitchen table with Elaine and Michael, like a real family, like a commuter on a train who'd come home at last. At bedtime, Archer still dabbed some of the oil on his thumb, then drew it in perpendicular lines on Michael's head while the boy slept, in the sign of a cross. Some habits he wasn't yet ready to quit.

Archer slept better. Lost weight. Stopped yelling in impotent fury at cars that drove slow in front of him, or politicians on television. Anger dissolved from him so fast he didn't notice at first, like a teaspoon of sugar stirred into an ocean. At night, he'd sit in the rocking chair in Michael's room while the boy slept and relish the silence. No beeps, no overhead pages, no one checking vital signs every hour. Better still, no sirens, no diesel exhaust, no rooms filled with cigarette smoke and screaming relatives, no phone calls on Christmas morning, no missed meals, all of it now a memory.

He and Elaine took Michael to visit Julio's grave on weekends, although Archer knew it wouldn't last. He didn't want the visits to become rote, or routine as getting an oil change. When it stopped hurting, Archer knew he'd stop coming, at least for a bit. That was the way of pain. It was like an explosive vapor, building and building until there was too much of it in such a small place to detonate. All that remained was a dull ache and no hope of relief. Worse, Archer thought, than the original pain, this ache that couldn't be salved or even felt.

Archer checked in on Maria often. The new house in Northborough was wonderful, she said, but not the same without Julio. She said she didn't blame Archer for Julio's death, but he wasn't sure he believed her. He wasn't sure he believed it himself, but he tried. That was the best gift he could offer his friend these days.

Archer began going to church. He tried them all— Catholic, Protestant, an evangelical congregation that rented out his old elementary school. None of it seemed quite right, as if everyone was on some radio frequency that his receiver couldn't get. But he went anyway, smiled at everyone, dropped a buck or two in the offering plate.

Archer figured it was part of his duty, to repay a grace he might or might not have been granted from a God who might or might not exist. He was inclined to think there was a God, but that the thing He created in His image was an inconsistent reflection of Him, at best.

At one church, the congregation held hands during the recital of the Lord's Prayer. When they finished, Archer slipped out the back door and vowed never to return. He wasn't looking to participate. He wanted to sit in the back, soak it all in, drift on the periphery like a ghost.

A patient whose heart Archer once restarted had told him that he'd seen the whole thing from above the ambulance stretcher, that he'd died for a few minutes and drifted up to watch Archer work on him. The man was scared, spoke like he'd seen a ghost, that the ghost was him, and Archer envied anyone who could detach and watch the world and not have it demand anything of him, even for a moment.

In the weeks after, the wanderlust of Archer's younger years returned, only now he prowled the city and its surrounding Roman hills. Sometimes he took Michael with him. Up and down and through neighborhoods good and bad, Archer often drove for hours, waving at ambulances as they rushed from call to call.

"That used to be you, Daddy," Michael said one day, not long after returning from the hospital in Boston.

"We both used to spend a lot of time in hospitals," Archer said.

"I'm glad that's over," Michael said.

He cashed out his 401(k), brought coffee to cops working road details, pizzas to firefighters in the station, boxes of pastry to his old ambulance mates. By day, Archer ate at the Bully and watched the retired wiseguys pinch each other's cheeks, studied the city's architecture, bought an annual pass to its art museum, enrolled in courses in literature and pottery at the community college, but dropped out of each. He wasn't as ready for change as he'd thought.

Archer remembered the old couple shuffling to Evangeline's window in search of healing, not able to touch the girl but certain that a nearness to her, to the miracle they believed in, that such proximity to God or God's vessel would unwind the years that accumulated on human bodies and spirits, rendering them stooped and broken and supplicating at a comatose girl's window. Archer brought his own offerings too, not in hope of miracles, but in visits to her grave to give thanks for the things he'd witnessed in her house, things that might or might not have been miraculous. It was his own penance and his own escape. He'd never be one of them again, but he'd never be free of them, either.

One day he stopped at the junk store in Leary Square, not looking for anything in particular. He found a painting of a Maine lighthouse, standing sentry above a roiled coastline taking a beating from angry white waves. Something about the painting in its beaten wood frame, painted in a flaked and scratched gold leaf, caught Archer's attention. He paid his fifteen bucks, took the painting home, hung it over Michael's bed.

Late at night, while Michael slumbered and took long, luxuriant breaths, Archer looked at the painting and settled harder into the cushion on the wooden rocking chair. This was a place for staying. He'd been gone long enough.

ACKNOWLEDGMENTS

FIRST AND FOREMOST, I want to thank my family for their love, support, and encouragement throughout the years of writing this book: my wife, Jen, our sons, Brendan and Kevan, and our daughter, Ainsleigh. I love all of you dearly and could not have written this without you!

I need to also thank Jim Baker, who has been a father to me longer than my own, and Andy and Megan Baker, along with my nieces Molly and Abby. There is nothing that means more to me than family, and I couldn't have asked for better!

Thanks also to Julie Stevenson, agent extraordinaire, who believed in this book from the first and whose encouragement has meant the world to me throughout the process. I can never thank you enough, Julie!

Ben Leroy is an editor whose works I'd admired long before I was lucky enough to work with him on this book. He is one of the great people in all of publishing, and I learned so much from working with him. If there's any part of this book that strikes a chord with anyone, it almost certainly has Ben's fingerprints on it.

I need also to thank Wiley Cash for his tireless efforts to help me tell the story I wanted to tell. Without Wiley, this book simply never would have happened. One could not ask for a better advocate, teacher, and human being than Wiley Cash, and I am forever indebted to him for everything he's done to make this a reality.

If you're lucky as I have been, you get to spend time working with a wide variety of writers who support and improve your work. I am absolutely one of those people, and I am forever grateful to Mark Sundeen, Leslie Jamison, Merle Drown, Ann Garvin, Jo Knowles, Ben Nugent, Lydia Peele, and Craig Childs for their insight, not just on this novel but also on how to be a writer in the world today.

Great mentors aren't the only thing a successful writer needs—they also need compadres. Fellow travelers on the same path. First readers who will be honest even when you want them to lie and tell you everything you write is gold. Most of all, sympathetic ears who celebrate your success and shake their fists at the world with you when you fail. I am humbled and privileged to call the novelist John Vercher my buddy and thank him for being that presence in my life.

There are dozens and dozens of additional people I could thank. Portions of this book were written over the years on an aircraft carrier, in Children's Hospital Boston during a blizzard, on ambulances and, for part of one scene, in the back of a helicopter. Making time and space to write is itself an art form, and over the years I've become pretty decent at carving out that time and finding that space. I close my acknowledgments with a word to anyone reading this book who's struggling to write while working at other things. It's simple, but this book you're holding in your hands is proof that sometimes the simplest choice is the correct one: never give up.